GODZILLA
vs.
KONG

GODZILLA
VS.
KONG

THE OFFICIAL MOVIE NOVELIZATION

NOVELIZATION BY **GREG KEYES**

TITAN BOOKS

GODZILLA VS. KONG – THE OFFICIAL MOVIE NOVELIZATION
Print edition ISBN: 9781789097351
E-book edition ISBN: 9781789097368

Published by Titan Books
A division of Titan Publishing Group Ltd
144 Southwark Street, London SE1 0UP
www.titanbooks.com

First edition: April 2021
1 2 3 4 5 6 7 8 9 10

A CIP catalogue record for this title is available from the British Library.

Printed and bound in the United States of America.

To Sandy Kay White

ONE

"Are you kidding? What *can't* you do with it? Pharmaceuticals, bioweapons, food—hell, there isn't a country or a company on the planet that doesn't wanna get their hands on one of these suckers. I mean they're basically living atomic weapons."

Dr. Richard Stanton, Monarch scientist, on why anyone would attempt to steal the Mothra Larva

Sea of Okhotsk, Three Years and Two Months Ago

Manchaary Rybekov put his rifle back on safety as he watched the helicopter descending toward the oil platform. He exhaled a puff of white vapor into the freezing air.

"Put away your weapons," he told his men. "I know who this is." He gestured at Serj. "Go down and tell the gunners to be easy, too. But everyone stay on alert."

His second, Proctor, sidled up to him, a bit of his unruly

red hair peeking out from beneath his wool cap.

"Who is this guy, Manch?" Proctor asked, dropping his pistol into one of his deep coat pockets.

"He is the money," Manch replied. "Come to see what we've been doing with it."

"Think he'll be pleased?" Proctor asked.

Manchaary shrugged. The night, as usual, was cold but clear, and the three-quarter moon rippled light on the surface of the sea. In the distance, the mountains on the mainland were a ragged shadow against the starry sky. For the moment, this was all his. Eventually the Russian state would regain the wind it had lost in the Titan attacks and look back to its peripheries, where men like him had taken advantage of the chaos to carve out territory. In a few months, maybe. Not yet.

His little kingdom wasn't all that large, but it was rich in oil, and he had managed not to kill the bulk of the workers on the rig, and even convinced most of them to join his "profit sharing" plan. Production was up, and he was making a decent return on the black market. But maintaining his territory cost money in bribes and military equipment, which cut into profits. A little discovery—well not little, really—beneath the waves had secured him help with both.

"I think so," he said.

"And why should we care what pleases some banker?"

"Eventually we'll have to give this all up," Manch said. "We need to get everything out of it we can. We have something this man wants, and he's willing to pay very well for it."

"And then?" Proctor said.

"The world may settle back down; it may not. If it does, maybe we'll move into some legitimate enterprise, eh? And this man can help with that, too. He has important connections."

"And our cause?" Proctor asked. "What of that?"

"Causes need money," Manch replied. He smiled at Proctor and slapped him on the shoulder, thinking that it might be about time for his second-in-command to have an accident of some sort. Things happened, out here. People fell off oil rigs all the time. Ten minutes in these waters was more than enough to bring about an untimely end.

The helicopter landed, and a man got out, followed by two more.

"Who is it?" Proctor said. "Some mobster from Moscow?"

"No, worse," Manch replied. "An American businessman. He is to be referred to as Mr. Rosales. Understood?"

"Is that an alias? He some sort of superhero?"

"No," Manch replied. "He's just careful of his reputation around trash like you and me."

They watched the man and his bodyguards draw near.

"You are Rybekov, I assume," the man said. His smile was a crooked little thing. His heavy parka looked expensive— and brand-new.

"Yes. It's good to finally meet you, Mr. Rosales."

"It's very brisk here, isn't it?" Rosales said.

"It's warmer inside," Manch said. "Come along."

"That sounds great," Rosales said. "And as much as I would like to get to know you two and your merry band, I'm afraid time is pressing on me. So if we could get straight to the show."

"Of course," Manch said. "I wouldn't want to waste your time."

"Don't take offense," Rosales said. "I'm sure you're far too busy to spend your time entertaining me, as well. So let us skip the tea and board games and get right down to it. No one offended, no one insulted."

"You think like me," Manch said. "That's good. Come along. As it happens, you came at a good time. The submarine is down there."

"Submarine?" Rosales said. "That's quite impressive. Where did you get one of those?"

"There is—was—a naval port not far from here. We borrowed one from there, along with a sympathetic crew. Your money in action."

"I see," Rosales said. "You will send me the invoice?"

"Wait," Manch said. "You really—"

"Kidding," Rosales said. "Just kidding. How you distribute my charitable contribution to your orphan's fund is quite up to you."

"Ah," Manch said. "This is what I thought."

The helipad opened directly into the offices and control room, all of which Manch had deemed a little cramped for company, so he had set up one of the large screens in the rec room to display the feed from the submarine.

Rosales took a seat when invited, but his men remained standing. Manch put on a pair of headphones with a speaker.

"Mizuno," he said. "Manch here. Can you give our visitor a view?"

"Just a minute," the sub's captain replied.

The screen went blank, then came up again, revealing an underwater view of a large, amorphous presence covered in minute glowing points, as if a pile of leaves had been covered in stars.

"It looks like a giant jellyfish," Rosales said. "Not what I was expecting."

"That's the containment field," Manch said. "We … ah, borrowed one from one of the ruined Monarch facilities. Underneath the field, it's quite another story."

Rosales gazed at the image of the monster on the monitor. He stood, walked over to it, seemed on the verge of stroking the screen.

"It's beautiful," he said. Then frowned. "He? She?"

"Both," Proctor replied. "It can change sex as needed and can be both at once."

"I see," Rosales said. "Even better, I suppose. Does it have a name?"

"I worked at its containment facility," Proctor said. "Before it was destroyed. I was on the crew that found it, all curled up on an old Soviet submarine. We called it Kraken, but the official name is Titanus Na Kika."

"You worked for Monarch?" Rosales said.

"As a contractor," Proctor replied. "Nearly cost me my life."

Rosales nodded, studying the monitor. "Na Kika," he said. "I like it. Where does that name come from?"

"Kiribati," Proctor said. "It's an island nation. The people there worshipped it for centuries before European explorers showed up. Some still do."

"So underneath all of that, it's more like an octopus?"

"Something like that," Proctor said. "A cephalopod, anyway."

Rosales peered more closely at the screen. "What's this greenish cloud coming up from it?"

"That's its blood," Proctor said. "We wounded it in the capture. Nothing serious. It will heal."

Rosales smiled. "This is wonderful," he said. "I'll have a team come in to assess this situation and prepare for extraction. Now that I've finally got one of these in hand, I would hate to make a misstep. Congratulations, gentlemen, you have just received funding for the immediate future. And who knows? I might be able to pull some strings in Moscow when things become more—stable."

"How large a team are you bringing?" Manch asked. "There aren't many empty beds here."

"A handful," Rosales said. "You'll hardly know they're here. I—Say, what's going on?"

The image had suddenly shifted. The microphone was still on, and Manch suddenly heard a lot of shouting from the submarine.

"Mizuno!" Manch demanded. "What's happening?"

"We're coming up!" Mizuno said. "He's cutting him free."

"What the hell are you talking about?"

"Godzilla! He just—he's there, with the squid."

Manch paused for a second. "Evgeniy, did you hear that? Drop the depth charges. Drop them now!" He turned to Proctor. "Dump the oil, too."

"Wait!" Rosales said. "What are you doing? That's my Titan down there."

"Depth charges won't hurt them," Manch said. "But they might blind Godzilla, dampen his sonar or whatever."

"Until what?" Rosales demanded.

"We have another net," Manch replied. "On the sub. How would you like to have two Titans?" He switched on his transmitter. "Mizuno, do you have a shot?"

"We've dropped it," the voice came back. "And now we're—" The man broke off and began swearing in Japanese. They suddenly had a visual: a glowing net, floating down, and something huge and dark moving into it; flashes like chain lightning. Then, abruptly, a column of blue-white light stabbed up through it; and an instant later in the submarine's floods, a reptilian face, filling the entire view. Mizuno screamed, but the shriek of metal rending drowned him out. Then the screen went dark.

"Oh, shit," Proctor said.

Rosales stood up. "If you gentlemen don't mind," he said, "I believe I'll catch the rest of this show streaming." He gestured to his men and they all exited onto the helipad.

"Go ahead," Manch muttered after him. "I've still got a trick or two up my sleeve. Proctor, are the choppers up?"

"They are."

"When he surfaces, give him the gas."

"Okay," Procter said. He sounded dubious.

The door to the radio room banged open and Serj stuck his head out.

"What is it?" Manch demanded.

"Sir, I've got a Monarch jet approaching. They have ordered us to stand down."

Manch bolted out onto the helipad just in time to see Rosales's helicopter leave. Ignoring them, he climbed up to where they had installed their heavy weapons battery. His own choppers were all in sight, converging.

From the pipes below, oil was pouring into the water, spreading over the sea, like liquid glass in the moonlight. Everything was ready. He had considered the possibility that Na Kika would somehow call help; he had never imagined Godzilla himself would show up, but he had been prepared for another Titan.

The last bubbles from the depth charges surfaced, and for a moment, everything was quiet and still.

Then the sea broke in half, and hell came up from the rift. The moonlight gleamed on reptilian scales as Godzilla heaved into the air and arched against the moon-bright sky. In a heartbeat, Manch's gunners responded; tracer rounds from heavy-caliber guns streaked through the night; shells and missiles bloomed on the Titan's armored hide like anemones as the heavier-than-air gas poured out of the choppers.

It's going to work, he thought, *as it did on Na Kika.* But deeper down, he heard another voice. The voice of his grandmother, telling him the stories about the *abasy* who lived below the world, the spirits of darkness, and their chief, a huge giant with iron skin...

Two fireballs appeared in the sky, where a pair of his helicopters had been. A jet shrieked overhead.

"Take that down," he told his men, before returning

his gaze to Godzilla. The gas was clinging to the Titan, as predicted. Only his back was visible now, and to Manch's eye, Godzilla appeared to be sinking as the remaining helicopters dumped more of the virulent stuff onto the surface of the water. He grinned in satisfaction as a missile took out the Monarch jet. The first of the two burning helicopters hit the water, igniting the oil, and the sea was suddenly aflame as Godzilla sank from sight.

"We got him," Manch said. "Deploy the other net."

"That will take a few minutes," Procter said.

"Quickly," Manch said. "Who knows how long it will take him to recover?"

"I'm on it." Proctor started down the ladder.

Manch stared at the burning sea below. It was beautiful to him, and for the first time since coming here, the wind was warm.

"Screw you, Grandmother," he muttered. "And your scary stories."

Then the light of the burning sea was suddenly over-shadowed by a blue-white glow. That, too was beautiful, but Manch felt his heart clot inside of him as he turned.

From the center of the rig, a pillar of blue light stabbed into the heavens like a beacon.

"Ah, shit," Manch said, as the rig exploded, heaving him and everything else skyward. He had a single searing glimpse of the demon from the deep, rising amidst the ruin, and then the past and future closed in on him, and he winked out like a candle flame.

Apex Offices
Pensacola, Florida, Two Years Ago

"I'm impressed," the man said, once he was in Walter

Simmons's office and the door was closed. "I didn't think you would meet with me in person."

The man didn't look impressed. He looked hard, his dark eyes cold. The wrinkles on his face had not gotten there from smiling or laughing. Not a pleasant fellow, surely. But he was here to do business, and Simmons understood business.

"Why wouldn't I?" Simmons said. "I have no reason to suspect you mean me harm, and if you do, my security detail is, I assure you, very efficient. May I get you something to drink?"

"No, thank you," the man said.

Simmons stood and walked over to the window of his Pensacola office, turning his back on his guest.

"The view isn't as nice as that from my Hong Kong office," he said. "Yet I find it pleasing. Have you been here before? Seen the local sights?"

"I haven't much use for local sights," the man said. "I've seen about as much as I want to, over the years."

"That's too bad, I—Wait, what the hell is that?"

There was a ship in the docks, drawn up right behind one of his, with a bunch of people, half of them in tie-dye, lined up at the rails. And now that he was looking, there were a bunch of them on land, too, with signs and banners.

"I should say those are environmental crusaders," the man said. "I passed through them coming in."

"These guys," Simmons muttered. "A thorn in my side." Then he brightened. "Well, not so much a thorn as a little stitch, or maybe a mosquito bite. You didn't come here with them, did you?"

"God, no. They're a bit feeble for my taste."

"So I understand. And speaking of that, you are really the one at risk coming here, aren't you? Wanted by Interpol and at least twenty governments?"

"I'm not counting anymore," the man said. "But as you say. I am, let us say, outside of my comfort zone. Can we get down to it?"

"Of course," Simmons said. "What do you have to offer me? I know something of your history, but I must warn you, I have my own sources for the sort of things you deal in."

"You don't have a source for this," the dangerous man said. He laid what looked like a photograph on the table.

"Seriously?" Simmons said. "Is that an instant camera picture? You contact me on the dark web, and then you show up in person with a cheap photo? Why didn't you just draw it out on a clay tablet?"

The man didn't answer.

Simmons reached for the photograph and turned it over. He picked it up and held it closer.

"Is this really what I think it is?" he said.

"Yes," the man said. "It is."

Simmons sat down, still staring at the image, and he knew. He could see the circuits in his head, already, or some of them, anyway. It was the missing piece. Or *a* missing piece.

"Astonishing," he said. "And yet, what would I do with such a thing?"

"Don't play games." The man spoke quietly, without apparent emotion. The hiss of a viper.

"Well," Simmons said. "It would be better—"

"—if I had two?" the man said.

"Now that you mention it."

"I have two."

"What?" Simmons said. "Not all three?"

"Just the two," the man said.

"And for this you want…?"

"Money. A lot of money."

"Really? I should think a man like you—"

"You don't know what a man like me is," the man said.

"You will never know." He pulled a bit of paper from his shirt pocket.

"The money goes to these three accounts," he said.

"I have to hear your price first," Simmons told him.

"You don't, actually," the man said. "Send the money. If it is enough, I will deliver. If not, I have other options."

"No, hang on," Simmons began, but the man stood up, took the photograph, and left the office. Simmons watched him go, following his progress out on the security cameras. Then he took out his phone and tapped a number.

"Yes," he said, when he got an answer. "I need you to see how much money we can come up with. Completely off the books, you understand?" He stood and went to the window as he listened to the reply. He looked out at the ship and the protesters.

"No," he said. "That's not enough. Yes, I understand you may have to liquidate some offshore accounts. That's fine. What do I pay you for? That's right. Just do it." He paused. "And another thing. I'm going to set up a press conference downstairs in about half an hour. I'll be cutting a handsome donation to whatever organization is out there protesting. It might not shut them up, but it will make them look bad. Yes, of course we're reporting that one. Don't get these two things confused. Right."

He touched the phone off and looked back out the window.

"Environmentalists," he muttered under his breath.

TWO

It may be replied, that the idea of a world within a world, is absurd. But, who can assert with confidence, that this idea is, in reality, nothing more than the imagination of a feverish brain? How is it shown that such a form does not exist? Are there not as strong reasons for believing that the earth is constituted of concentric spheres, as the court of Spain, or any man in Europe, had to believe that there was an undiscovered continent? Has not Captain Symmes theoretically proven his assertions of concentric spheres and open poles, and embodied a catalogue of facts, numerous and plausible, in support of his opinions? And who has confuted his assertions? I *dare* to say, that none can be found, who *can* fully disprove them, and account for the facts which he adduces as the proofs of his theory. Is there not the same reason to believe, that the earth is hollow, as there is to place implicit confidence in the opinion, that the planets are inhabited? And yet the one has been ridiculed as the wild speculations of a madman, while the other receives credit among the most enlightened.

If it can be shown that Symmes's Theory is probable, or has the least plausibility attached to it—nay, that it is even possible—why not afford him the means of testing its correctness? The bare possibility of such a discovery, ought to be a sufficient stimulus to call forth the patronage of any government. And should the theory prove correct, and the adventure succeed, would it not immortalize our nation?

From *Symmes's Theory of Concentric Spheres,*
James McBride, 1826

A Carrier in the Pacific, One Year Ago

"Mercury," Nathan Lind told his older brother Dave. "Not Apollo."

Dave settled his paper cup of single malt Scotch on the metal counter.

"Why not Zeus?" he said. "I mean, if we're talking Greek gods, why not go for it?"

"I'm not talking about Greek gods, dimwit," Nathan said. "The space program. Mercury. Gemini. Apollo."

"Oh," Dave said. "That makes more sense, I guess."

"It's an apt comparison," Nathan replied. "In 1961 the unknown frontier was space; no human being had ever been there. We had a lot of science, but we didn't know for sure what to expect. So we took it slow."

"Right," Dave agreed. "So slow the Soviets beat us to the punch."

"This isn't a race," Nathan said. "We're not in competition. We practically had to beg the press to show up. We don't have anything to prove."

"Well, that's not true," Dave said, wagging his finger at Nathan. "We've spent years wrangling funding for this expedition. If we don't have anything to show for it, we won't get any more. Half of the scientists at Monarch think it's bullshit, and almost half of those that *do* think it's real believe we ought to leave well enough alone, especially after that ... bat thing—"

"Camazotz," Nathan said. "Yeah. He kind of put a damper on things."

"Right. Since that mess, they want to shut us down. Fortunately, I still have enough pull to make it happen. As long as it happens *soon*. If we put on a good show, bring back some goodies, we'll have plenty of people writing us checks. If not, we're done. Years of working and planning, down the drain."

"Monarch was practically founded on the notion of the Hollow Earth," Nathan said. "Bill Randa, Houston Brooks—"

"Randa was crushed by a Skullcrawler some fifty-odd years ago," Dave said. "And Brooks, well, everyone likes him, but he isn't taken all that seriously by most people. Not anymore."

"I take him seriously," Nathan said.

"Most *sane* people," Dave said.

"Hey, who volunteered to pilot this thing?" Nathan said.

"I never said I was sane," Dave replied. "We have the same genes, you know."

"Hah," Nathan said. "You'd never know it to look at us."

"Yeah. That's why we've been explaining that we aren't twins since you were eight and I was ten. Remember that time in Sao Paulo, in that bar?"

That was true, although in the details he knew Dave

was better-looking; his eyes deep blue instead of gray, his jaw a little more manly, his locks a shade closer to true blond than Nathan's sandy hair.

"That's not what I meant," Nathan said. "What I meant is, you're the guy who broke Mach 10 in an experimental Monarch aircraft, while I was looking at grains of basalt under a microscope. You summited Everest while I was tracing shifts in paleomagnetism and writing articles in obscure journals about bioelectrical sensory organs in trilobites."

Dave put his hand on Nathan's shoulder. "Nathan," he said. "Shut up. I might have flown a fast plane, but I didn't develop it. And at this point climbing Everest is, at best, tourism. What you've figured out—what you've *proven*—I never could have."

"There are people who still think I haven't proven anything," Nathan said. "They think I'm as nuts as Darling back in 1926, when his expedition started out to find Hollow Earth—and never returned."

"Sure," Dave said. "And together, we're going to show them they're wrong. In about, what? Eight hours. So let's have our one shot of decent whisky, get some rest, and change the world. Together."

Nathan nodded, and reached for his drink. But he frowned.

"Okay," Dave said. "What is it?"

"We can always delay this," Nathan said. "Get a little more data. Let me crunch the numbers again."

Dave sighed. "Like I said, if we wait too long—poof. The funding goes away. We've already lost pilots and aircraft, and we haven't even tried to get in yet. Important people are trying to pull the plug. Like your friend Andrews."

"I understand that," Nathan said. "But ... maybe not *there*. Maybe not Skull Island. There are too many complicating factors now. The storm. And the entrance, it's too unstable. I don't trust it. There's always Antarctica—"

"Which *you* said we couldn't enter. Not with the vehicles we have. Right?"

Nathan nodded. "Yes. But we can improve the planes. I have some ideas."

"That's more time and more money," Dave said. "A lot more money. I'm just doing the math here, brother. It's now or never." He put his arm around Nathan's shoulder. "I believe in you, little brother," he said. "You've got this. Anyway, Mercury, not Apollo, right?"

"You understand what I meant by that?" Nathan asked.

"Yeah," Dave said. "The first Mercury mission just dipped our toes in space. We didn't try to go all the way to the Moon. Or even orbit the Earth. Just up and down."

"So tomorrow…?"

"Wet toes," Dave said. "No Moon landing. I'll see what I see, we'll get better readings, I'll come back. And next time—we'll go together. All the way. Now." He lifted his cup. "Unto the breach," he said.

Nathan raised his own whisky. "Unto the breach," he said. "And *Sláinte mhath*."

"Fancy," Dave said. "Where did you learn that?"

"A phrasebook," Nathan said. "I did a book signing in Glasgow—"

"Just drink," Dave said.

"Fine." He drank, then made a face as the stuff went down. "Oh, God," Nathan said. "What the hell is that?"

"The smokiness? The peat?"

"If by that, you mean acid and dirt," Nathan said. "Wow. That was awful."

"Maybe an acquired taste," Dave said. "I guess you didn't have any Islay whisky in Glasgow."

"No," he admitted. "A beer now and then is more my speed."

Dave nodded and knocked his knuckles on the table. "What are we going to find down there, Nathan? In Hollow Earth."

"You've read the briefing. And my book, I assume."

"Yes, well, I've also been busy training," Dave said. "The briefing is boiler-plate nothingspeak, and I haven't had a chance to read your book. So what do you, the expert, think we're going to find down there?"

Nathan swallowed again, trying to get the taste of the whisky out of his throat.

"Another world," he said.

"Godzilla?"

Nathan cocked his head. "Brooks thinks so. He believes the Titans originated from there. And since Godzilla has vanished from sight, maybe that's where he's hiding out."

"And you?"

He knew Dave was probably just trying to mollify him. But it was hard not to get going anyway, especially after spending weeks on a tour where hardly anyone was listening.

"Do you know how many times life on Earth nearly became extinct?" Nathan asked.

"Well, there were the dinosaurs, I guess—"

"Many, many times," Nathan said. "The end of the Permian was a big one. Ninety percent of everything died. But even earlier—there was a period when the entire planet froze over. We call it Snowball Earth, because that's what it would have looked like from space. Not a regular ice age, mind you, when you still have liquid surface water in the oceans. I mean totally frozen over. And there were other times, right after we think life formed, that the Earth was pounded with asteroids, covered with volcanic lakes. An inferno. And yet, life kept coming back. Every time. After every massive die-off, something poked its head up and started to evolve, diversify, build an ecosystem."

He paused, let it sink in a moment.

"You think life hid out down there," Dave said. "In Hollow Earth. And when the worst of it was over, it just came back out of hiding. But how? Without sunlight—"

"The first life on Earth probably didn't depend on the sun at all," Nathan said. "Photosynthetic organisms like cyanobacteria and algae were latecomers to the party. In fact they caused an extinction of their own because of all the oxygen they produced, which was pure poison to the world's earliest life. Even now, there are plenty of organisms that need neither sunlight nor oxygen. What life does need is *some* sort of energy source; there are living things that subsist on the heat and chemicals in deep-sea volcanic vents, where no sunlight can penetrate. And I think there is plenty of energy in Hollow Earth. More than we can dream of, maybe. It's just the form of it that I'm not certain of. But if there is energy, life will find a way to use it, unlock its potential."

He leaned forward, feeling the whisky in his veins.

"I don't think life began up here at all," he confided. "I think it may have *originated* down there. Made its way up here through volcanic vents and so forth. And yes, when times got tough up here, maybe surface life migrated back down there. Cross-pollination. An exchange that's been happening for billions of years." He looked seriously at his brother. "And maybe one of those exchanges included some of our own ancestors. Australopithecines, or *Homo habilis*, but more likely some form of hominin that we've never found fossils of—because they're down *there*. Do you know how many human cultures, scattered all over the globe, have legends that their ancestors emerged from the ground? I think when we get down there, we won't just find the origin of the Titans, but possibly of ourselves."

"Wow," Dave said.

"I know, right," Nathan replied.

"I mean, wow, what a lightweight," Dave said. "One shot and you're drunk off your ass."

Nathan smiled. "Yeah. I'm rambling. Who knows what we'll find down there? That's what this is all about, right?"

"Absolutely, brother," Dave said. "Which reminds me."

He pulled something out of his pocket and held it in his palm.

Nathan stared at it incredulously. "My spaceman," he said. "How—"

"*My* spaceman," Dave replied. "We made a bet, remember?"

"You cheated," Nathan said. "You still *have* that?"

"Sure," Dave said. "I took it to college with me. To remember my little brother and his crazy ideas. It's been my good luck charm. But now I want you to have it back."

"But—why?"

"I don't need it anymore," Dave said. "I've got you now."

"I can't—"

"Sure you can," Dave said. "You were right. I did cheat. It belongs to you."

"Dave, I don't know what to say."

"Say goodnight," his brother replied. "I'd better get my beauty sleep. I want to be sharp when I get behind the stick."

"Right," Nathan said, taking the little plastic doll and looking at it. Remembering. "See you in the morning."

The next morning, Nathan watched nervously as Dave and his team went through their checklists and their craft were fueled on the deck of the carrier.

The press corps arrived, and it was showtime.

There were more of them than he had imagined, which he supposed was good news.

Once he thought they were ready, he cleared his throat.

He waved at the three aircraft.

"Good morning," he said. "The, uh, expedition consists, as you can see, of three state-of-the-art Monarch hover jets. They have been modified, reduced from two-seater to single-seater craft to accommodate a variety of scientific instruments. I know they aren't all that impressive in terms of size, but they are exceptionally maneuverable, capable of supersonic flight, and equipped with the specialized communications equipment they will need for their descent into the Hollow Earth."

"Dr. Lind," one of the reporters interrupted. "You speak of the Hollow Earth as if you have evidence for its existence. But surely you know the vast majority of Earth scientists consider your theory as ridiculous as that of a flat Earth."

"Yes," Nathan said. "I am aware of that. But I can assure you, we would not have mounted this expedition unless we were quite sure there was a place for these aircraft to explore. I am aware that my claims are unorthodox, but I think that in a very short time you all will see them borne out. This is what science does; it tests predictions."

"You're saying there is a hole big enough to fly aircraft through that goes through the crust of the planet," another reporter said. "How can such a passage resist the intense pressure, the temperatures that most surely melt stone?"

"Both of those objections are based upon false assumptions," Nathan said. "The data I have collected, and my calculations based on them, demonstrate there is a sort of membrane, an electrostatic-gravitational anomaly that separates the Hollow Earth from the upper parts of the planet. The mathematics predict a sort of acceleration vortex. It will be something like slipping into a jetstream and will carry our explorers very far down in a very short time. When they come out the other end of it, they should be at their destination. Their instruments might get wonky during that time, but communication ought to resume when they reach the other side. Just to be sure, they will release a series of relay devices as they descend."

"And supposing all of this is true," another reporter asked. "And there is some vast system of caverns down there. Some have rumored that Godzilla and the other Titans may have their origins down there. What will your team do if they encounter … monsters?"

"Then we come back," Dave said, from right next to him. Nathan jumped a little. He hadn't seen his brother walk up.

Dave gestured at their exploration craft.

"We couldn't make room in these beauties for weapons. Even if we had, we know they wouldn't be too useful if we run into Titans. So we stay alert, we fly true, we come home. And hopefully, we'll have some fantastic images for you."

"So where is this happening?" a reporter asked. "Are they going to dive down into the ocean?"

"No," Nathan said. "The opening—we call it the Vortex—is on land and nearby, but the climactic conditions are rather extreme, so we'll be monitoring the expedition from this carrier. The exact location is secret, for obvious reasons, which is why we have been jamming any GPS equipment you might have. You will all be allowed on the bridge to watch things as they develop. If you go above deck you won't see much, but if you do you might want to dress for wet weather. We have a storm coming in."

The storm wasn't coming to them, of course—they were going to it. Nathan watched as the black clouds grew until they blotted out the eastern sky. They came to a stop just outside of the storm's radius, at Dave's request.

"We won't have a problem flying through all that," he said, waving at the cloud. "But taking off in a full-on thunderstorm—why take the chance."

"Once you've taken off, we'll ease in closer," Nathan said. "I want to be as close as possible to the relays."

"That's all you," Dave said. "I'll feel better knowing you're watching me."

Nathan had compared their endeavor to the space program, with some justice, he thought. And yet it started with considerably less fanfare. There was no countdown, no spectacular lift-off. The three aircraft simply rose up on their under-jets and flew off toward the standing storm. As promised, the ship started forward almost immediately, nudging into the tempest. As sheets of rain swept across the deck, the last of the reporters came onto the bridge.

Dave's plane had forward-mounted cameras, and what they showed now was nothing but clouds. Nathan knew the pilots had radar and other instruments working for them, but he felt claustrophobic just looking at the screen.

Once he'd been driving in a rainstorm when an eighteen-wheeler passed him and doused his windshield with so much water it took his wipers what seemed like an eternity to clear it. He hadn't been able to see anything—not the taillights of the cars in front of him, not the shapes of the cars, nothing. If he'd slammed on the brakes, he'd known he might be rear-ended, but how could he keep going when he might smash into a car in front of him at any moment? He had barely managed to control his panic, and that was nothing compared to rocketing along through a superstorm, aiming for a freaking hole in the ground…

He closed his eyes. *Come on, Dave.*

"Little light precipitation," Dave's cheerful voice came over the intercom. If you will look off to our port side—

that's to the left, folks—you'll be able to see—well, nothing. But if you keep your eyes straight ahead, I think I can promise you—there we go."

The jungle suddenly appeared, the tallest trees jutting into the clouds, the planes so low to the treetops Nathan found himself involuntarily pushing imaginary brakes on the floor. They were going so fast…

In an instant, the cave mouth was there, a gaping wound in the world.

"In we go!" Dave shouted. "Unto the breach."

There's gonna be T-shirts with that on it, Nathan thought. *This is going to change everything.*

The jets turned on floodlights as they whipped down the tunnel. It was harrowing, but somehow not as bad as the storm. This was more like watching a roller-coaster ride, maybe with a Wild West silver-mine theme. There wasn't anything to see here that was too far out of the ordinary. Everything weird was much further down the tunnel. Monarch had sent drones in, of course, and the data they had provided had added significantly to his calculations, but there was a point beyond which the signals weren't strong enough to maintain the sort of contact that made remote piloting possible. That was especially true when they hit the Vortex itself, where gravity appeared to do funny things with time, so outside signals were out of synch with the drones' experience of reality. Human pilots were necessary.

"Looking good, control," Dave said. "Outside temperature elevated, but nothing crazy. This looks like a cakewalk."

"You're coming up on the Vortex," Nathan said. "Once you enter, you'll have to switch to your G-pulse signal for us to stay in touch."

"Acknowledged, control."

Nathan watched the feed from the forward cameras.

The tunnel tilted down now, not vertical but not that far from it. Up ahead, weird colors scintillated, cutting off visibility of anything beyond.

"Switching to G-pulse," Dave said. "Going in, brother. See you on the other side."

The screen went black as the transition happened. Then it flared back on, a chaos of rapidly shifting pixels. He knew the data was now coming in discrete bundles every few seconds, but the receiver should be buffering it, piecing it together, synchronizing the disparate flows of time.

"Dave?" he said. "Do you read me?"

"Copy," Dave said. "Trippy. Really trippy ... could probably sell tickets..." his voice stretched out into a long squeal, then a groan, lowering in pitch until it was inaudible. As if the signal was red-shifting, moving away from him at incredible speed. How fast were they going? No telemetry was coming through.

"Shit," he muttered under his breath. "Shit."

This was not supposed to happen. He'd missed something. Yes, he had expected acceleration, but not nearly to this order of magnitude. He had told the reporters it would be like going into a jetstream; this seemed more like a railgun.

"Dave," he said. "If you can hear me, abort. Abort now. Put on every brake you have and come back."

He listened desperately for an answer, but none came.

No, no, no, no...

It should still be all right. When they came out the other end of this, they should have space to slow down, right? If it was like he thought, there should be dozens of miles of open space in front of them, hundreds maybe. A world-sized cavern.

It was going to be all right. It was...

Abruptly everything was back—telemetry, sound, the forward cameras. He had a glimpse of open space, a curved horizon, a storm or something, in the distance, coming closer with incredible speed.

"Wow," Dave said. "That was intense. But we're—"

Then everything went black. Nothing.

"Dave!" he shouted. "Dave!" He switched frequencies, tried again. Nothing from any of the planes. It was as if they had simply ceased to exist.

Trying not to panic, he pulled up the last image, the last set of data. The picture showed nothing but what might be a thunderhead with lightning shining from its core. Mountains in the distance, upside down. He scrolled through the other readings until he got to the readout of speed, velocity—deceleration. He went back over it again, desperate to believe it was wrong. That he had read it wrong.

"Dave," he said. "Oh, God, Dave."

THREE

They believe, in all this country, that there is a kind of gorilla—known to the initiated by certain signs, but chiefly by being of extraordinary size… Such gorillas, the natives believe can never be caught or killed; and also, they have much more shrewdness and sense than the common animal. In fact, in these "possessed" beasts it would seem that the intelligence of man is united with the strength and ferocity of the beast.

From *Explorations and Adventures in Equatorial Africa*, Paul B. Du Chaillu, 1861

Skull Island Eleven Months Ago

White light scorched across the dark heavens, leaving a jagged streak of red behind Jia's eyelids as she blinked them shut against the pouring rain. An instant later, she felt the shiver the light made in the earth and air. The water sucked at her ankles, climbing higher toward her calves. She clung to Sister-Mother's hand, felt the calluses there, the strength that kept her going, the grip that forced down her terror. Everything was wrong, and she knew it. She did not know the wind speech of her people, and they rarely used it anyway. But she knew it by their expressions, by the way they held their hands, the set of their shoulders, tilt of their hips when they paused, struggling through the jungle.

She knew that they expected to leave the world soon, to join the bundles of their generations in the What-Always-Is.

The blue-white light came again and again, incandescent serpents coiling in the sky and striking down toward the earth. She could smell the breath of the rainsnakes—like copper, like blood and yet not quite like either. And she could smell salt in the rising waters of the stream. She liked the scent of the ocean; she remembered long days overlooking the Eternal Waters that surrounded the Land-World, staring across the waves. Back then the black sky and lightning snakes had been out there, surrounding the Land-World. Protecting it, the elders said. Keeping the great enemy at a distance. But now the salt water had come ashore, and the black sky covered the island, and the once-gentle winds had become malevolent spirits, breaking the trees, pushing waves across the lowlands, scouring the highlands. And the things from Below-The-Land, those dark recesses where the bad things came from—they were rising, too. Things were stirring, the elders said, things were mixing that ought to remain separate. The Iwi counted time in bundles of generations, each a bundle of four. And they counted back many thousands of bundles to the start of things, when the Iwi and animals were the same, before they crawled out of the moist earth and became what they were now.

Perhaps because the Iwi tradition was so ancient, they were slow to react. Many of her kin were already gone, buried beneath a mudslide. The village of her birth was now sunken beneath roiling waters. The ancient wall that kept out the predators was filled with debris and became a dam, holding the waters in as they had once kept the enemies out. And now she and a handful of her kin were fleeing toward the high ground of Hanging-Fish-Calls-There, where some said the caves could offer them shelter, shallow as they were, with no deep trails to the Below-The-Land and its dangerous inhabitants.

Now the water was to her knees, and she did not yet see the skyward-yearning earth that led up to the high country. They were still among the ferns and rushes and Make-A-Fist trees that formed intertwined thickets too dense to travel through.

She felt her own heart beating, quick, like a bee. She felt the pulse of Sister-Mother's fear in her fingers.

And she felt something else, in the water.

She stopped, squeezing Sister-Mother's hand, then pointing behind them, where a cluster of trees and bushes drifted in the rising waters.

Koru lifted his spear, and Hiu, too, but they might as well have been wielding twigs. The huge jaws opened, filled with teeth: the Sirenjaw clamped down, and now they were four fingers of kin rather than a handful-and-one.

Sister-Mother lifted her bodily and began to run through the water as best she could. Without her feet in the water, Jia could no longer tell what was happening behind her. She tried to look over Sister-Mother's shoulder, but the rain was now so hard it felt like a shower of stones, and it was *cold*. Jia began to shiver. She felt Sister-Mother's breath, so hard it felt like something tearing inside of her, and she squirmed, trying to get down.

Finally Sister-Mother did put her down, and to her surprise, she felt not water, but soil beneath her feet. It was wet with rain, but she smelled moss now, and the rain-bruised leaves of needleleaf, which only grew on high ground.

She looked up at Sister-Mother, who flashed her a smile-that-wasn't-really-a-smile, but Jia smiled back, a sign of her trust.

There was no one else behind them, Jia saw. Two fingers of kin, now.

They twisted their way through the trees and across rocky meadows. Normally at this time of year, Jia remembered, these open places would be blood red with Ichor Blossoms, and the wind full of their rotting-meat smell, which attracted flies and more noisome insects and even leafwings, supplementing their diets with the liquor of half-digested insects that the funnel-shaped blossoms contained. The Iwi came here to hunt the creatures for their wings. The smell was here, fouler than ever, but the flowers were black and rotten, destroyed by months of rain.

She felt another turning in the earth below her. A trembling, growing stronger, nearer.

Sister-Mother knew it, too. She could probably feel it in the air, with her ears, as Jia could not. Once again, she grabbed her hand, pulling her along, no longer running uphill, but parallel to the gradual slope.

And then, suddenly, in a moment, Sister-Mother grabbed Jia around the waist and lifted her up, pushing her into the closely spaced, sturdy limbs of a Friend Tree. Confused, Jia, looked down at her, saw the smile-that-wasn't-a-smile, the farewell in Sister-Mother's eyes.

Then a wave of water swept down from the high ground and took her away. Jia glimpsed her hand reaching for a branch. Then nothing.

The tree shook, despite its thick trunk and deep roots.

Panting, her mind bright with fear, Jia climbed up, this branch to the next. But the water was still coming for her. Too soon, she reached the most slender, upper branches of the tree, which bent beneath her weight.

She realized she was staring at her knuckles, pale from her death grip on the tree, at the water rising up the trunk from below, and at nothing else. How tiny her world had become.

So she turned her gaze out and was astonished.

The black clouds piled against the mountains, full of light, glowing red and purple with inner fire. The water cascading down from hills, the birth of a new river, however short its life might be. The trees all bent one way, as if bowing in worship to an unseen spirit in the deep distance. The furious rush of the wind itself. It was terrible, and frightening and beautiful. That was everything about her home at once. There was no mercy in the water, the winds, the clouds, but there was no hatred either. No animosity.

She wondered, not for the first time, if what she saw and felt would be more beautiful if she could do the thing with her ears that other people did; if the "talking air" would tell her something she was missing. She would never know.

She glanced back down. She was still afraid, of course, but her fear seemed a little more distant. She wondered what it would be like to see her ancestors.

The tree shook in a way it had not before. Not from the wind, not from the rising water, but from something else. Something familiar, comforting, but at the same time so much bigger than her.

As the water touched her feet, she saw him, in the distance, coming her way. She waved, she shook the branches of the tree, watching as he waded through the flood. He did not see her, she knew; she was too tiny. His head was almost in the clouds, and his eyes were searching for something far distant, like the bending trees.

She closed her eyes. She knew the words to his hymns, although she could not say them. In her mind, they had their own shapes, taken from the lips of her kin, from their gestures, their expressions. She began to move her hands, to make those shapes.

Though you pass me by, O Kong, we are kin. Though you are great and I am small, we are one. Remember me, if only as a leaf fluttering in the wind.

Then she felt a warm wind on her face and opened her eyes.

He was there, his face filling her entire universe, his eyes, almost as big as her, full of concern. Below her, his hand rose up until it was level with her, within her reach.

He waited. It was her choice.

And it was no choice at all. Her most ancient kinsman, her god, had come for her. What could she do but accept?

She climbed into the huge cup of his hand. He closed it partway, shutting out the worst of the wind and the rain. And then, like a mountain walking he started off. And Jia was relieved, and she was sad, and she knew everything about her world was changed, and would never be the same again.

In His Sanctuary, Present Day

He remembered the glimpse of a tiny creature, one of his, reaching to touch him, the obliterating light that followed. Renewed, he had risen, and fought, and triumphed. He proclaimed himself and the others bowed to him. But no war is won so easily. He knew this from his own memories, but also from other recollections that came to him from a far deeper place, from the darkness before his eyes first opened. They were not the same recollections as those he had experienced himself; there were no colors or remembered shapes or even places, but instead a deep certainty. As his senses stretched to encompass the wind that blew from the heart of the planet and encircled the world above to meet the winds from the sun, as he could feel the slow rivers of molten rock flowing, colliding, swallowing land, giving birth to it, the cycle of hot rise and cold fall in the waters, the pumping heart of the oceans, everything that was *now*, so too did he feel what was, when the surface of the earth was liquid rock, when waters came, when ice covered everything, when the green life came and clawed its way onto bare rock. When many of his kind lived, fighting always, and the New Ones came to try to claim dominance.

He had settled the latest war. And then he had sought his own place to rest. But the same light that had given him the energy to fight had also destroyed that place. So he searched for another, and found it, wrestling it from a terrible adversary. He called the others to their places of rest. And there, in the warmth, in the hollow bones of the earth, he had rested his weary, battered body, knowing that eventually the planet would call him back. He drifted into the half-dream, where present and past were the same.

Time passed, no more than a single blink of his eye, it seemed. Then came an itch, a taste on the back of his tongue. Familiar but not familiar. Out of place and wrong. He tried to ignore it at first, because it seemed so insignificant; a tiny parasite trying to burrow into his scales.

But it grew, and as it grew, so did his anger. They should not dare. They should know better.

He broke from the half-sleep, his dreaming ended. He reached out to the other Titans, those woken by Ghidorah and all of the others, too. They were all still where they were supposed to be, quiet, at rest.

All but one; one that should be there but was not.

He pulled himself up. The time for rest was done. His gaze rested on the gigantic skull of the enemy, the ancient adversary his kind had once driven from this place but never completely defeated. He shrieked his warning, his threat, his growing rage.

And then he began his long journey back to the surface, to find the itch in his scales and end it forever.

Skull Island, Present Day

Kong woke to the sound of leafwings overhead, his arms aching as if he had been climbing. He could not remember what he was pursuing, but it had drawn so far ahead of him he could neither see it nor remember anything but depths and darkness—and a light, of some sort. A light that stung his eyes and flesh and had color like the brightest of skies. And there was an outline, a shape in the clouds. He should know what it was, but he could not quite remember. But he somehow felt it was out there, circling his territory, looking for a way in.

And he felt *wrong*. Slow. Everything slow, and not bright enough. Nothing exactly the right color, and the smells all wrong.

It had been like this. He remembered the rain, the fire in the sky, the water rushing across the land, the stink of everything dying, rotting. Everything darker, wetter, every day. The land bleeding like a wounded thing into the dark waters all around. The enemies from beneath came up, and he killed them, one by one or several at a time. And though they tasted foul, he ate them, for there was little left to eat.

Then, one morning, the sky was clear, the jungle green and alive, as he remembered it. But small, somehow. Not the way it had been. And the colors, the smells…

He looked up at the sky, clean and blue, and for some reason it made him angry.

Jia woke, shivering, pushing a dream away, trying to keep it from her waking thoughts. She didn't want it here, with her, in Mother's house. Let it stay in the strange place between true sleep and waking where it belonged, with the other bad things.

But then she knew; her dream had not been about herself; it had been about Kong.

She went to the window, pushing aside the drapes and looking out into the jungle, but she didn't see him. She glanced at Ilene-Mother, sleeping, and then made her decision. She grabbed her unfinished Kong totem, slipped out the front door and ran, barefoot through the jungle. Here she knew all of the trails, and she had no fear of the bad things. She remembered them, of course, but they were gone now, or far away. She had not believed it at first, but then she had come to understand. The bad things were gone. Along with everything else.

Kong was starting to understand, too. When he did, he would be upset. When that happened, she should be there. And although she could not remember her dream, or the sound that had wakened her, she had a feeling about it. That today might be the day.

She found him, but he seemed okay. She noticed a little clearing, and a rock to sit on. She waited there, working on the little Kong totem. Just in case.

Kong shook the last of the dream from his eyes, from where it had settled like dust on his fur and limbs. He found the running water and waded through it until he came to where it fell in a great rush from high above. He put his head into the falling water, then his whole body, let it beat down on him, flow through his fur, cooling him, bringing him further out from the place he sank into when his eyes were closed.

He looked at the sky again, at the bright light of day. He scowled, thumped his chest once. The sky and the sun did not respond to his threat. That was nothing new, but somehow, today, it felt as if they might. As if they were somehow an enemy that had sneaked up on him.

In the nearby forest, he picked out a tree of the right size. He grasped it and heaved it from the dark soil, tested its weight. He twisted off the part that went into the dirt and then he stripped off the limbs and broke off the top part, which was too thin. He began grinding the light end of the shaft against a stone, until it formed a point. He hefted it again.

Then he saw her, the little one. She stood looking up at him, holding up an even smaller thing toward him. For a moment, he felt his anger lessen. He remembered her kind, the little ones. Finding her in the tree and taking her under his protection. He leaned down near, making eye contact, so she would know he saw her and was glad that she was there.

But even she could not make him forget his purpose. He stood back up, lifting the thing he had made from the tree. Then he took aim at the sun.

When he was smaller, he had done that many times, and also thrown things at the dimmer orb of night. He did not like things that were out of his reach, and although he had always been disappointed his missiles fell short of their radiant targets, he had thought one day he would hit them. When he was bigger and could throw further.

Then he'd had other concerns and stopped thinking so much about the round-sky things and how to hit them.

But he was bigger now and had taken a dislike to the bright circle and the sky that held it aloft.

He let the tree fly, grunting as he put his whole body into the throw.

Up it sailed, high above the trees, the cliffs, far into the blue sky. He watched, concerned it would fall short once more, but hoping it would not.

Then the tree hit the circle light of day, with a sound like stone cracking.

Kong stared for a moment, unsure what had happened. Weird patterns of light flickered above, and the dead tree stayed where it was, stuck in the circle of daylight.

He roared in anger, staring at where he had wounded the sky, at the strange way it bled.

Jia stopped, looked up to where the tree was stuck in the sun. Even though she knew, even though she understood, it was still strange to see. Kong kept looking at it, making angry, uncertain noises.

She ran up close and got his attention again by shaking a sapling near him, then waving her arms. He resisted looking down at first, but then he noticed her. He tilted his head, and his expression softened a little.

I know it's strange, she signed. *It's okay. It's okay.*

His hand came down near her. He extended one of his fingers, carefully. She placed her hand on it.

Try not to be mad, she signed, touching his hand. He looked at her, then back at the fake sun he had stabbed, then turned his head to take it all in.

She hadn't understood at first, either. She had seen the ships, the flying machines, the odd houses the Awati built. But this had been more than she could imagine, at first. A house so big it looked like the jungle. Outside, the sky was dark, even in the day, and the storms never stopped. Inside, the sky was blue, and the sun shone down.

But it was not real. She had known it for a while. And now Kong knew that, too.

Dr. Ilene Andrews had only been asleep for an hour when her phone began to ring. She considered ignoring it for a moment, until it entered her sleep-fogged brain that—in this remote location, with this degree of security—she couldn't be receiving an outside call. Something was wrong, here, and now. She sighed, rolled over, and picked up.

"Andrews," she said.

"Dr. Andrews," a voice came back. She thought it was Forteson, one of the techs. "There's been a problem. Kong breached the biodome."

She was fully awake now.

"Breached? What do you mean 'breached'?" She went to her bedroom window and threw open the shade, but the jungle outside closed off her view of most of the valley.

"He, uh, made a spear out of a tree and threw it at the ceiling. He put a hole in it."

"In the ceiling," she said. "Is he still in there?"

"Yes," Forteson said. "But I think he's figuring it out."

"Yeah," she said. "I'll be right there." She was about to hang up when another thought jolted through her.

"Jia!" she called. "Jia!" Phone still in hand, she bolted to the second bedroom. The bed was empty. She put the phone back to her ear.

"Do you know where Jia is?" she demanded.

"She's with him," Forteson said. "We spotted her a few minutes ago."

Of course she was.

"Should we send someone in there after her?" the tech asked.

"No," she said. "Absolutely not. I'll handle this. Get Ben and have him meet me there."

"Yes, Doctor."

She pulled on pants and a shirt, then grabbed her blue jacket. She had let her long brown hair down for the night. She preferred it tied up in a bun, so it didn't get in the way, but she didn't have time for that.

She saw Kong almost immediately, long before she saw Jia. He was the tallest thing in the place, with the exception of the cliff with the waterfall. He was at or near his full growth now, over three hundred feet tall.

When she spotted Jia, Ilene slowed down; the girl was standing in front of Kong. Her best guess at the girl's age was that she was about ten; she had light brown skin, black hair, and a heart-shaped face. She was wearing a white shirt and dark pants that Ilene had given her, but she had tied her red maiden shawl over the shirt so it formed a cross on her chest. That, the leather circlet on her head, and her necklace of leafwing teeth were all that remained of her original wardrobe, and she rarely went anywhere without all three of them on.

She had seen Jia and Kong like this before, silently communing, and she had wondered if the bond was merely emotional or if they were somehow conveying real information to one another. Whatever they were doing, Ilene was afraid that if she moved nearer, it might upset the delicate balance of Kong's mood. He tolerated Ilene, indulged her attempts to teach him sign language. But if he was in a bad mood, he was not necessarily at his best around those he considered strangers. And although she had been working with Kong for ten years, she knew that in his mind she still fit that category.

Not so Jia. Jia was a member of the Iwi, the indigenous people of the island. It had once been Ilene's dream to study their language, or what was left of it, even though it was exceedingly hard to coax the Iwi into speaking it. They seemed to have little use for vocal communication to the point that some early observers had reported they had no spoken tongue. However, a few Iwi had demonstrated the ability to learn English, and an earlier linguist had determined that they did have a spoken tongue, but concluded that the Iwi had replaced almost all of their verbal communication with signs, facial expressions, and body language.

In her decade on the island, Ilene had confirmed that. It was a fascinating and possibly unique situation among human groups, most of which communicated primarily through the spoken word.

In the last few years, and especially since taking Jia under her wing, she had begun to develop a theory, although she wasn't yet sure enough of it to commit it to writing, much less present it for peer review. It seemed possible that their extensive use of non-vocal communication might stem from their close relationship with Kong. The Titan's vocal cords weren't suited to producing anything like human language, but his facial and body expressions were as versatile as those of humans. It might be that in emulating their god, and in learning to communicate with him, they had developed an interspecies pidgin that had no verbal component and had gradually adopted it as their day-to-day language. Of the few words recorded before she came along, a few showed Oceanic origins, almost certainly brought to these shores relatively recently by Polynesian wanderers. But the core of their language did not seem to be related to any other Pacific languages, or indeed, any known language whatsoever. It was a puzzle she had been excited to tackle. She'd had a little success, recorded about a hundred words, and worked out a descriptive grammar of their tongue. But that took years. She'd begun to realize that the spoken language was more like a fossil than anything else, that the truly relevant questions should be about the way they actually communicated and their relationship with Kong—and then tragedy struck.

The storms that had once hidden the island from the outside world had intensified and moved inland. Massive flooding and mudslides ensued, and the dangerous species of the island went berserk for the several months it took most of them to die off from lack of sustenance. She had tried to get the Iwi to relocate, either to the biodome they were building for Kong or to another island. They resisted, and when she returned to their village for one final try at persuading them, she'd found that the whole lot of them had vanished. Since that time, no member of the Iwi had been spotted alive, and she had reluctantly come to believe that they were extinct.

Except for Jia. The way the girl told it, Kong had rescued her when some of her people were trying to make it to higher ground. Ilene had found her with the Titan and brought her to live with her.

The girl was deaf from birth. She used her own sign language based on Iwi non-verbal communication, but there were limits to that. She was a quick student, however, easily mastering the American Sign Language that Ilene had learned in graduate school, and together they were able to communicate with a mixture of the two.

Like all of her people, Jia had a connection to Kong, a complicated one. Early visitors to the island had seen that the Iwi worshipped Kong as a god, and that was true enough. But it went deeper than that; they believed that Kong was Iwi, and the Iwi were Kong. Symbiotic; one people with different forms. It was not unheard of to find such belief in indigenous cultures—the idea that animal spirits and gods were also relatives—but the Iwi–Kong bond seemed especially tight. And Jia's connection to Kong was another thing again. At times, she swore the girl and the Titan could read each other's minds. At the very least, Jia often had a calming influence on him.

But at times like this, when Kong was agitated, Ilene worried, nevertheless.

The Titan could crush the girl with his pinky and might not even notice until it was too late. The size difference was just too great, and Kong's mood too mercurial. Jia never seemed to feel in danger, but children were often unaware of the dangers around them, especially when they were trusted, familiar, and had been a part of their lives since birth.

She turned her gaze up to where Kong's makeshift spear still hung at the top of the dome. The illusion of a "sun" was broken. It could be repaired, but Kong would remember. His cognitive level was high, and his memory had proven to be very good indeed—especially when it came to things that had caused him pain or pissed him off. Kong had been born with a chip on his shoulder. He could hardly be blamed for that: his parents were killed by Skullcrawlers just as he came into the world. So he knew how to hold a grudge.

She heard the sound of an automobile approaching, and moments later a Jeep came to a screeching halt. Her assistant Ben hopped out, wild-eyed, looking from the damaged dome, to Kong, to her. He adjusted his glasses.

"Dr. Andrews, did you see that?" he asked.

"This habitat's not going to hold much longer," she told him.

"No kidding." He ran his fingers through his short black hair. "I mean … look at that."

She watched him pace nervously.

"We need to start thinking about off-site solutions," Ben said. "Someplace where he can't, you know, break the freakin' sky."

"The island is the one thing that's keeping him isolated," she said. "It's his territory. Most of the other Titans seem to recognize that, including the big guy."

"Except that bat."

"Camazotz was different. He was challenging Kong for the island itself. And that was our fault. If Kong leaves here, it's like he's signaling he's in the mix for the planet at large. If he leaves, Godzilla *will* come for him. There can't be two alpha Titans. The whole theory of an ancient rivalry stems from the Iwi mythology."

"He's gotten too big, over time," Ben said. "This environment won't sustain him much longer. It's too unstable."

Ben was right about that. Cut off from the sun by the perpetual storm, the landscape stripped by constant flooding and deprived of the sunlight, the once lush island was a rotting mess. The flora and fauna in the biodome were all that remained. The biodome provided full-spectrum light to sustain the plant and animal life in the dome at healthy levels. But an animal the size of Kong required an enormous amount of food, far more than the limited ecosystem could naturally provide. Already they had to ship in meat to satisfy his hunger, megatons of it. Clearly the Titan suspected something; he had attacked the "sun" on purpose. The illusion wasn't good enough to fool him anymore. Once it really sunk in, what would he do next? Probably find one of the walls and start pounding on it. The structure could handle that for a while, but between the relentless storms and Kong's attack on the artificial barrier that sustained this place … well, it was only a matter of time. But what she'd said about Godzilla was also true. It was an impossible situation, and she couldn't see a clear way out.

To her relief, Jia had noticed her; she'd left Kong and was coming their way. Ilene smiled, trying to keep her troubled thoughts to herself.

She gathered Jia in a hug. She didn't have any children of her own, but she had started thinking of Jia that way, and she believed the girl reciprocated, at least to a certain extent. She realized she was hugging almost too tightly; she had been more frightened for the girl than she had been willing to admit to herself.

After a few seconds, Jia pulled free, stepped back and started signing.

He's angry, she said.

Ilene glanced over at the scowling Kong.

Go wait *for me, sweetie,* she signed. She didn't want to continue her discussion with Ben with Jia nearby. She was learning to read lips, Ilene knew.

Jia's face shifted subtly into an Iwi expression that Ilene interpreted as, "Whatever, Mom." But she did as she was told and got in the jeep.

Ilene glanced at Ben. "Off-site would be a death sentence," she said.

"You don't think the King could take care of himself?" Ben said.

"Beat Godzilla in a fight?" she said. "Maybe." Probably not, given what she knew of the other Titan. Either way, she did not want to find out. Kong was the last of his kind. She could not tolerate having the extinction of his species—or the death of him as an individual—resting on her shoulders. Her job was to keep him from harm, not to mention shield the world from the kind of collateral damage a Titan battle could produce. She would do her level best to do both of those things.

"There has to be another way," she said. But even to herself, she did not sound convincing.

FOUR

So listen up, class. Way back in the day there was this
guy named Odysseus. He got caught up in the Ancient
Greece version of the military-industrial complex,
went all the way overseas to fight in a war that did not
make one lick of sense. And when it was over, all he
wanted to do was get home to his wife. But the gods,
you know, were pullin' the strings behind the scenes,
so it took him ten years to get home. And that's on
top of the ten years he was fighting in this nonsense
war. So—trying to get back home—he comes across
this island where everybody eats this lotus plant,
this drug that keeps them mostly asleep and feelin'
good. They don't know what's going on, and they
don't care. They're happy that way, even if some lion
or something comes and eats one of them once in a
while. So all you listening to this—that's you. Most
of you. Lotus Eaters. Your lotus is video games,
television, social media, videos on the internet. For
some of you it's actual drugs. Most of you are asleep,

and you like it that way. I am not here to talk to the sleepers. I'm here for the ones half-awake. Who want to know. Who want their eyes wide open.

I had this teacher in sixth grade. If you said you were mad, she would say, "You aren't mad, you're angry. I've seen real mad people. They eat pillows and such."

She was a good teacher. One of the few I liked. But she was wrong.

This is Mad Truth, Mad as in all-in, Mad as in crazy, Mad as in for real—but also Mad as in angry, because I was asleep myself, and I slept right through the end of my world. And this shit is gonna get crazy, and it's gonna be angry, it's gonna be out of your comfort zone, and it's gonna be real. This is the first, but it ain't gonna be the last. I'm here to stay, ya'll. Buckle in for the ride or get off now.

Mad Truth, *Titan Truth Podcast* #1

Pensacola, Present Day

Mark Russell woke from an uneasy sleep and lay in his bed for a few moments, trying to remember exactly where he was. It was dark, the only light in the room the digital clock that told him it was five-thirty. So he still had thirty minutes of sleep before he had to wake Madison...

That made everything click into place. This was Pensacola, Florida. He and Madison had been here for almost a year. After he had returned to Monarch—after the battle in Boston—they had been shifted around the globe, sometimes moving four or five times a year. When the position in Pensacola had come open, he had insisted upon it. It was stable, long term. Madison could attend the same school for the remainder of her secondary years, settle in, make some friends, have something like a normal life. And he had family here, his older sister Cassidy. Her kids were grown and gone, and she didn't mind pitching in to help him with Madison from time to time.

As he sat up, he realized he smelled bacon. He followed the scent into the kitchen, where he found Madison cooking.

"That smells good," he said. "What are we having?"

"Morning, Dad," she said. "I'm working on my omelet skills today." He watched as she tilted a little non-stick skillet full of egg and then flipped it to form a half-moon shape. For an instant, he saw her as the little girl she had been not long ago, with the short haircut that flipped up at the ends. It was his default image of her, the one that came to mind when he was away from home. He wondered if it was like this with all parents, to have a younger picture of their child stuck in their heads. The image was no longer a good fit; she was fifteen now, and she'd grown her brown hair out long in the last year, not to mention sprouting up six inches.

"You know, you don't have to do this," Mark said. "I'm capable of making breakfast for us."

"Sure," Madison said. "I'm a big fan of your fabulous cereal and milk. And you make a mean … toast."

"Hey," he said. "I can cook."

"It's fine," she said. "I like doing it. It reminds me of…"

She didn't finish, but he knew where she was going with it. When Madison had lived with her mother, he gathered that they had become more like roommates than mother and daughter. Not in a bad way; Madison had always liked to pull her weight and Emma had encouraged a certain amount of independence in their children.

53

And, boy, had she succeeded. Madison had shown that back in Boston, three years ago. He was still surprised to this day that he hadn't dropped dead of a heart attack during that whole business. He still woke with the cold sweats sometimes, from nightmares of finding her in the wreckage of their old house, not breathing, pale as death.

He felt like he was still playing catch-up in a race where he had only one leg, trying to find a balance with his daughter. He wanted to give her what was left of her childhood, if he could, but it was also achingly apparent that she was mostly beyond that now, or thought she was. She was fifteen and fully convinced she could take care of herself. In a couple of years it would be over. And he had missed so much, they had missed so much together. It felt like what they had left now was gold.

"How's work?" she asked, as she added a new batch of beaten eggs to the pan.

"You know, about the same."

"But he's been sighted, right? The first time in years?"

"What?" Mark said. "Where did you hear that?"

"Mad Truth," she said. "It's a podcast I listen to."

"Oh, right," he said. "The one about chemtrails and crop circles and tap water and all of that."

"And Titans," she said. "He claims Godzilla was sighted near Kiribati in the Pacific."

Mark sighed. "There was *a* sighting. Of something. We haven't confirmed that, and anything you see or hear on the internet is just speculation."

"Maybe," she said. "But Monarch is taking it seriously enough to look into it, aren't they?"

"What's your security clearance?" he asked. "I forget."

"Yeah. I thought so," she said. "You're not denying it."

"No," he said. "Like I said, we're not sure what the islanders saw. We're trying to get to the bottom of it.

You know, through observation. Facts. Not conspiracy theories on the internet."

"Right," she said. She flipped the omelet, placed two pieces of bacon on the plate with it, and handed it to him.

"You can go ahead and eat," she said.

"I'll wait until you're done," he said. "We'll eat together."

"Okay."

A few minutes later, she settled down and started poking at her food.

"Something else on your mind?" he asked.

She nodded. "Sort of," she said. "You remember you said we could talk about homeschooling?"

He sighed. "I know you're not one hundred percent happy at your school ..."

"I'm miserable," she said. "I'm way ahead of everyone. And they all hate me."

"Josh doesn't hate you."

"Josh doesn't count," she said. "Anyway, he and I could stay in touch."

"Madison, if I could just stay home all day, maybe. But you know I have to work. And you, of all people, know how important my work is."

"I know," she said. "But I've looked into some online stuff. And Aunt Cassidy said she could help. All you would have to do is sign off on some things, and you could do that in the afternoons."

"It's a good school, Madison. I just want you to give it a chance."

"I've given it a chance," she said. "It's not working."

"You're not in a position to make that decision," he said.

"Why?" she said. "Because I'm just a kid? Because you know so much better than me?"

"Madison, these are important years for you. You've spent most of your life around people far older than you are. You've never really developed the social skills to deal with your peers. I know it's not fun—"

"Dad, it's Lord of the freaking Flies."

"I know it's not fun," he pushed on, "but you need to try. I know you have that in you. And you are already so much in your own head, and your podcasts, and these conspiracy theories—"

"It's Godzilla, Dad," she said. "Something's happening—"

"And it's not your concern," he said. "Look, you grew up too fast. You had to. And you have been through things I can't imagine having experienced at your age. I know you feel … responsible. But honey, you did your part. You did more than anyone. Now you need to take a break. You have to believe me when I say Monarch's got this. *I've* got this."

"Like last time, you mean?" she said.

"Maddie—"

"You want me to trust you," she said. "But you don't trust me."

"It's not that I don't trust you, Madison…"

She shoved her seat back and stood.

"I've got to get ready for school," she said. "Make myself presentable, you know. It's all about the clothes at my age, right?"

Before he could conjure up some magical, cure-all response, she was back in her room. He lowered his head to the table and bumped it three times.

Monarch Office, Pensacola

The Pensacola office was far from the center of the Monarch universe, and Mark liked it that way. He'd had his fill of being in the middle of the action, at putting himself and those he loved in mortal danger. At the same time, he had most of the data available to him that anyone with his security clearance had, so there was plenty to do. And what he did mostly was look for trails and patterns. He was a kind of glorified Titan analyst.

His background was in animal behavior; he had started with cetaceans—orcas, dolphins, and such. After leaving Monarch the first time, he had worked with wolf packs. The common denominator was his interest not in the behavior of individual animals, but in how *groups* of animals acted. That was the perspective he had brought to the attempt to understand the Titans; while it was tempting to think of creatures like Godzilla as solitary, unique actors, he was certain that none of them could be fully understood without reference to one another—and to a lesser extent, to humanity. That point of view had come in handy when Ghidorah was running amok and Titans across the globe were breaking out of confinement. Mark had recognized that despite being wildly different species on the surface, all the Titans were behaving like a pack, with Ghidorah as their alpha, calling the shots. That, in turn had led to the conclusion that they needed another alpha to confront Ghidorah. Godzilla. It had paid off, but the cost had been high. Mothra, a Titan allied with Godzilla, had given its life in that battle. So had Vivienne Graham, Ishiro Serizawa, and Emma, Mark's wife—Madison's mother.

And now he searched for trails and patterns, and for the past three years there had not been much to see, but that didn't stop him from going back over old data, rethinking it, preparing for the day when they would come again. Preparing for a time he fervently hoped would never happen.

And yet, this yahoo Madison listened to through her earbuds might, for once, be right.

Monarch had re-tasked several satellites overnight, along with tuning up the web of air and undersea sensors. The tale the data told this morning was unambiguous; there was no mistaking the twin bioacoustic and radiation profiles.

"Godzilla," he murmured under his breath. Not what he had been hoping for.

"You see it?" Chloe asked.

"Yeah," Mark said. "Have we had any movement?" Chloe was the intern on the night shift. She was young, but very good at her job. She had blond, curly hair that he suspected required a fair amount of effort to maintain. He usually missed her—she was almost always gone before he showed up in the morning—but Madison had left for school early, and he hadn't seen any reason to stick around the house with her gone.

"Yes, he's definitely cruising," she said. "Kind of exciting. This is the first time I've actually seen a Titan on the move. I was in high school, back in the day."

That made her, what, twenty-one? Twenty-two? Younger than he'd thought. A handful of years older than Madison.

"No worries," Mark told her. "That doesn't make me feel old at all. Let me have a look." He bent over her shoulder to examine the interactive chart showing several projections of the globe.

Madison was right; Godzilla had been spotted near the Micronesian islands of Kiribati two days ago. Now, after a global search expanding out from there, Monarch had located him. They were tracking him using various forms of telemetry, one of which was based on the passive bioacoustic characteristics of the ORCA that Emma had used to communicate with the Titans to devastating effect. This version could only receive, not transmit, and along with satellite surveillance, was one of their best early warning strategies against not just Godzilla, but all of the Titans.

He studied the Titan's meandering line. There was

no way of knowing where Godzilla had first started this journey, but extrapolating from the remnants of his trail, it looked like he'd taken a swing by Fiji, passing Kiribati on his way to a certain storm-covered island east of there. After that, he came near the South American coast, then followed it down to the southernmost tip of the continent. From there he had begun moving toward Antarctica before taking an abrupt turn north.

"He's patrolling again," Mark said.

"You mean for other Titans?"

"Right," he said. "Three years ago, right after the fight with Ghidorah, he did something we'll call 'the big cleanup.' Some of the other Titans didn't exactly stay in line. He went on a global walkabout and set them straight. He drove Scylla from Georgia. He ran Amhuluk out of the Amazon, and so forth. Not long after, they all ended up going dormant. We think Godzilla may have sent out some sort of silent signal, although we aren't sure how."

"He attacked humans, during that period, too, didn't he?"

"Yeah, but those were some very bad actors who were taking advantage of the chaos at the time. A terrorist group. They had taken over an offshore oil rig and had captured a Titan, Na Kika, using a stolen containment net, apparently with some sort of plan to mine her parts for use in bioweapons. Intelligence thinks it might have been an offshoot of Jonah's bunch, but I have my doubts about that. Monarch got wind of it and sent some jets to check it out. Then Godzilla showed up and wiped the floor with them. I think it fits in with the rest of his pattern during that time. It was like Godzilla was sorting things out, establishing himself as king, so to speak. And then he went silent. Disappeared. We haven't heard a peep out of him for almost three years. Or any other Titan, for that matter—Kong excepted, I guess."

"Looks like he checked on Kong," Chloe said, nodding at the map.

"We have him at Fiji first," he said. "That's where Rodan ended up. He cruised by Skull Island for sure. But he has never bothered Kong there—we're not a hundred percent sure why. And he checked on Quetzalcoatl, then Scylla. Then it looks like he was going to have a look at Methuselah, but he never got there. He went north instead."

"You think he's headed for the Amazon?" she said.

"Maybe," he replied. But it felt a little off. Godzilla had left Behemoth in the Amazon basin, where it hadn't been any trouble. It was hibernating like the rest of them, and the locals liked it a lot; some literally worshipped it. And why would Godzilla skip checking up on Methuselah when he was less than a hundred miles from it and head north instead?

Or maybe what felt "off" was the notion that he could predict what Godzilla was going to do. He had spent years of his life hating the Titan. His son Andrew had died in San Francisco during Godzilla's fight with the MUTOs—Massive Unidentified Terrestrial Organisms— and after that Mark had been a firm believer that the only good Titan was a dead one. It had taken a while for him to come around, to realize that Godzilla and humanity had a common enemy in Ghidorah. But how far did that go? With Ghidorah gone and the other Titans either submitting willingly to Godzilla's rule or being beaten into submitting to it, what was his agenda now? Godzilla wasn't just a big, dumb lizard. There was a brain in there, one Mark believed was pretty sophisticated. Emma had believed that the Titans existed as a check against the harm humans might do in the world; in releasing them, she had believed she would heal ecosystems devastated by pollution, deforestation, and climate change.

The thing was, Emma had been right. Not morally or ethically—dooming so many innocents was out of bounds, no matter how laudable the ultimate ends. But since the Titans had emerged, the rainforests were once more gaining ground, reefs were healing, climate change had ground to a halt and was even reversing. But now, humans were starting to put their thumbs on the scale again. People were forgetting, returning to the practices that had screwed up the global ecosystem so badly in the first place. The global ecosystem that Godzilla was apparently the steward of.

What if Godzilla came to see not another Titan as his competition for alpha predator, but the human race as a whole? Maybe three years ago he had seen humanity as the lesser of two evils, and one of those evils was now gone. Perhaps his priorities had shifted to meet the new reality. Maybe he had changed.

If so, then it was like Emma all over again, with Godzilla making the cold calculation that a certain amount of human death and misery was necessary for the good of the planet.

"Mark?" Chloe said. He realized he had been staring mutely at the screen for a long time.

"Sorry," he said. "I was just thinking. Your shift is over, isn't it?"

She nodded. "Yes, but Kennan is late."

"It's okay," Mark said. "I'll keep an eye on things until he gets here."

"Thanks," she said.

As she left, he poured himself a cup of coffee, then went back to his workstation and started doing his weekly report. But he kept glancing back at the map, and Godzilla's track.

You're thinking too much, Mark, old boy, he thought. *This obsession nearly wrecked you once. It nearly cost you everything. Do not let it happen again.*

But twenty minutes later, with the track still showing no evidence of veering toward any known Titan locations, he took the time to fire off a communiqué to command and control.

"Be advised," it said. "In my opinion, Godzilla tracking suggests behavior not in keeping with past patterns. Could indicate unpredictable outcomes. Godzilla may be off the reservation."

Skull Island

Ilene looked up as Jia padded almost silently into the room, wearing her moon-and-star pajamas and carrying her little Kong doll. She wore her red shawl like a cape.

You're supposed to be in bed, Ilene signed.

I couldn't sleep, the girl replied. *Are you still mad at me? I wasn't mad at you. I was worried.*

Jia tilted her head; her posture broadcast skepticism.

Fine. I was a little mad at you. Ilene admitted. *But mostly worried.*

Kong would never hurt me, Jia replied. *He and I are all that are left. All of the others are gone. He saved me.*

I know that, Ilene said. *I don't think he would hurt you on purpose. But he is so big, and he doesn't always pay attention, especially when he's angry. Haven't you ever stepped on a bug by accident?*

I watch out for bugs, Jia signed. *A lot of them can hurt you if you step on them, or if they bite you. If you step on a Blackstick bug, your whole foot can rot off.*

Don't pretend you don't know what I mean, Ilene said.

Okay. What are you doing? What are these pictures?

Ilene followed the girl's gaze to her desk, where she had two screens full of images and two dozen hard-copy prints overlapping one another on the desk.

Jia pointed at one of the images, a photograph of an "X-Ray"-style painting, an ancient trend in which people and animals were depicted with their bones and organs—and sometimes unborn offspring—showing through their skin. In prehistoric times, the style had spread to every inhabited continent and a number of islands. No one was sure why. The image in question looked something like a stylized man, but he also had a tail and an elongated face.

What do you think this is? she asked Jia.

Jia looked at it a little more closely. *Not an Iwi drawing,* she signed.

No, Ilene agreed. *This is from another people, far away. You tell me, then,* Jia said.

A lot of people think it's what's called a… She paused. There was no sign for it. So she spelled it out phonetically. *Chimera. That's when you combine different kinds of animal together, or people and animals. Some very smart people think this is a bear or lion and human chimera. A god of some kind.*

Jia scrunched her brows. *Then why does it have a star inside of it?* She pointed to a mark that resembled an asterisk, right along the backbone of the depiction. *And why these sticks on its back?*

A costume maybe? Ilene signed.

No, Jia said. *I think it's a bad lizard. He swallowed a star. Bad Lizard?*

Jia seemed to struggle. She closed her eyes, and then she, too, spelled something out phonetically.

Zo-zla-halawa.

Ilene blinked, wondering if she had seen that right, or if Jia had gotten it correct. The girl was, after all, deaf, and seemed to have been born that way. But she had a knack for connecting phonetic signs to spoken language, probably from lip-reading. It was often surprising how much of the spoken Iwi language she remembered, and how quickly she had come to understand English.

The first two syllables didn't mean anything to Ilene. But *hala* meant "enemy," and *wa* was an intensifier—meaning something like "great," or "superlative"—and also a verb conjugation that signified "eternal time" or maybe "forever." Great eternal enemy? The Iwi called Skullcrawlers *Halakrah*: "persistent enemy."

Zo-zla? she repeated, to be sure.

But Jia just shrugged. *I may have the word wrong*, she admitted. *Long ago story when I was little*.

"How much do you remember?"

Zo-zla-halawa, he lived in the Long Ago Below, like Kong, like us. He ate a star there and it made him evil. He could throw rays of the star out of his mouth and burn things. So it was decided he could not live in the Long Ago Below.

Iwi and Kong made bonds of friendship. Become one people to fight Zo-zla-halawa. They fought for a long time, trying to make him leave. Something went wrong, I think? Someone broke a taboo, maybe. Anyway, Kong and Iwi traveled together in darkness until we reached the light of this place. We left all of the bad people behind, and the Zo-Zla-halawa, with his stomach star, too. There was peace for a while, but then some monsters followed us. The Skullcrawlers and some others. Kong's parents fought them. So did Kong.

I didn't know you knew that story, Ilene said to the girl.

I was very little, she said. *I don't remember very well. But they told it with hand-shape-shadows at night around the fire. It was scary, but funny sometimes. There were other stories, too, like the one about the Mother Long Legs that raced the Mountain Turtle.*

Ilene nodded. Jia's account sounded like a children's

version of a story she had managed to get one of the elders to tell her years before. The version she had taken down had been much longer, much more complicated, and probably seventy percent of it had been an intricate Iwi genealogy which began in mythic time—in the "Long Ago Below"—but also involved incorporating later arrivals to the island into the Iwi people—that part of the epic was known as the Marrying of Strangers. The most prominent of these were a group of people led by a woman named Atenatua who arrived on the island around five or six centuries before; these people spoke a different language from the Iwi and had different customs, but by a series of marriages and rituals the Iwi and the newcomers eventually became one people, and Atenatua was an important ancestress, despite her overseas origins. Ilene's guess, based on the few words of their language that survived, was that these late arrivals had been Polynesians, speaking a language similar to that of Easter Island. The *atua* in Atenatua was almost certainly the word for "god" or "spirit." A fragment of this story had been recorded, in garbled form, by Aaron Brooks—but she had been the first to learn that the core of the Iwi claimed to have come together with the Kongs—there had originally been many of them—to the island from a lost paradise deep in the Earth.

I heard that story, too, she signed to Jia. *It reminded me that many people believe they emerged from beneath the Earth, in many places. And many believed they were leaving enemies behind them, under the ground. And, as with the Iwi, those bad creatures sometimes followed them to this world.*

It was true. The Navajo, for instance, the Hopi, the Choctaw.

Jia was leafing through the other images, stopping on one.

Zo-Zla-halawa, she signed again.

"Yes," Ilene said. This time the image was less ambiguous; drawn not by someone depicting a rumor of a creature but by someone who had almost certainly seen it. It was bipedal, like the first, but the tail was long, decidedly lizard-like, as was the snout; its arms were short and clawed, and it had fins on its back that at this point almost anyone in the world would recognize.

This was carved on a wall in a city under the water, she told Jia. *Some friends of mine saw this and took pictures. And see, with him?* She pointed to the much smaller figures clustered around the lizard-like giant.

People, Jia signed. *Not Iwi.*

Ilene nodded. *I think that long ago, the creatures you call Zo-Zla-halawa and the family of Kong fought a war. One of your elders said that, but there are stories from other places. Many people believe the gods fought a great war, long ago.*

They fight it still, Jia said. *I remember that now. It is sad. Why?*

What are they fighting about? Jia asked. *No one ever said. I don't think anyone knows,* Ilene replied.

There is only one Kong now, Jia said. *Must he go to war? Not if I have anything to say about it.*

Jia thought about that for a minute. *The Zo-Zla-halawa. What do the Awati call them?*

Awati was the Iwi word for anyone that wasn't Iwi. It meant "people from the sky," and referred to the pilots who had crashed on Skull Island during World War II and the later, Monarch-sponsored expeditions that had arrived by helicopter.

Godzilla, she signed. And then, aloud, putting Jia's hand to her throat and exaggerating the movement of her lips. "Godzilla."

Godzilla, the girl signed. *How many of them?*

I'm not sure, Ilene replied. *But I think just one.*

Jia held her Kong doll a little tighter. *I hope their war is over, then,* she said.

So do I.

Because if it is not, Jia went on, *I will have to fight with Kong and help him kill Godzilla.*

FIVE

From the notes of Dr. Chen

*The ancient Maori believed there were ten worlds
beneath the surface world. The lowest was the home
of the goddess Miru and her hordes of reptile gods.*
—TU-TE-WANA' *from* TU-PARI *gat* KAWEAU, TUA-
TARA,
PA-PA, MOKO-MOKO, *lords of lizards and of reptiles;*
O'er them MOKO-HIKU-WARU *rules as deity and
guardian,*
*Rules in peace!—a god of evil, he in darkness dwells
with* MIRU,
In the eighth gloom dwells with MIRU, *goddess of
three nether regions;*
Dwells in evil thoughts with MIRU...
TU-TE-WANA' *from* MAI-RANGI *gat the many gods
of reptiles*
That in darkness sit with Miru...
...Conflict endless, rends the dwellers in thy waters;
*Unremittingly thou warrest on the creatures made
by* TANE',

Slayest trees, and birds, and insects, preyest on thy
forest brother:
Internecine warfare shatters sons of thee on earth, in
ocean!

Excerpts from *Maori Life in Ao-Tea*,
Johannes Carl Anderson, 1907

Monarch Office, Pensacola

Mark spent the next eight hours reviewing Godzilla's last
known activities, all of which had happened years before.
He had told Chloe that he thought Godzilla was mopping
up the competition during that period, but maybe he'd been
wrong about that. People tended to anthropomorphize
animals and their actions, and it was possible that he and
the rest of Monarch had fallen into that trap.

Mark had been there in Boston, after Godzilla—with
the help of Mothra and the united military of the human
race—had defeated Ghidorah.

There were still a lot of questions about that fight.
The Titans seemed to be hierarchical in nature; they
had a pecking order, and whichever one was strongest,
whichever one came out on top, seemed to control the rest.
Godzilla and the three-headed Gidorah had been battling
for that top spot until the government made a bad call,
overruling objections from Serizawa and other Monarch
scientists. They had experimented with a weapon known
as the Oxygen Destroyer, trying to wipe out Godzilla and
Ghidorah with a single missile.

The missile had nearly killed Godzilla, and in fact at
first they thought it had—but it hadn't had any noticeable
effect on Ghidorah, and Ghidorah had then proceeded

to take command of more than a dozen Titans, many still in containment. The results were devastating, and it soon became clear that nothing in the human arsenal could stop Ghidorah, who seemed intent on stripping the world back down to its bedrock bones. Subsequent studies of Ghidorah's DNA had suggested that the three-headed dragon was so genetically different from the other Titans—and life on Earth in general—that it might not even be a native of the planet. Mark doubted that; it seemed extreme to invoke an extraterrestrial origin when there was so much they still didn't know about the evolution of *any* of the Titans. But for whatever reason, Ghidorah was different. While many of the Titans—Godzilla, Kong, Mothra, Behemoth—seemed to be dedicated to preserving some sort of global balance—part of a failsafe system to keep the environment from going too far off of the rails—Ghidorah was certainly not that. If it had been able to continue on its rampage, projections suggested that the only thing left alive on the planet at this point would be Ghidorah and certain bacteria.

But it had not succeeded; Godzilla had ended it, and soon after, more than half a dozen Titans, summoned by Ghidorah to kill Godzilla, had instead literally bowed down to him.

But that complete obeisance was short-lived; a few of the Titans had clearly had their fingers crossed behind their backs while they were bowing. Scylla, that truly weird chimera of arthropod and cephalopod, had attacked the coast of Georgia, apparently in an attempt to feed on an A-bomb that had been lost at sea there for decades. Godzilla had kicked Scylla so badly it had fled all the way down to an island near the tip of South America, where it had hibernated in a freezing lake. Behemoth, who had broken out of the containment center near Rio de Janeiro, had settled peacefully down in the Amazon, where its presence was clearly a healing influence on the human-ravaged rainforests there. When Behemoth was attacked by Amhuluk—another Titan that refused its Godzilla-mandated bedtime—the big lizard showed up and weighed in on that too, tipping the confrontation in favor of Behemoth. Then he had gone into the deep sea, reappearing to deal with a rogue human operation in the Sea of Okhotsk and freeing the octopus-like Titan Na Kika to return to her rest at the bottom of the sea.

And then, someplace in the South Pacific, Godzilla had vanished.

It was not the first time. It was well established by that point that Godzilla and other Titans could use parts of Hollow Earth to take short-cuts in their journeys. But this time Godzilla stayed away, out of sight, as he had been in the decades, and perhaps centuries, leading up to his appearance in 2014, when he had come from some deep hiding place to destroy the insectile MUTOs in their rampage from Japan to San Francisco. After that emergence, Monarch had been able to keep tabs on Godzilla, tracing a fairly stable pattern of patrol through the vast currents of the world's oceans. He had briefly emerged to battle yet another MUTO, a fight Emma had been involved in, but other than that he had remained quiet, but visible, at least to Monarch.

But these last few years, nothing. Houston Brooks and Nathan Lind conjectured that Godzilla had returned to the deeps of Hollow Earth. It seemed to Mark as plausible an explanation as any, and as far as he was concerned, good riddance. Godzilla might have proven he was nominally an ally of humanity, but whatever his motivations, the collateral damage of any Titan contest was devastating. He no longer believed that the only good Titan was a dead Titan, but he certainly believed in letting sleeping Titans lie.

And now Godzilla was awake. That could not be good.

He spent most of the day confirming the status of the other Titans. A few, like Godzilla, had gone somewhere off the map, but most of them were right where they were supposed to be, according to Monarch surveillance. He could not rule out the possibility that one or more of the Titan locations had been compromised by terrorists, and that the surveillance data was misleading, but everyone he shouted out to came back with the right answers.

So he did the only other thing he could do—continued tracking the one Titan that *was* out there and on the go.

But off the coast of French Guiana, about seventy klicks east of the Îles du Salut, Godzilla vanished without a trace. The bioacoustic and radiation signatures just vanished, and the underwater drones tracking him at a distance also lost contact.

By that time, Chloe had come back in for the night watch. He thought she looked tired and disheveled; she had put her hair up in a band. He hadn't seen her wear it like that before. He felt for her. He remembered his first experience with a Titan.

"That's past the mouth of the Amazon," she noted. "So he's not likely checking in on Behemoth. Do you think he's headed for Isla de Mara?"

"Nobody home there," Mark said. "Unless Rodan laid eggs or something. Nothing left of the outpost. But there are still people in the area, so put it on the map. But at this point he could literally be going anywhere. I'm putting out an all-points bulletin, and then I'm going home. Call me if anything comes up, and I mean anything."

"Yes, sir," Chloe said.

The night passed peacefully, with no sign of the Titan. When he returned to work, Kennan was on duty. He was a tall, serious fellow around thirty who retained only a whisper of his native Jamaican accent.

By noon Mark was starting to believe he was being overly paranoid. The big fellah had come out of hibernation or whatever to stretch his legs a little, check on some old pals, and maybe now he was all tucked in again for another three years. Or ten. Or a thousand. He had almost turned his mind back to other projects when Kennan said something under his breath.

"What was that?" Mark asked.

"Look," Kennan said. He was pointing to a video playing on his screen. It looked like it had been shot with a phone from a small watercraft of some kind. It showed an expanse of blue sea, and in the distance, what looked like a stony ridge rising from the water. Except that the ridge was moving, leaving a wake—and although shot from a considerable distance, there was hardly any doubt that the "ridge" was Godzilla's dorsal fins.

"When was this?" he demanded.

"It was posted about twenty minutes ago," Kennan said.

"Where?"

"It was taken from a yacht, the *Ima Outahere*," Kennan said.

"Cute," Mark said. "Where is she?"

"En route from Galveston to Veracruz," he said.

"The Sigsbee Deep," Mark said. "Deepest part of the Gulf." That was spitting distance from Isla de Mara, so it looked like Chloe had been right.

"Headed west?" he said, to confirm the suspicion.

"The *Ima* reported him headed northeast," Kennan said.

"Northeast? Bring up a chart."

Kennan complied.

"If that's true," Mark said, studying the map, "He's not

going to Isla de Mara. If he is topside, we should be able to reestablish a fix. Set bioacoustics and radiation signature scans from the Deep to DeSoto Canyon and everything in between. Find him."

"On it," Kennan said.

It was six-thirty in the evening when they picked up the trail again; by then Godzilla was less than a hundred miles from the northern rim of the Gulf. Mark upgraded his message to command and control. By seven, they finally scrambled some jets from the nearby Naval Air Station and diverted nearby coastguard ships to have a closer look. Alarmed, Mark called command and control and was referred to a fellow named Clermont.

"Don't let them engage," Mark said. "Whatever you do. You know what he is capable of. I don't know why he's headed for the Gulf. It might be something inland. Do you guys have any other Titan activity, anywhere?"

"No," the Monarch official, replied. "Nothing. What do you advise?"

"His path has been wobbling, like he's triangulating on something," Mark said. "Right now he could come ashore—*if* he comes ashore—anyplace between Biloxi and Panama City. We'll know more in an hour or so. We should start evacuating everything in between."

"That's a lot of territory," the man said. "I don't think I can make that case. And as far as we know, Godzilla is still a friendly."

"It doesn't matter how friendly he is," Mark said. "If he comes ashore, for any reason, he's going to break things. Like buildings and highways. People are going to die."

"Look," Clermont said, "we're doing what we can, for

now. When he gets closer, if you still think he's coming ashore, we'll be ready. We've got relief staff on their way already."

"Prevention is way better than relief," Mark said.

"Look, most likely he'll turn, right? We're running projections, and none of them have him coming ashore. He's avoiding human populations, just like he's been doing for the last three years."

"I think something's changed," Mark said. "I feel it in my gut. Something new is happening."

"Just keep us updated," Clermont replied. "And stay away from the press. The last thing we need at this point is a panic over nothing."

What about a panic over something? Mark thought. But he knew when he was at the wall. Yet as the next hour passed, and then the next, it became clear that Godzilla was headed straight for Pensacola.

Why? Because there was a Monarch base here? Could the Titan somehow be aware they were tracking him? Maybe. Or at least he might have noticed the aircraft surveilling him, even if they were keeping their distance. Had Monarch escalated an innocent situation by putting things Godzilla recognized as weapons into play? Mark had seen that happen once, in the Monarch base near the Bahamas. Maybe if they called everything back… But Godzilla had been on his way here long before they sent out the jets. He was overthinking.

"Enough of this," he said. He called Clermont back and told him that if he didn't evacuate the waterfront, he would call the Federal Emergency Management Agency himself. The official made noises that sounded agreeable but didn't really amount to much. Godzilla was now only twenty miles offshore and showing absolutely no signs of turning. If anything, the Titan was speeding up.

Mark took out his cell phone and called Madison.

Russell House, Pensacola

It was sometimes possible for Madison to close her eyes and just *sleep*. But all too often what she saw on the back of her eyelids made that impossible. Ghidorah, stalking her, destroying the ball park around her. Scenes of mass carnage. Her mother, in the distance, Ghidorah stooping over her, ending the woman who had sung her to sleep at night, nurtured her, mentored her. The therapist her dad had sent her to had said it was post-traumatic stress disorder, and she figured he was right. She had seen monsters, a lot of them, up close and personal. And she had known monstrous people, who murdered without conscience. And for a time—a short time, but still far too long—she had been on the same side as them.

So maybe she was a little messed up. But she could not just give in to that. That could not be her identity. She refused to be a victim.

She sat up, looking around her room. Her command center. The many computers, the maps, the incident charts, the newspaper clippings.

Clearly this was going to be one of those nights when sleep would not come easily. She didn't let it upset her anymore. If she occupied her mind with something else for a while, she could try again later. She had some homework; maybe she could turn her attention to that. Like most of her homework, it was just time-wasting drivel, guaranteed to bore her into unconsciousness.

Then she remembered. Mad Truth was about to drop his latest podcast.

She grabbed her phone and navigated to the site; saw he was uploading in four minutes. She went to the kitchen, filled a water bottle and returned to her bedroom. Her earbuds in, she took the pen and legal pad she kept by her bed for taking notes.

Mad Truth—also known as the Real Deal, Titan Truth, Weathervane, and Godzilla Watch—had a low, confident, and obviously digitally altered voice.

Hello, loyal listeners, welcome to TTP, Titan Truth Podcast episode 245. Today is the day. Maybe the last podcast I ever record. And look, I know I said that last week ... and maybe a few other times, but the point is this—I'm sick of waiting for the right moment. Five years of deep cover at Apex Cybernetics is enough. I'm about to walk in and download hard evidence and expose a vast corporate conspiracy. If I walk out of this at all. And if this is my final broadcast, no regrets.

Madison listened intently, parsing every syllable. A lot of what Mad Truth said was a sort of code; if you hadn't been following him from the start, you might not get half of it. She had all of his podcasts archived, so she could cross-reference them whenever she needed to.

She had been skeptical of him at first, and still was, to a point—maybe half or more of Mad Truth's speculations were nonsense. But at the core of it—and especially when it came to the Titans—she thought he was probably on to something. Because she had been inside of a conspiracy, a big one. One that had almost destroyed the world, and her mother had been the architect of it. So, yes, she believed in such things. Like Mad Truth.

Don't call me a whistleblower, he went on. *I ain't whistling. And this ain't a leak, either, this is a flood. And you better believe I'm gonna wash away all of Apex's lies. You can believe that.*

She waited for more, but then realized he had signed off.

That was a short one, Madison thought. Too short, given how he liked to rattle on, building his case, piling up evidence until his conclusions made themselves. Maybe this time Mad Truth really was about to do what he had been planning all along, to go through with it. But he had said it himself, this wasn't the first time he'd been right on the verge of blowing everything wide open, and so far, he had never followed through.

She sighed and put the phone in the charger. She wasn't ready to sleep yet. Maybe it was time to see about that homework.

Then her phone rang. She saw it was her dad and rolled her eyes. Why did he always call when he was coming home late? Why couldn't he just text like a normal person?

"What is it, Dad?" she answered. "I'm kind of busy here at the opium den."

"Yeah," he said. "That's great, honey. But listen, I sent Jeanne—you remember Jeanne?"

"The Jeanne you work with? Seaman Baskin?"

"Yes. She's coming over to give you a ride, okay?"

"A ride? Why? To where?"

"Look," he said. "I can't really explain over the phone. She'll probably be there in about ten minutes. Grab whatever you need for an overnight."

"Overnight? What's going on?"

"Probably nothing," he said. "I just want you here, with me, okay? I'll feel better."

"Well … okay," she said.

"I love you, honey."

"I love you too, Dad," she said.

She put down the phone and started stuffing things into her duffel bag. The only place to sleep at her father's work was in the bunkers underneath it. That could only mean one of three things: hurricane, tornado, or Titan. And it wasn't a hurricane or a tornado, because a) the weather was clear, and b) Dad wouldn't hesitate to mention either of those over the phone.

Shit, she thought. *Mad Truth.* Did this have something to do with him? With him going after Apex tonight? It was hard to believe it was a coincidence.

A few minutes later, Jeanne showed up, or rather, Seaman Baskin, part of the military detachment in the Pensacola office.

"Have they started evacuating the waterfront?" she asked Baskin.

Baskin frowned, clearly hesitant.

"Dad called," Madison said. It wasn't a lie.

"Oh, so you know, then," Baskin said. "Don't be scared. You'll be safe where we're going. And your dad sent someone for your aunt."

"Which one is it?" Madison asked. "Scylla? Rodan?"

"No," Baskin said. Then she got it. "You didn't know, did you? You tricked me."

"Dad wouldn't say over the phone," she said. "But I'm not an idiot."

"No, that would be me," Baskin said. "But I guess it's too late now. No, it's the big one. Godzilla."

"That can't be right," Madison said. "Godzilla doesn't attack for no reason. One of the others must be near."

"If they are, I haven't heard about it," Baskin said. "And I sincerely hope you're wrong. One of these things is plenty for me."

"You don't have to worry," Madison said. "Whatever he's doing, he didn't come here to hurt us. Or anyone. You'll see."

SIX

The atheling of Geatmen uttered these words and
    Heroic did hasten, not any rejoinder
    Was willing to wait for; the wave-current swallowed
    The doughty-in-battle. Then a day's-length
elapsed ere
    He was able to see the sea at its bottom.
    Early she found then who fifty of winters
    The course of the currents kept in her fury,
    Grisly and greedy, that the grim one's dominion
    Some one of men from above was exploring.
    Forth did she grab them, grappled the warrior
    With horrible clutches; yet no sooner she injured
    His body unscathèd: the burnie out-guarded,
    That she proved but powerless to pierce through
the armor,
    The limb-mail locked, with loath-grabbing fingers.
    The sea-wolf bare then, when bottomward
came she,
    She grabs him, and bears him to her den.

The ring-prince homeward, that he after was powerless

(He had daring to do it) to deal with his weapons,

But many a mere-beast tormented him swimming,

Flood-beasts no few with fierce-biting tusks did

Break through his burnie, the brave one pursued they.

The earl then discovered he was down in some cavern

Where no water whatever anywise harmed him,

And the clutch of the current could come not anear him,

Since the roofed-hall prevented; brightness a-gleaming

Fire-light he saw, flashing resplendent.

From the Anglo-Saxon epic *Beowulf*, date disputed,

circa 700–1000 AD

Apex Facility, Pensacola

Bernie Hayes stared at his laptop screen for a few more heartbeats, at the button for uploading to the SoundCloud. Then he clicked it.

No turning back now, he thought.

But of course, there was. No one knew who Mad Truth was. He hadn't yet blown his cover at Apex. Maybe he wasn't ready for this yet.

He turned on the car light, pushing night out of the cramped vehicle.

An itch in his sinuses suddenly turned into a sneeze.

Yeah, he thought, fishing out his sinus spray. *I'm a real international super agent.* He opened the glove box, spilling out empty chip bags and food wrappers, crammed his laptop into it and closed it up. It wouldn't help if someone was really on to him; they would search the car from end-to-end, probably take it apart. But it was an expensive piece of equipment, and he didn't want to tempt anyone to smash his window in to take it. If that happened, it would probably end up being sold to a hacker who would wipe it so they could re-sell it—and in the process find more than they bargained for. That might create a trail, leading back to his car, to him…

Good thing I'm not paranoid, he thought. Maybe he should just take the damn thing with him.

No. That was even riskier. His car was a blight. No one was going to break into it unless they saw something valuable on one of the seats. He was pretty sure a bunch of empty chips bags wouldn't attract anyone's avarice.

As he reached for his fanny pack, he caught a glimpse of himself in the rear-view mirror and thought how different he looked—from back then. Just a few years ago. Would she even recognize him now?

Of course *she* would. Sara. In some way or other, he felt like she was looking down on him right now. And if she was, what she would see—better than anyone else ever could—was how freaking scared he was.

"You got this," he whispered to himself. "You got this. You got this."

Eventually you had to either give up or take a stand. And he was not giving up. The stakes were too high. Maybe he wasn't some kind of superhero. But he could do this. For Sara. For everyone.

He got out of the car and paused for just a moment to look at his destination, the Apex facility, and industrial blight blocking his view of Pensacola Bay. Years he had been working there, trying to make it look like he had his head down, that he wasn't paying attention any more than the other worker bees in the building. They ground out their product, they didn't ask questions, they took their paychecks home and pretended everything was fine. They never asked what they were making or why. They didn't care. He hadn't cared until his eyes were opened. When Sara died. Working for Apex.

They had been married about a month when Godzilla and the MUTOs duked it out in San Francisco, but while terrifying and fascinating, it hadn't seemed connected to them in their tiny flat in Port Huron. And then Godzilla ... went away. And like a lot of people, they'd tried to pretend that was the end of it—the age of monsters had ended as quickly as it had begun.

But over the next year, he began to see Sara wasn't over it, exactly. She would drop odd comments about the Titans during mealtimes, or when they were watching TV. Eventually, he came to believe she was a little obsessed with the subject. That hadn't worried him so much. He had his own obsessions. He even joked with her about it, and she joked back.

But at a certain point, her laughter stopped. The jokes weren't funny to her anymore.

And then she had quit her job at Apex. At the time, it seemed to come out of the blue. It was only later that he began to remember the little things she'd said about work, about how she wasn't sure she could take it anymore. She worked a lot, too much, and he had assumed it was about that, and her dislike for her coworkers.

When she quit, they had had a fight. His income wasn't enough for them to live on, and he'd felt ambushed by her decision. She told him she needed a break, that she needed to think about some things. He'd been terrified she would leave him, but after a difficult few days he'd come home to find a present wrapped for him on the kitchen table, and a note saying she was sorry, that she had her head straight and wanted to talk about some things, but that she loved him and it would be all right. That she would bring takeout for supper.

He had got the call two hours later. She had been involved in a three-car collision. She was still alive when he got to the hospital, but she never regained consciousness. He was holding her hand when she died.

The next two weeks were a blur, largely spent in a drunken stupor. The third week he had finally worked himself into going through her things. In the desk drawer in her home office he had found a single note.

Godzilla > Apex > Monarch Contract > shipping manifest > component for bomb.

The next day he had brushed up his resume, quit his job, and applied for a position at Apex.

I go in there almost every day, he thought, still staring at the building. *This is not a problem. No one will even notice you.*

Feeling a little more confident, he started walking.

One of the perks of working at Apex was that you were exposed to a nearly constant barrage of propaganda about how great the company was, how essentially altruistic they were. Even in the employee locker room, where a television screen was running the latest company ad. It began with scenes of three years ago, after the Titans ravaged much of the planet, followed by scenes of Apex helping rebuild. The voice narrating the video was that of the company's CEO, Walter Simmons.

When we started Apex cybernetics, he said, *our dream*

was to extend the power of cutting-edge technology to everyone around the world. Then the world changed. We learned monsters are real. And we knew we had to dream even bigger. We dreamt of strengthening our cities against the Titan threat and making our homes safe. We dreamt of new ways to defend ourselves and keep the human race in full control of our destiny. Robotics, automation, artificial intelligence.

Images of wheat fields, next-generation windmills, robots playing chess, some dude in a helmet with wires, and the latest satellites were replaced by a new well in an impoverished African village. Nice touch.

Who knows what brave new future we'll dream up next?

Then Bernie was looking at the man himself, Walter Simmons, surrounded by the happy children of the village, well-hydrated with disease-free water.

I'm Walter Simmons, he said. *And it is my privilege to lead Apex into humanity's bold new era. We're not going anywhere, and neither are you.*

The children cheered, Simmons laughed, and Bernie bit his tongue.

You knew, he thought angrily. *You knew what was going to happen three years ago. And you capitalized on it.*

That had been the subject of his third podcast: How Big Tech knew the Titans were coming. How Apex had the contract to supply certain elements for a secret weapon known as the "Oxygen Destroyer" and how the whole thing had been covered up after a failed attempt to use the weapon, an attempt that had directly resulted in Ghidorah's reign of terror.

After being betrayed by one of their own, Emma Russell, and after losing more than half of their number to the Titans, there were plenty of disgruntled Monarch employees ready to talk, at least off the record. The picture some of them painted of Apex's role in the disaster wasn't pretty. But with Simmons's money and influence, and with the government itself complicit in covering up their own screw-ups, the relationship between Apex and Monarch had been swept very far under a very deep shag rug.

Just wait, Simmons, you jackass, he thought. *I'm gonna nail you. You think you're immune, but nobody is immune to the truth.*

For an instant, he was afraid he'd said it out loud, but, if he had, none of the other employees starting their days around him seemed to have heard him.

He clipped on his badge and fanny pack.

Just be cool, he thought. *Just act like you know what you're doing. Most people don't ask questions, and especially not these people. It's why Apex likes them.*

Yeah. Of course, it was also why they got rid of anyone who was on to them. By whatever means necessary.

Horace pulled up the shipping manifest and the routing map. The logistics of this shipment were complicated, and this was going to take the better part of an hour to work out, but that was what he liked about the job. He got to work puzzles all night, and he got paid for it. He excelled at his work, and because he was so good at it, people generally left him alone, and they let him work the night shift, which was very quiet and exactly how he liked things.

Studying the manifest, he reached for the apple he'd brought to snack on.

"No!" someone said behind him, causing him to jump a little. "It's incredibly unhealthy!"

Horace looked at the doorway of his Plexiglas cubicle and saw a stout African American fellow in coveralls and a tool belt staring at him as if he wasn't even aware he was interrupting something. What was his name? Ernie? Bobby? No, Bernie, one of the guys from engineering.

"All those GMOs?" Bernie went on, obliviously. "Growing a second head could be useful, you'll have to let me know. Myself? I can barely handle the one head I got."

"Bernie," Horace said, trying to smile politely, "you're not supposed to be in here." *There*, he thought, turning back to his screen. He figured that was the end of it.

It wasn't.

"You ever wonder about what we're doing here?" the guy blathered on. "What we're *really* doing here? From what I hear they've inlaid nano-circuitry in a field of turnips in Idaho."

Why one earth would anyone just walk up and start babbling like this? What was wrong with this guy? Horace was starting to feel crowded, with Bernie blocking the door like that. Not threatened, exactly, but extremely uncomfortable.

"Why are *you* here?" he asked. "This isn't engineering."

"Because, you know, they're rendering these new specs which is going to take over…" Bernie paused and looked at his watch. "Oh, this is stuck in calendar mode," he said. Then, before Horace could even flinch, Bernie reached out and grabbed *his* arm, twisting it so he could see *his* watch.

"Over an hour," Bernie continued. "Maybe even more. So my foreman told me to take a walk, make some new friends."

Oh, crap, Horace thought, as Bernie got even deeper into his already highly compromised personal space.

"Now that we're friends," Bernie pushed on, "I can share something with you, right? Okay, cool, you're going to love this because when I found out, it blew my mind."

Horace had been wondering if the nightmare could get any worse, and it immediately did. Bernie emptied his fanny pack onto Horace's desk.

"Oh," Bernie said. "Um, can you hold onto these things? They're very important to me. This is hand sanitizer I made from my own garden, it's really amazing. A compass because I get lost around here, it's a big place. Do you have any oils on your hands? This is a battery I made that is very sensitive to that. Ah!"

He picked up a tiny circuit board. "See this? Check this out."

Horace looked at it.

"Yeah?" he said.

"You see that?"

"I do."

"That right there is radio mesh networking with a voice-record sub-processor … guess from what, c'mon."

"I don't care," Horace said.

"A toaster!" Bernie said, with a weird air of triumph. "Look at this thing. You know my Sara, she said this is how it begins. Robot uprising, right here."

That was it. There was no way he could be near Bernie for another second. Horace got out of his seat. He felt like he had termites all over him.

"I have to go to the bathroom," he said.

"Oh," Bernie said. "Is it one or two? Because if it's two it's probably from those apples. Hey, you want to use some of the hand sanitizer that I made? Okay, I'll just … stay here."

Bernie's voice faded with distance as Horace fled the scene.

Santa Rosa Island, Florida

Jenny Tuazan swam in darkness, enjoying the gentle pressure of the water enveloping her. Other nights she might have walked a few hundred feet south and enjoyed the surf rolling in from the Gulf of Mexico to break on the thirty-mile-long spine of Santa Rosa Island. Those nights she would ride the waves, sometimes fight them, like some ancient goddess of the sea. So she had pretended when she was a girl, and secretly did so even now as she approached thirty. When she was a child, her family had come here often to camp and swim and beachcomb. It was less than a hundred miles from where she had grown up in Louisiana, but it had always seemed so different, so exotic to her. So far from the family business, which also involved the sea, but there it was all work, long hours on the boats and then mornings pulling the heads off shrimp. This place, with its white beaches, restaurants, hotels, and National Park had been all about fun, relaxation, family time.

When she grew up and became a park ranger, she had managed to get a job here, on the westernmost end of the island. After nine, the general public was locked out, but she had the run of the place and full communion with the beach and the bay and the memories they contained for her.

Tonight she wanted solitude and quiet, so she swam on the bay side of the island, across from which the city of Pensacola glittered like so many strings of Christmas lights.

She came up for air and felt the wind; in the distance thunder rumbled; a storm was rolling in. She smiled, thinking how her father would have made her get out of the water at the first sign of bad weather for fear she would be electrocuted by distant lightning. She figured she would take a few more moments here, then walk over to the Gulf side and watch the waves get wild. She was already wet, and she didn't mind a little rain.

Four fighter jets shrieked by overhead. Pilots from the

Naval Air Station training, probably. It seemed like a weird night for it, with the storm rolling in, but maybe the pilots needed to be certified for rough weather, or something.

She took a breath, and went back down, hands searching for the bottom.

And heard something.

There were plenty of things to hear in these waters, even at night. Shrimp boats going out, tourist ships cruising the harbor, comings and goings at the port. Tonight thunder, rolling along the surface of the bay, and the fading sound of the jets. And … helicopters? But this noise she heard now was none of that; it was something different. A sort of deep thrumming, like a heartbeat. She surfaced again and blinked water from her eyes and looked around but saw nothing unusual.

But then the sound—more a vibration, really—changed. She was feeling it now from below her. She went a little shallower, and there it was; the submerged earth beneath her feet was pulsing, very slowly, boom … boom … boom…

Maybe someone was using explosives to generate tremors and search for oil? But they weren't supposed to be doing that, not in these waters.

She turned back toward Pensacola, and when the earth shuddered again, she noticed waves spreading across the bay in the reflected light.

"What the hell?" she muttered. Could it be an earthquake? She had never been in one, and down here she had never expected to be.

Then the stars in her peripheral vision were blotted out. And the resulting darkness … moved.

She stared off west and saw him then, rising from the sea with each step, a massive, unmistakable outline she had seen hundreds of times in stills and videos. And even so, he was so much bigger than she had imagined.

"Godzilla," she breathed.

And as if he'd heard her, the massive, craggy fins on his back flickered with blue light, and then began to glow. She watched in amazement as he moved through the entrance to the bay. Not an animal, not a monster even. A god of the sea, from before the times when any human eye had laid eyes on the world. She saw the jets coming back now, and helicopters drawing near, and wanted to laugh. What could they do to *him*? Piss him off, maybe. If even that.

And then it occurred to her. Godzilla hadn't been seen in years. If he was here, that might mean another Titan was too, like when he'd shown up in Savannah to drive Scylla away from the city.

The prospect of a Titan fight was almost as exciting as it was terrifying.

The water started to pull at her, like when one of the big container ships came in, creating an artificial tide dragging her into the bay.

But this was stronger than that, much stronger, and already her feet were no longer touching the bottom. Gasping, she put everything she had into swimming toward shore, only to watch it recede. She felt panic well up.

She tried to stay calm. Panic killed more swimmers than anything else.

Jenny let go, floating on her back, and allowed the bay to pull her out. Godzilla was already mostly out of the water. Soon the pull would end and even reverse. Then she could easily swim back to the beach and watch whatever was going to happen from there.

Mist rolled in, and then the rain, as if Godzilla was pulling them, too, in his wake.

Apex Facility, Pensacola

That should keep him away for a while, Bernie thought, as Horace's footsteps receded. He slipped a thumb drive from his tool belt and into the CPU tower, began typing commands, and took a bite of Horace's apple.

In moments he had what he was looking for, or at least he thought so. It was a shipping manifest, something being sent to Hong Kong from here, the Pensacola facility, from sub-level 33.

"What are they shipping to Hong Kong?" he wondered. "And what's sub-level 33?"

And also, how? He couldn't find the name or ID code of a ship. Were they maybe sending it by plane? Whatever it was looked heavy for that, but maybe they were in a hurry. Either way, this facility wasn't equipped for that kind of shipping. Maybe they were sub-contracting with someone else in the port. Or they might be using one of the big troop carriers at the Navy base; Apex and the government were tight, after all. The manifest had an entry for maglev data, which also did not make a damn bit of sense. Unless it was an acronym for something he wasn't aware of, maglev usually referred to the magnetic levitation technology used in trains. Which they did not have here in Pensacola.

"What's this?" he muttered.

There was a sort of schematic on the screen. It was circular and looked like a dynamo or a reactor chamber, but it wasn't either. There wasn't enough detail to figure out *what* it was.

It was all very weird, but absolutely something he could investigate. He just had to find sub-level 33.

Before he could follow up on that thought, the alarm went off.

For a horrible second, he thought he had been caught,

that there was a safeguard against copying files that he hadn't known about. He lifted both hands in surrender before realized that it was the facility-wide alarm. If he'd been noticed, or if Horace had reported him, they would have probably sent security to quietly drag him off someplace, not alert everyone in the building. He lowered his arms sheepishly, pulled the USB key and hurried out.

Everyone else was already obediently forming lines. Bernie merged into one, trying to look like he belonged in this part of the building.

"Proceed toward the fallout shelter in a single-file line," a security guard said.

Fallout shelter? What was this? If the place was on fire, or if there had been a chemical spill, they should be headed outside, right? There had been a storm coming in, but could it really be that bad?

Or maybe it was something else. Maybe Apex wanted all of its employees locked underground, where they could easily be scanned, searched, questioned, exposed to certain chemical agents…

The woman in front of him glanced back. Maybe she saw he was nervous. She had a friendly, round face and bangs.

"It's going to be okay," she said.

"You know," he replied, "back in the day they used to use cyanide capsules instead of fallout shelters, keep the secrets in. But that's neither here nor there so don't listen to … me."

Her brow creased, and she acted like she was about to say something. Instead she turned back around.

Again, he thought. No one was listening to him. They were all intent on getting to the shelter, away from whatever threat the alarm portended. No one was paying attention to anything. There would never be a better time than now to figure out what Apex had hidden away on sub-level 33.

And to escape whatever diabolical fate awaited those who stayed in the line.

He watched a few guards and guys in white lab coats run through sliding doors marked "Authorized Personnel Only."

"That way," he said to himself.

As the line turned a corner, Bernie slipped out of it and through the sliding doors.

SEVEN

Loyal listeners, I'm gonna start with another history lesson. This one's about pirates. Yeah, the real thing, not what you see in the movies. Most of 'em started out as privateers. What does that mean? It means they worked for the government. Unofficially. Off the books. So English privateers robbed French and Spanish ships, but never English ones. And the privateers from France and Spain, same rules. And everybody was sort of okay with it, for a while. Then comes along the first multi-national corporations, like the East India company, and they say, this piracy thing is bad for business. And yeah, they're Freemasons, they operate across national lines, we've talked about that before. The point is, it's not the kings and queens and parliaments that have the real power anymore. It's the corporations. And all of a sudden, English privateers are being hung by the English government—that they worked for. In a couple of decades, the pirates are all gone. Because this Company wanted it that way. They want trade to be free, predictable, and profitable. That's what they still want, these corporations. You think they have an allegiance to any country? Think again. They want their stuff to ship on time and get where it's going. And you know what can throw one hell of a monkey wrench in that? Titans. You can't bribe a Titan, you can't lobby a Titan. Like the Tea dudes, Apex can control governments. If Walter Simmons can figure out a way to control Titans, he will. And take it from me, he is trying. But if he can't, then he will absolutely do everything in his power to snuff them.

Mad Truth, *Titan Truth Podcast* #115

Apex Facility, Pensacola

Ren Serizawa watched the storm as it crossed into the bay. The wind was already here, buffeting the rooftop and the helicopter warming up for flight, at times trying to steal off the titanium case he carried from his grip.

A storm at night could be a wonderful thing to see. It could bring with it many surprises. Of course, in this case, there would be no surprise. He knew what was coming. Monarch had ordered the evacuation a few minutes ago, but Apex had known a half-hour before that, because they still cultivated sources inside Monarch. Simmons had been worried about this eventuality; Ren had thought him paranoid. But Simmons had not gotten where he was by being stupid.

After three years, Godzilla was back. Coming *here*. It was not—could not be—coincidence. It was inevitable that he and the Titan would meet. His father had seen to that.

You are out there, aren't you? he thought. *And you, Father? Are you with him?*

Ren did not believe in ghosts, not literally. But he did believe that people left things behind them when they were gone. Memory. Consequences.

And what could be more consequential than a son? A literal, biological legacy?

He knew it was a tired story, the father who never had time for his son. There had been songs written about it. He was not one to bring it up in conversation, or cry about it to a lover when he felt weak. He would not be a stereotype to be pitied and inevitably mocked. He had managed to keep his resentment even from his mother.

He supposed that was because he had always imagined they would reconcile, he and his father. That the old man would have a moment of *satori*, that the fish scales would fall from his eyes, and he would understand what he had been neglecting in the pursuit of his obsession. In pursuit of Gojira.

Of course, his grandfather Eiji had set the pattern. A sailor in World War II, he had lied to his son Ishiro for thirty-five years, claiming to work for a cargo company when in fact he had been drawn into working for Monarch. Eiji had come clean to *his* son, before he died in 1981, and they had had at least a little time to reconcile, for father to pass the torch to son.

But he would never get any such catharsis. His father had all but ignored him in life, but Ren had worshipped Ishiro, nonetheless. He had studied hard, learned to build and create in hopes that his father would someday understand him—or at least take note of him. It was on Gojira that Ren focused his anger. Gojira had felt almost like a big brother to him—the older brother his father truly loved and doted on. And in the end, his father had died for Gojira—a monster who had killed thousands—rather than come home alive to his only son.

His father had made his choice. Ren had made his. What father worshipped, the son would revile. What the father saved, the son would destroy.

That was how it was. That course was now set. His father had chosen to side with monster. Ren chose humanity.

"It's time! We need to evacuate now!" Simmons shouted to be heard, approaching from the facility below.

Ren followed Simmons and Hayworth, the security chief, to the helicopter. Ren caught Hayworth's eye, then looked back at the approaching mist. He thought he could make out a shape there, *the* shape. And then, there he was.

Jets screamed by, and explosions billowed against Gojira's hide.

Hello, brother, he thought. *They don't learn, do they? Those pitiful weapons can't stop you. But I can. I will.* Then he climbed in.

Santa Rosa Island, Florida

The rain was cold, so when Jenny made it back to shore, she took shelter under the eaves of one of the buildings. Godzilla was revealed by his glowing dorsal fins and by flashes of lightning that burned the sky white.

And then—another kind of light, like fireworks, but all the same color.

She blinked as her perspective shifted. Jet fighters, firing missiles at Godzilla. But why? Wasn't he supposed to be humanity's ally? What was going on?

Even as she wondered that, Godzilla's fins suddenly glowed with heat, and a bolt of blue energy erupted from his mouth, stabbing into Pensacola.

Apex Facility, Pensacola

"Okay," Bernie said, as he ran through the corridors. He needed to find an elevator, and he figured there should be one around the turn ahead. "Okay ... not okay."

Because the two armed guards watching the elevator ahead were staring at him.

"You!" one of them said. "Where's your clearance tag?"

Bernie drew himself up. Showtime.

"You know what?" he said. "The fact that you're talking about clearance tags right now in a time of crisis is incredibly unprofessional. We should be talking about evacuation!"

But the show closed as soon as it opened. The guards drew their Tasers.

"Freeze!" one of them shouted.

"Okay," Bernie said, holding up his hands. "Okay."

It had been a nice try. Well, no, it hadn't been, had it? Even that was wishful thinking. He had completely bungled this.

Sorry, Sara, he thought.

They were still pointing their Tasers at him. Were they going to use them anyway?

Bernie heard a dull thud, and the building shook. The guards looked around warily, fingers still on the triggers of their weapons.

Another much closer explosion shuddered the building. Bernie took a few shallow breaths. The guards were a little distracted. Maybe if he made a break for it—

The wall exploded in a shower of sparks. The lights went out as Bernie was slammed into the floor.

I'm dead, he thought. Then: *Wait, am I?* He wiggled his fingers. They seemed to be alive.

The lights came back up, red. The room was completely trashed, rubble everywhere. The guards were out of it, and he—he wasn't dead, but was he injured? He'd heard people in shock sometimes didn't notice fatal wounds until they cashed out. He patted his hands over his body, scanned for wounds.

He seemed to be all right.

Gazing around, trying to understand his situation now, his attention was drawn to a gaping hole in the wall. Through the jagged concrete frame, he saw a round mass of circuitry suspended on scaffolding. Attached to it was a flip-out screen scrolling data, going so fast he only caught a little of it—*running defensive gait analysis … updating predictive algorithm…* And this all came with a soundtrack, too, an awful rhythmic pulsing. He stared, wondering what the thing could be, somehow knowing at the same time that whatever-it-was was why he was here.

And it opened its eye and stared at him. His heart seemed to wiggle in his chest. It wasn't an eye, but a mechanical aperture with something behind it, something glowing red…

"What the hell is that?" he said.

Then he became aware that the whole building was coming down around him. Time to get out.

Skull Island

Kong had been increasingly restless since he had speared the "sun" in the biodome enclosure, but he seemed especially agitated as the new day wore on. As Ilene feared, he had begun testing the other boundaries of his containment. When building the structure, where possible, they had hidden its limits behind natural features, so he wouldn't be suspicious. He was familiar, after all, with cliffs and canyons as barriers or at least impediments to movement. But given the breadth of his reach, there were a few spots they'd had to hide with nothing more than dense vegetation or the illusion of sky, and he had zeroed in on one of those.

But he didn't start pounding at it as she feared he would. Instead, he tore out the tall bamboo and pressed himself against the unnatural barrier—more like he was listening for something than trying to get through. And he seemed—uncertain.

And then, in the afternoon, he suddenly stood to his full height and began hooting, pounding his chest.

A threat display. She hadn't seen that since—well, not since Kong's battle with the Titan Camazotz. What the hell was going on?

Maybe Zo-Zla-halawa, Jia signed.

Probably not, Ilene replied. But it might very well be something outside of the barrier, a surviving Skullcrawler, maybe. She should probably look into that.

She and Jia went back to their little prefab cottage near the entrance of the dome. They had larger quarters in the facility, but crossing through the storm was a pain, and sometimes they spent a day or two on-site. And Jia was more comfortable here, in the little fragment of the world she had lived in for most of her life, near the Titan who had adopted her just as surely as Ilene had.

She went to her workstation and began going through the perimeter camera footage and motion sensor data, but nothing bigger than a squirrel showed up.

Then she noticed the alert on her phone. It was a silent one, so it probably wasn't an emergency, but it was marked urgent.

It turned out to be a Monarch general mailing for her clearance level, and urgent didn't begin to cover it. She threw it to her larger screen and watched in horror as the footage displayed Godzilla crashing into a coastal community. Where was this?

The answer was Pensacola, and the footage was in real

time. It was dark, night-time in the States.

Moments after she started watching, Godzilla stopped his advance into the city and returned to the sea. The cause of his retreat was as much a mystery as his attack. But that was for someone else to work out; she had a puzzle of her own to worry at.

Kong. He must have somehow sensed Godzilla was active again. It couldn't be a coincidence.

But how? Pensacola was half a world away. And why was Godzilla attacking there? The lead report was by Mark Russell, maybe the greatest surviving expert on the Titan, but he didn't seem to have discerned any motive behind the attack.

Whatever the reason, Godzilla was back from his vacation. And if the past was a prologue that meant he was likely to start seeking out threats to his alpha status.

The only Titan that currently fit that description was Kong.

A quick check on Godzilla's trajectory showed he had made a swing by Skull Island earlier and given it a pass. That was a relief, because it meant that the island was still somehow protecting Kong from Godzilla's attentions. But it made her wonder...

Further inspection confirmed her suspicions. Kong had hurled his spear at the "sun" during Godzilla's nearest approach to the island. It might be a coincidence, but Kong had spent a long time in the biodome without losing control. Maybe the fact that Godzilla was out there, on the prowl, had triggered his fight-or-flight instinct. Well, except Kong did not have the "flight" component of that. Or maybe it wasn't that extreme; maybe he had the vague sensation that there was something dangerous out there, beyond his island.

One thing she did know. If Monarch tried to move Kong

off of the island, Godzilla would know instantly. And given what she suspected about the relationship between the two Titans, that would not have a happy ending for anyone...

Tallahassee Magnet High School, Pensacola

Normally, Madison wouldn't have been bothered very much by the intentionally audible snickers from Lara and Alicia as she walked by them. She'd stood toe-to-toe with a three-headed dragon, after all, so what were a couple of mean girls compared to that? Of course, if she was honest with herself, she knew those two things didn't go together. Yes, Titans were objectively more frightening than teenaged girls; Ghidorah had terrified her nearly beyond reason. She had dealt with that because she had been on a mission, and because there had been no option. Coping with kids her own age—that was an option. She had been homeschooled for years, and her memories of elementary school hadn't prepared her for high school. She had assumed making friends would be easy. But if you were even slightly weird here, it was a problem, and she was more than slightly weird. But that was okay. On most days, anyway.

But today was different. She'd spent the night in a Monarch bunker with her aunt, watching her phone obsessively, viewing videos of Godzilla's attack, reliving her oh-so-fond memories of being holed up in a similar bunker outside of Boston, wondering whether or not her mother's associates would slit her throat while she slept.

Back then, at least, she had been able to *act*. She had stolen the ORCA and used it to disrupt Ghidorah's rampage of terror.

Today, with Godzilla's attack over and the Titan already far out to sea, she had something far worse to deal with.

School.

She wandered through the halls, only half paying attention, watching the tiny screen of her phone, trying to find something, anything that could explain Godzilla's behavior. But if it was there, she was missing it.

It had been her own mother who unleashed the Titans on the world. She had believed that doing so was the only way to correct the damage human beings had done and were continuing to do to the environment. And for a while, Madison had been right there with her. She knew it was hard to understand, and she had had difficulty explaining it later, even to her dad. But a huge part of it had been that Mom trusted her with all of her secrets, including her mad plan to use the Titans to save the world. With all of Monarch's data at their fingertips, it had been easy to see the problem—the vanishing rainforests, the mortally wounded Great Barrier Reef, the steady rise of carbon dioxide in the atmosphere, the melting polar ice. Not to mention the extinctions of plant and animal life, all on track to match even the worst extinction events the planet had ever known. But while most of those prior extinctions had happened over periods of thousands or even hundreds of thousands of years, the Anthropocene extinctions were occurring at a much faster pace of a few hundred years. And this wasn't privileged knowledge—everyone knew it. The big oil companies knew it. Big Tech knew it. Politicians knew it.

And they did nothing. Would do nothing until it was far too late.

And then her mother had noticed something. In the places devastated by the MUTOs and Godzilla, life was on the mend. Deserts were blooming, ecosystems recovering. Titans were hard on human beings, but they were good for the planet. So Madison had believed that her mother was doing a good thing. That *they* were doing a good thing.

She understood that some people might die. A few. But the way her mom put it, more people would be saved. And the death of her brother, Andrew, would not have been in vain.

It all made sense right up until the moment that Mom's co-conspirator, Jonah, started murdering people right and left. People Madison knew. And it kept getting worse; Mom had planned to let only a few Titans loose, but in freeing Ghidorah first, she'd made a terrible mistake. She hadn't known that Ghidorah could awaken the rest, release all of the Titans at once—and control them. The result had been a bloodbath.

And still her mother had tried to justify it. And rationalize nearly killing Madison's father. That's when Madison had realized she couldn't be complicit any longer; she had to act against her mother, against Jonah. And finally her mother had come around, sacrificing her very life to try to atone for her mistakes.

And after that, the world had actually gotten better. People were rebuilding, in most cases smarter and better than before. In Boston, Godzilla had shown that he was an ally of the human race. Afterward he was seen a few more times, herding recalcitrant Titans away from human populations, returning them to places of rest. And for three years, there had been peace, and healing.

But now Godzilla was back, and *he* had broken that peace, attacking Pensacola in the night.

Why? she wondered, as she stared at cable news on the TV the teacher was playing in her next class.

"A world at peace, shattered a mere twelve hours ago when the massive Titan, once thought a hero of humanity, made landfall in Pensacola, doing significant damage to the Southeastern headquarters of Apex cybernetics. CEO Walter Simmons had this to say."

The scene cut to Simmons, walking through the

wreckage of the Apex facility.

"This time is about working together," the CEO said. *"To ensure a safer world. From this day forward, I will stop at nothing to destroy Godzilla."*

The other kids in the class were whispering, glancing back at her. Some uneasily, some with suspicion, some outright hostile. The Godzilla girl. The weird girl who had been homeschooled by the woman who tried to destroy the world. Who hung out with monsters and never did anything fashionable with her hair.

More stares. Whispers getting louder, meaner. She frowned, staring straight ahead. She wanted to bolt, but she didn't want to give them the satisfaction. Or get in trouble with the principal again.

She looked down, and noticed a note folded on her desk. She picked it up and slipped it in her pocket.

The day was a loss, in more ways than one. When the bell rang she launched out of her chair. Only then did she unfold the note and read it.

It was from Josh, of course.

You okay? It read. And he had hand-drawn a concerned-face emoji.

She smiled and put it in her pocket. Then she got out her phone and pulled up Mad Truth's podcast as she made her way out of the building.

"Oh loyal listeners I was there! Oh, man, I was there! Godzilla's Apex attack, I saw it go down! You don't think it's a coincidence that he reappears, and just so happens to curb-stomp that specific facility? Ha! No such thing as coincidence."

No, there isn't, Madison thought. If Godzilla attacked Apex, he had a good reason. And Dad would know that, too.

Monarch relief camp, Pensacola

Running on caffeine and adrenaline, Mark had once again concluded that he would rather be wrong about these things than right. Wrong meant people left him alone, he could do his job, go home and listen to Madison complain about how boring her homework was, get a good night's sleep.

Right meant everyone wanted a piece of him: everyone in the office, the volunteers with the relief effort, the press, the Monarch director. He felt like a creature with a hundred limbs and only one head to control them all.

And once the press realized who he was, it was all coming back. All of the stuff about Emma and her associate Jonah, the ecoterrorist who was, by the way, still at large, somewhere out there. Was he responsible for this? Was there another ORCA? Were the events of three years ago about to repeat themselves? Was it true Ghidorah had reappeared at the North Pole?

He didn't blame them. They had every right to be frightened, to demand answers from the organization that claimed to oversee the monsters lurking in the shadows, that claimed to have all of the answers.

And maybe someone at Monarch did have those answers, although given his conversations with his higher-ups he had his doubts. But *he* did not have many answers at all. Godzilla showed up. Godzilla broke things, mostly belonging to Apex, Godzilla left.

"Is it possible Godzilla is being controlled by eco-terrorists?" one reporter asked him.

"I…" Mark began. "Seriously? That's what you're asking me?"

"Dr. Russell," another interrupted, "given his attraction to human-caused environmental change, is it possible Godzilla hates artificial beaches?"

Mark looked at that reporter for a moment.

"Okay," he said. "Does anyone have questions about the relief effort? No? Good." He turned and ducked back into his command tent.

"Somebody at Monarch command wants to talk to you," Chloe said. "He said you aren't answering your phone."

"Enjoying the day shift?" he asked.

"Not so much."

"Me either," he sighed. "I'll talk to whoever it is."

He pulled out his phone and returned the missed call.

"Sorry, Clermont," he said. "I've been a little busy with … things here. It's sort of a madhouse."

"I'm sure," a strange voice said. "But this isn't Clermont. This is Director Guillerman."

"Oh," Mark said. "Director. Nice to talk to you."

"To you as well. Let me come to the point. I need you here, Dr. Russell."

"Here?" Mark said.

"In command and control. Castle Bravo. You're the only one who called this right. I need you."

"That's—ah—flattering," Mark said. "But I have obligations here. I can't just drop everything."

"We can staff up Pensacola," Guillerman said. "But we need you."

"You did fine without me for years."

"Well, that was before Godzilla decided to wipe out random cities for no obvious reason," the director said. "You predicted that."

"I didn't," Mark said. "I only said his pattern had changed. I didn't know what it meant. I still don't."

"And we need you to figure that out. Here."

"Okay," Mark said. "I understand. But until the new staff arrives, I need to be here. And I've also got to make arrangements for my daughter. So if we can just hold off—"

"Understood," Guillerman said. "You don't have to be here tomorrow. This is just notice that you're on call. So make whatever arrangements you have to. If that big lizard resurfaces, I will want you on site ASAP."

Too tired to protest further, Mark agreed and ended the call. He was about to pocket the phone when he saw another missed call, from a different number.

It was Madison's school, with a recorded message that she was truant.

"Dammit, Madison," he muttered. He knew she had gotten there. Her driver had confirmed it.

This, he really didn't need right now. Not on top of everything else.

Monarch Relief Camp, Pensacola

Godzilla was not a precision weapon. His goal might have been the Apex facility, but he had trampled plenty of other buildings as well. Madison knew as well as anyone that when Godzilla was around, there was always collateral damage.

She knew that Monarch would be on the scene, and they were, near the water, setting up relief tents, passing out rations, giving first aid. It was the kind of scene Madison had hoped to never see again. Godzilla had created peace. She'd thought it would last.

But she hadn't come here to gawk; her father was in charge of this region, and he would be at the center of all. All she had to do was head toward where the most yelling was.

She found him without much trouble. But he looked decidedly unhappy to see her.

"What are you doing here, Madison?" he demanded. "You're supposed be in school!"

"Dad, I'm trying to tell you that there's something provoking him that we're not seeing here. I mean, why else would he flash an intimidation display if there wasn't another Titan around?"

"That podcast is filling your head with garbage," her father snapped. "You should be in school!"

"I'm just trying to help!"

"I don't want you to help," he said. "I want you to be a kid! I want you to stay safe."

There was that again. Her mother and father had been separated when the Titans rose. When her dad figured out what was going on, he had done everything he could to save her. And he was still doing that, determined to give her as "normal" a life as possible. Normal house, normal school, everything just right. Except it wasn't, and it never had been. Not since Andrew died, and probably not before.

They reached a mobile office tent, where Monarch employees scrambled around like ants whose nest had just been kicked.

"We needed a plan to keep peace with these things," her father went on, "and the best one we had just went down in flames. The whole world is screaming at me for answers, and I don't have any." He paused and took a breath. "The last thing I need to do is be worried about you."

"Godzilla saved us," Madison said. "You were there … with Mom. You saw it. How could you doubt him? There has to be a pattern here—"

"There doesn't," he said, in a low, flat tone.

"A reason why he—"

"There isn't!"

"How do you know that?" she demanded.

"Because creatures, like people, can change! And right now Godzilla is out there, hurting people, and we don't know why. So cut your pop some slack, would ya?"

Madison had developed a pretty thick skin. She had been threatened by professional murderers. She had stolen the

ORCA device from them and used it to disrupt Ghidorah's control of the Titans. And she had been right to do it. Who knows, if it had not been for her, the world might be a smoking ruin right now.

But her father didn't seem to remember any of that. He didn't want to hear what she had to say, and he didn't trust her, because he wanted her to be some kind of normal kid.

And that hurt, even through the thickest skin. What was the point? There wasn't one.

"See you at home, Dad," she said.

He softened a little. "Yeah," he said. "We've got some other things to talk over. I'm just—this isn't a good time."

EIGHT

From the notes of Dr. Houston Brooks

Two brothers, One Hunahpu and Seven Hunahpu, are invited to Xibalba, the Underworld, by the Lords of Death, who send very strange owls to guide them there. Some living Mayan informants claim to know where the entrance to Xibalba is, although no one has definitively nailed this down.

—H.B.

One Hunahpu and Seven Hunahpu left immediately, the messengers guiding them as they descended down the path to Xibalba, the Underworld. They traversed a steep slope until they came out on the banks of the canyons called Trembling Canyon and Murmuring Canyon. They passed through turbulent rivers. They passed through Scorpion River, filled with uncountable numbers of scorpions, but they were not stung. They came to Blood River, and were able to pass because they did not drink of it. Next they arrived at the River of Pus, which

112

they passed, undefeated. Finally they came to the Crossroads, and there they were defeated.

From *Popol Vuh: Sacred Book of the Quiché Maya*,
written down circa 1554–8

Denham School of Theoretical Science, Philadelphia

"The seemingly unprovoked Godzilla attack on Pensacola has left the world in a state of shock. Monarch officials are scrambling for a response but as of now there is no official directive. Civilians are advised to shelter in place."

Nathan Lind shook his head as he listened to the report on the radio. Shelter in place? What did that even mean when it came to the Titans? Hiding in an inner hallway or doing the old duck and cover was not going to offer much protection if Godzilla stepped on your house, even if your house was built to withstand a hurricane, which many in Pensacola were.

But then what did he know? Just enough to get his brother and two other pilots killed and himself thoroughly discredited. If he didn't have tenure, he would have been out on his ass; instead the Denham School of Theoretical Science was content to let him rot away in this dark office, with a minimal workload of intro courses where they figured he couldn't do any harm. He glanced around the cluttered, unkempt office at his diagrams of the Hollow Earth. The picture of his brother, as he had last seen him, in Monarch flight gear, his helmet with "Unto the Breach" written on it. The piles of manuscripts and books he hadn't looked at in months.

He had dreams, almost every night. Everything happened as it had: their last drink together, the press briefing on the carrier, the planes entering the tunnel.

And at every point in the dream he tried to stop it, make something else happen, say the right thing. But it always ended in that last moment, hearing Dave's last words.

Everything had imploded after that. Monarch, already tender over how they were perceived by the public, left him to hang. No one blamed him by name. But there was a lot of talk of how the calculations had been wrong, that the Hollow Earth theory had not passed the verification test. Other academics reacted with predictable *Schadenfreude*, blasting him as a fringe theorist and holding him up as an example of a pseudoscientist whose nonsense had gotten people killed. There were still people at Monarch who knew better, but they weren't talking. Houston Brooks had retired, and as far as Monarch was concerned, two major debacles on the Hollow Earth front were enough. Pure research for the sake of research was out, replaced by what they considered to be more "practical" projects. At that time the Titans were sleeping; why risk waking more of them up, as they had Camazotz? What if there were a thousand Titans below their feet, just waiting to be riled up like a nest of skyscraper-sized hornets?

He tried to fight it at first, to salvage what he could of his reputation. The fight hadn't lasted long; he didn't have the will or the stamina for it.

He heard a faint sound and turned. He was shocked to see a man standing in his office, a man in a very expensive-looking black suit. His dark hair was styled so it almost covered one eye, and he sported a thin mustache. He wasn't looking at Nathan but was casually surveying the contents of the office. Like he belonged there and was taking inventory.

"Uh, can I help you?" Nathan asked.

The man didn't answer but continued his review of the various news clippings, diagrams and photographs in the room.

"Look, if you need an appointment, my office hours are nine to five—"

"Oh, please, Dr. Lind," another voice said. "Guys like us don't do normal hours, do we?"

Nathan wondered if his jaw had literally dropped, or if it just felt that way. There was another guy sitting across the office—*his* office. From him. How had he come in within him noticing? Had he been that preoccupied?

And this guy wasn't just anyone. He still didn't know who the first man was, but the man who had just called him Dr. Lind was one of the most famous people in the world. There was no mistaking the widow's peak, the salt-and-pepper beard, the slightly crooked smile. Inventor, entrepreneur, a man who thought so far out of the box that boxes were now all but obsolete: Walter Simmons, founder and CEO of Apex Industries. Nathan watched, struggling to understand what was going on, as Simmons approached his book, the one with the ungainly title *Hollow Earth Gravity Paradox and Our New Frontier.*

"I've been fixated on Hollow Earth as long as you have," Simmons said. "Your theory that it's the birthplace of all Titans is fascinating."

"Your book was very impressive," the other guy said, finally proving he could speak. "Brilliant ideas."

"I've got about thirty unsold boxes in my apartment if you want some," Nathan replied.

"Walt Simmons," Simmons said. "Apex Industries."

"Y-yeah, yes, sir," Nathan stammered. "I know who you are. It's an honor."

"The honor is mine," Simmons said. "As is the urgency. Godzilla has never attacked us unprovoked before. These are dangerous times, Dr. Lind. Allow me to introduce Apex's Chief Technology Officer, Mr. Ren Serizawa. He has an … interesting thing to show you."

Nathan watched as Serizawa pulled something up on a pad and then placed it on the table. A holographic globe appeared above the pad—the Earth but depicted in MRI imaging. As Nathan studied the digital globe, he began to pick out density representations, lines of magnetic force—and something else. An energy signature that was substantially different than anything else he had ever seen— but which was also oddly familiar. He had seen similar data before, but it hadn't gone nearly as deep into the planet.

Oh, Lind thought.

"Magnetic imaging from one of our new satellites penetrated the Earth's mantle," Simmons said. "You know what this is."

"Hollow Earth," Nathan breathed, his gaze still picking over it, now identifying hollow spaces, some very large, others smaller but nevertheless distinct.

Simmons nodded. "An ecosystem as vast as any desert or ocean, beneath our very feet."

Nathan continued tracing the contours of it, hardly believing what he was seeing. His theory predicted this, all of this, right down to the global electrostatic barrier, the boundary that certainly marked the gravitational reversal, the Swiss cheese nature of the interior of the world. Although that one central pocket was a little larger than he had imagined.

And that unknown energy represented … he couldn't be sure what it was exactly, but the sheer power it signified agreed with his prediction that there must be some vital force to sustain life in lieu of sunlight and chemical outflow.

"This energy signal," he said. "It's enormous."

"And almost identical to readings from Gojira," Serizawa said.

"As our sun fuels the planet's surface, this energy sustains the Hollow Earth," Simmons said, "enabling life as powerful as our aggressive Titan friend. If we can harness this … life force … we'll have a weapon that can defeat Godzilla."

That was it. That made it all snap into place. Monarch scientists had been debating the nature of Godzilla's metabolism since he had first reappeared in 2014. It was clearly linked to radiation—after all, Ishiro Serizawa had used a thermonuclear bomb to jump-start the Titan—but many speculated that Godzilla *converted* conventionally understood radiation into some other form of energy, which manifested into the beam of unknown energy he discharged from his mouth. *Which did not closely resemble the nuclear particles and waves discharged by a fission or fusion reaction.*

Here was the proof, another sort of energy, perhaps not nuclear in origin, but tied more closely to quantum states…

He noticed Serizawa and Simmons exchange a quick glance. Then, as if they had reached some tacit agreement, Simmons met Nathan's gaze.

"I need your help to find it," Simmons said.

Nathan's first reaction was stunned disbelief, followed quickly by suspicion that they were mocking him. But that seemed like a weird thing for a billionaire tech giant to do, slum down to a basement office just to make fun of a has-been geologist. That left him with the possibility that they were—as impossible as it seemed—*serious*.

Hell, yes, Nathan wanted to say. What came out instead was a bitter laugh.

"I don't know if I'm the right guy for the job," he said. "Did you read the reviews?" He picked up one of his books. "'A sci-fi quack trading in fringe physics,'" he quoted. Then he nodded at their surroundings. "Look where they put my office—I'm in the basement right across from the flute class. Besides, I'm not with Monarch anymore. And Hollow Earth entry is impossible. We tried."

His throat caught on those last words. Simmons softened immediately and glanced at the news clipping about Dave.

"I'm sorry about your brother," Simmons said. "He was a true pioneer."

"Thank you," Nathan said, trying to put on a polite smile, but it was, in fact, all he could do not to break down. He took a steadying breath. Simmons gave him a moment, then motioned toward the holographic globe.

"All forward scans suggested a habitable environment down there. So … what really went wrong? Your brother's mission."

Nathan took a moment to try to distance himself from the subject. To try to explain it dispassionately.

"When they tried to enter," he finally said, "they hit a gravitational inversion. A whole planet's worth of gravity reversed in a split second. Like flying a Volkswagen into a black hole, so … they were crushed in an instant."

Simmons nodded, as if he'd just heard something he already knew. "What if I told you that we at Apex have developed a phenomenal craft that could sustain such an inversion?" He nodded at Serizawa. The technology officer pulled up something on the tablet that turned out to be specs for some sort of machine.

"The Hollow Earth anti-gravity vehicle," Simmons said. "HEAV."

"The right tool for the job," Serizawa added.

Nathan stared at the specs, instantly overwhelmed by the design. This was his dream vehicle, the one he'd seen the possibility of but could never harness the technology to build.

And Simmons had built it.

"We can make the Hollow Earth entry possible," Simmons said. "We just need you to lead the mission." Simmons sat down next to him. "Help me," he pressed.

"Help everyone. Finding this needle in a haystack is our best shot against Godzilla."

Nathan's mind had already shifted into overdrive, something that hadn't happened in a long time. He had theorized on an energy source in Hollow Earth, but it had not been the point of the expedition Dave had spearheaded. That had been pure science, a voyage of discovery.

But he could work with this. If Simmons's objective was to find the energy source, that was okay. It was still a path that led to Hollow Earth, to everything he and Dave had been trying to accomplish. But it did present a bit of a problem—they would have to find it. And it wasn't likely to be obvious to human senses or to the machines that they had created to enhance those senses.

A green plant, an anole lizard—most life on Earth had evolved to perceive the presence of the sun, to react to it. A plant bent toward the light, trying to maximize the energy it could draw from it. An anole warmed its blood in the sun, moved to shade when it was too hot, buried itself and hibernated when the luminary's warmth was no longer enough to power it. Nocturnal animals reacted negatively to the sun, staying hidden when it was out, emerging when darkness came. But, as the surface world's chief source of power, the sun was *salient*, and living things recognized that.

Even if you could not perceive the sun, you could use a sunflower to find where it was; the sunflower would turn toward it.

By that logic, what would turn toward the power source of Hollow Earth?

Nathan stood, walked over to a pile of papers and magazines, and dug out his copy of *A Scientific Future* magazine and the cover article "Kong: Genetic Memory and Species Origins" by Dr. Ilene Andrews.

"I have an idea," he told Simmons. "But it's crazy."

"Love it!" Simmons said. "Crazy ideas made me rich."

Nathan waved the magazine. "Are you guys familiar with the concept of genetic memory? It's the theory that all Titans share an impulse to return to their evolutionary source."

"Like spawning salmon," Serizawa said.

"Exactly," Nathan said. "Or a homing pigeon." He pointed at the holographic globe. "So if this is the Titans' home, and this ... life force sustains them——"

"A Titan could show you the way to the energy source," Serizawa said.

"Yes," Nathan agreed. "With a little help from an old colleague."

Skull Island

Ilene hadn't seen Nathan Lind in almost a year. Back then, he had been sincere, energetic, charming in a clueless sort of way. He had come to Skull Island pursuing the same leprechaun that Houston Brooks and a half-dozen other scientists had come for in the last fifty years—a path from Skull Island to Hollow Earth. She had been caught up in it herself at the time; Iwi mythology suggested that much of the life of the island—including most of the people themselves—had come up from some ancient, mythic underworld. The biological reality of the island seemed to confirm the mythology. If you looked at a continent like Australia, which broke off from Pangaea before the dinosaurs became extinct, you could see that tens of millions of years of isolation had encouraged life to diverge quite radically from the rest of the world; marsupials dominated the megafauna instead of the placental mammals that ruled the other continents, for instance. Monotremes, egg-laying mammals once found everywhere, had survived and continued to evolve in Australia and New Guinea, but nowhere else, exemplified by that weirdest of creatures, the duck-billed platypus.

Biologists and geographers recognized a famous demarcation called the Wallace Line, separating Borneo and everything west of it from Sulawesi, New Guinea, and Australia—all of which had once been a part of or very near a Greater Australian continent known as Sahul that was now partly submerged. East of the Wallace Line was like an alternate universe, an alternative Earth. A place where things evolved differently. And yet, the genetic roots of everything in Australia could be found, both in the fossil record and in living species, on other continents, most notably South America and Antarctica, to which Sahul had been most recently connected.

You could trace a similar line around Skull Island. Call it the Lin Line, after the scientist who first formally described much of the island's flora and fauna. But if the Wallace line seemed to mark a border between what was "normal" in most of the world and the weirdness that was Australia, the plants and animals of Skull Island were a whole different degree of strange. Some looked like odd, often gigantic versions of more widely known animals, but in most cases, these seemed to be cases of convergent evolution, superficial resemblance based on similar adaptations—the way that marsupial moles and placental moles resembled one another, although a placental mole was far more closely related to a whale or a giraffe than to any marsupial. Similarly, though a Skull Island leafwing might superficially resemble a bird, it most decidedly was not.

And unlike the fauna of Australia, it was sometimes difficult to find any close or even very distant relatives on other continents. Skullcrawlers were an excellent example. Genetic analysis suggested that they split off from the amniote line that led to modern reptiles, birds, and mammals before those groups diverged from one another. Yet besides that very distant reptiliomorph heritage, there were no other fossil or living relatives of the Skullcrawler lineage known from anywhere else on Earth. So how and where had they evolved?

One obvious answer, the one Ilene herself favored, was to take the Iwi at their word: they had come from beneath, along with the other animal and plant inhabitants of the island. Isolated, Skull Island had made its own, divergent way. Skull Island, she had famously claimed, was like the Hollow Earth brought to the surface.

When they discovered what was to be charmingly called the "Vile Vortex," Brooks's speculations—and her own—had been vindicated. Nathan's older brother David Lind had become the spearhead of a Monarch expedition to enter Hollow Earth via the Vortex. Nathan, whose theories about Hollow Earth seemed to straddle the plausible and the avant-garde, and who had just published a popular book on the subject, was brought in to consult. It was Nathan who had identified and mathematically described the electrostatic barrier separating the surface of the Earth from the maze of chambers and tunnels underneath, as well as what he called the probability of a "gravity inversion."

Things hadn't gone as planned. Prior to the proposed expedition, the storms that surrounded and protected the island had intensified and begun to creep toward shore. At first, they thought this had something to do with the widespread environmental destruction wrought by Ghidorah, perhaps also linked with climate change, but in blasting the caverns beneath Skull Island—wide enough for planes to go through—they had inadvertently released Camazotz, a bat-like Titan who had apparently "called" the storm to shield it from the sunlight it abhorred. Kong and the pilots training for the Hollow Earth expedition had managed to defeat Camazotz, but the Vortex had been destabilized—and worse, Camazotz had drawn the tempest ashore and sustained it there.

In any case, Nathan's dream of finding a path to Earth's secret depths on Skull Island had been dashed when his brother and two other pilots lost their lives trying to enter the Vortex. Soon after that, Nathan had cut his ties with Monarch. Ilene had made a few attempts to check in on him and how he was doing. None had gotten past a few perfunctory comments, and finally he quit returning her calls and texts entirely. She hated to admit it, but it had been something of a relief; it was hard to watch someone she liked self-destruct.

And now, suddenly, here he was, requesting a video conference. She had agreed, and after working out their very different time zones, they had set up the call.

He looked thinner, hollow around the eyes. He'd grown a beard, and not a well-groomed one. His demeanor was more jaded, or perhaps he was simply exhausted.

"Nathan, you're looking well," she lied. "It's been a long time."

"Yeah," he said, nodding. "It has. I've been, you know, busy. Becoming a laughingstock."

She sighed. "I haven't seen you since … well. I wanted to tell you, I think what happened to you was unfair."

"I got three people killed," he said. "One of them was my brother. I lost over a billion dollars in equipment, and I made Monarch look ridiculous. I can't really blame them for pushing me off the cliff."

"Priorities were changing," she said. "Theoretical work like yours and mine got the shaft. I'm only here because of the investment they made—continue to make—in Kong."

"How's that going?" he asked.

"There's a lot I can't tell you," she said.

"How about this?" Nathan said. "I'll tell you what I already know, and we can go on from there."

"Fair enough," she said, cautiously.

"I know after the Vortex anchored the off-shore storm to the island, you built a containment facility for Kong."

"It's not a containment facility," she said. "It's a biodome. A haven."

"So he hasn't tried to get out?"

She hesitated, unsure what to say. Instead, she changed the topic.

"What's this about, Nathan?"

"I've been offered a job," he said. "By Walter Simmons. Apex. They want to fund an expedition to Hollow Earth."

"Nathan—"

"I know what happened last time," he said. "I know how to fix it. The aircraft we used before were not suited to the job. Apex has the goods."

"And why are you telling me this, Nathan? You concluded Skull Island wasn't a viable entry point. The Vortex is too unstable, not to mention the storm."

"It isn't viable," he said. "But that's not why I called you."

She paused for a moment, trying to read his face.

"Tell me this doesn't involve Kong," she finally said.

"Do you remember what you wrote about genetic memory?"

She frowned, ran the sentence over in her mind.

"No," she said.

"You haven't heard—"

"I don't have to," she said. "The answer is no."

Nathan paused and looked down at his desk. Then he looked back up, and she thought she saw some of his old energy there.

"It's important," he said. "Listen, I don't want to

discuss this anymore long-distance. Monarch and Apex are doing this as a joint operation, with Apex providing the equipment and expertise. Monarch has taken me back on, and, uh—I'm in charge. I'll be flying out this evening to meet with you. All I ask is that you keep an open mind."

"Is that an order?" she said.

"Look," he said. "I understand. I'm not here to railroad you. But I do hope to convince you. Kong is your baby, I know that."

"That's right," she said. "And as long as you keep that in mind…" She pursed her lips on the rest of the sentence, then nodded.

"I'll see you when you get here," she said.

"It was nice talking to you again, Ilene."

"The same, I'm sure, Dr. Lind."

Ilene had worked with several so-called "language apes" when she had been in graduate school, teaching and learning to communicate with them in sign language. One of them, a chimpanzee named Puck, had been a third-generation signer; another, a young gorilla named Fancy, was learning sign from the ground up.

As an anthropological linguist, Ilene had found Puck the most interesting. He had learned his sign vocabulary and grammar from his mother, who had learned it from her mother, and while humans were involved in the process, Ilene was certain she could see a unique language developing, something with striking differences in grammatical construction and semantics than the original language. The meaning of some words had shifted in three generations; the word order was different from English. In Puck's pidgin sign language, she thought she might learn something about how humans invented language in the first place.

Fancy, on the other hand, had mostly been frustrating. With her, language use was still tied mostly to reward, and at times Ilene felt she was merely complicit in teaching an animal to do a fancy parlor trick.

When trying to teach Kong to sign, she wished that she could even get that far, but in more than a year she had not had the slightest of successes. She had begun the attempt when she noticed the Titan watching her and Jia communicate. He still did that; he seemed to be fascinated by their signing. He seemed less interested when she tried to teach him, but it did not stop her from trying. Intelligence was a messy, awkward thing to measure, but there could be little doubt that Kong was at least as intelligent as a chimpanzee. His brain was gigantic, of course, but to understand its capacity, you also had to factor in the size of his body. Intelligence, generally speaking, had to do with the *relative* size of brain and body. Chimp brains were not just absolutely smaller than human brains but were smaller in proportion to their body mass as well. Radar and sonar brain scans taken while he was unconscious suggested Kong's brain was closer in relative size to that of a human than that of a chimp or a gorilla. Yet it wasn't just about size alone, but about how the different parts of the brain were arranged, and Kong's brain was … strange.

Today had not started out more hopeful than any other. But Ilene felt a touch of desperation. Nathan was on the way, and whatever he wanted—whatever *Monarch* wanted—it probably was not going to be good. Some part of her felt that she needed a breakthrough immediately. She needed to get into that huge head. To be able to talk to him.

And today, he was following her—she was sure of it.

Watching her fingers, listening to her voice, amplified over the loudspeaker.

You: Kong, she signed. *Me: Ilene. She: Jia.*

His eyes shifted with the words.

Yes, she signed. *Good. Can you talk with hands? Say "Kong"?*

That was easy. All he really had to do was point to himself. Bonus if he made the sign Jia had made up for "Kong."

At first, he didn't do anything, so she went back through the whole rigmarole.

Then to her shock and delight, Kong lifted his hand. His lips parted, not threatening, not showing teeth. A convivial gesture, a greeting even.

Come on! she thought.

Kong then scratched his nose, let out an extended, windy yawn, and turned away.

She closed her eyes and sighed. When she opened them, Jia was there between them.

Ha, ha, she signed.

It's not funny, she said. *Jia, this could be important. If we could communicate with him, really talk to him—that could be huge.*

Jia shrugged. *He doesn't talk,* she said.

"Tell me about it."

NINE

Soon after the Earth (*yahne*) was made, men and grasshoppers came to the surface through a long passageway that led from a large cavern, in the interior of the Earth, to the summit of a high hill, Nané chaha. There, deep down in the Earth, in the great cavern, man and the grasshoppers had been created by Aba, the Great Spirit, having been formed of the yellow clay.

For a time the men and the grasshoppers continued to reach the surface together, and as they emerged from the long passageway they would scatter in all directions, some going north, others south, east, or west.

But at last the mother of the grasshoppers who had remained in the cavern was killed by the men and as a consequence there were no more grasshoppers to reach the surface, and ever after those that lived on the Earth were known to the Choctaw as *eske ilay*, or "mother dead." However, men continued to reach the surface of the Earth through the long passageway that led to the summit of Nané chaha, and, as they moved about from place to place, they trampled upon many grasshoppers in the high grass, killing many and hurting others.

The grasshoppers became alarmed as they feared that all would be killed if men became more numerous and continued to come from the cavern in the Earth. They spoke to Aba, who heard them and soon after caused the passageway to be closed and no more men were allowed to reach the surface. But as there were many men remaining in the cavern he changed them to ants and ever since that time the small ants have come forth from holes in the ground.

The Choctaw of bayou Lacomb, St.
Tammany parish, Louisiana
by David I. Bushnell, jr.
Related by Emma Pisatuntema, 1910

Skull Island

The more Ilene thought about Nathan's visit, the more nervous she felt. Nathan was an old friend, and an interesting guy, but he had his obsessions, coupled with an energy that often led him to go very far out on very thin limbs. That included publishing papers and books peers would consider insane, before he had the proof to back it up, and it sometimes involved doing very dangerous things in order to get that elusive proof. But his brother's death and the failed attempt to validate his Hollow Earth theory had knocked everything out of him. He had been a husk of his former self, with no motivation to do anything. The dynamo that had once churned inside of him was dead. But in her short phone conversation with him, she had heard it in his voice—the electricity was back on. And while that was good for him, it worried her. Because if he was coming to see her, it almost certainly had to do with Kong. He hadn't quite said so, but he hadn't denied it. And that … might not be good, especially given that he had mentioned genetic memory. He wanted Kong to remember something about the Hollow Earth. Kong had never been down there, so it was something he would not consciously know but which might be lodged in the genetic memories he had inherited from his ancestors. What could that be?

On top of that, she couldn't find the book she was looking for.

"Where is it?" she murmured.

"Dr. Andrews," the loudspeaker in the hall announced, "you have a visitor waiting at security."

She looked over at Jia, who was pulling the book from beneath a pile of stuff on the bed and holding it toward her.

Thank you, she signed, and sat down next to her so they were eye to eye.

You're nervous, Jia signed.

Everything's fine, she replied.

You can't lie to me, Jia said. *I'm not a kid anymore.*

Ilene couldn't help but smile. Jia was constantly surprising her.

A few minutes later, she met Nathan at security. He looked better than he had on the video call. He had shaved the beard, for one thing, so the dimple in his chin was visible again. His light hair had been trimmed back, too, and his grey eyes seemed livelier. She tried to hide a grin as he pulled off his rain jacket; underneath he was wearing a brown puffer vest, just as he had when she first met him. She had remarked at the time that she hadn't seen anyone wearing one of those since the eighties. He had just shrugged and smiled.

He noticed her expression and glanced down at the vest.

"It *is* a new one, at least," he said.

"I didn't know they still made them," she said.

He smiled and they exchanged a perfunctory hug. Then he looked questioningly at Jia.

"This is Jia," she said, signing along with her spoken words. "Jia, this is Dr. Lind."

Kong isn't sick, Jia signed. *Neither am I.*

Ilene smiled. "He's not that kind of doctor," she said. "He's like me. A scientist."

"I don't do house calls," Nathan said, smiling at the girl.

Ilene translated. *He doesn't travel around giving people medicine.*

Jia frowned. *You won't hurt Kong,* she signed.

Nathan looked to Ilene, confused.

"She just said she's feeling fine," she replied.

"Oh," he replied. "I'm glad."

"Can I get you something to drink? Do you want to see your room?"

"I'll just get settled in," he said. He nodded at the doors he had come through from the helipad. "I knew it was bad," he said. "But this…"

"And it's getting worse," Ilene said. "And it's our fault, you know."

"I think I can help," he said.

"Help?" Ilene said. "Help who? Kong? The Iwi? Because Jia is the last of them."

"I know you're skeptical," he said. "But surely, if it really is getting worse, you must be willing to at least hear an alternative."

She sighed. "Tell you what," she said. "Let me show you where you'll be staying. Then we'll go."

"Go where?" he asked.

"To the biodome," she said. "To see Kong, up close. Get his opinion."

While Nathan got settled and changed, she pulled a security clearance for him to visit the enclosure.

Is he a bad man? Jia asked.

No, Ilene said. *He's a good man. But sometimes he makes bad mistakes. Like all of us.*

"Do you walk through this every day?" Nathan half shouted through the driving wind and rain. As Ilene watched Nathan struggle with the downpour, she realized how much a fact of life it had become for her. Like Kong, it had been a long time since she had seen the real sun.

"Not always," she said. "Jia and I have a little prefab in the biodome. Sometimes we stay over. But the room in the Monarch facility has most of our stuff. So, tell me, now that you're here. You want Kong for something. What?"

"Godzilla is active again," Nathan said. "He attacked Pensacola."

"I'm aware of that," she said. "Godzilla doesn't attack without reason. Maybe you should be looking into that."

"Looks like this time, he did," Nathan said. "If he did it once, he'll do it again. We have to stop him."

She turned and jabbed a finger at him.

"If you're even thinking what I think you're thinking—"

"No," he said. "This isn't about Kong stopping Godzilla. It's about *us* stopping him. It's about Hollow Earth."

"Then I don't follow," she said, pulling the hood of her rain slicker to better protect her face from the downpour. "You said this has something to do with genetic memory. I assumed you meant Kong's memory of an ancient feud with Godzilla's species."

Nathan shook his head. "I don't want to throw Kong into a fight with Godzilla any more than you do. I've seen some new satellite scans of Hollow Earth. Good ones, taken by Apex. Life needs energy, Ilene. Plants use sunlight. Animals and fungi and bacteria break energy out of chemical compounds, from either living or non-living material. Like slow-burning fires. But in Hollow Earth, well—there's an energy source, almost unimaginably powerful. I think the wellspring of life is down there, at least some of it. Waiting for us to discover it."

Honestly, at the moment, she wouldn't have been that unhappy if a flood swept Nathan off and buried him in the salt marshes. She'd been right about not liking what he would have to say.

"A power source?" she snapped. "In Hollow Earth? This sounds nuts even for you, Nathan."

"It's there," he insisted. "We just need Kong to bring us to it."

"The second you bring Kong out of containment Godzilla is going to come for him. You know that. Camazotz proved that beyond any doubt."

They reached the biodome, cycled through the airlock. They were out of the rain, albeit soaking wet. Nathan gazed around, his face full of wonder. And purpose.

"This is amazing," he said.

"Don't change the subject."

"You said yourself, you can't keep him here forever," Nathan said.

"No!" she said. "Our meddling has already wreaked havoc on Kong's habitat—no way am I letting you drag him halfway around the world to use him as a weapon."

"An ally!" Nathan insisted. "To protect us—lead the way down there."

"And what makes you think he'll go in?" she demanded,

holding her palms up toward him. "And how do we get him there?"

Nathan paused. "I've seen what's going on out there," he said. "The storm is here to stay. This island will not recover from this, not as it was. Life will survive and adapt, as it always has, but the ecosystem that nourished Kong—it's gone, and it isn't coming back. And there is no place like it on Earth, at least not above ground. You always believed Skull Island was like the Hollow Earth come to the surface. This could help him find a new home. And it can save ours." He glanced meaningfully at Jia. "And hers. That power source may be our only hope. Please, we've gotta stop Godzilla. This is our only chance. We have to take it."

She sighed, then turned her gaze up to where Kong's makeshift spear was still hanging from where it had punched into the dome. Nathan was right. This place was and had always been a temporary measure. And Godzilla was on the move again, which meant there was a good chance politics was about to become involved once more. Walter Simmons and Apex had a lot of political clout, maybe enough to have Kong taken away from her whether she agreed or not. Worse, there were plenty of people in important positions who still held to the idea that the Titans should all be summarily executed. Godzilla's seemingly heroic actions had muted their voices, but now that Godzilla was public enemy number one, they would be heard again. Some would demand Kong be put down while he was still Monarch's captive.

Nathan was right about another thing. Skull Island was ruined. Even if things returned to normal this afternoon, it would take decades for its ecosystem to recover.

"Okay," she relented.

"Yes!" Nathan said.

She stuck a finger in his face. "But when it comes to Kong, what I say goes."

Nathan's face lit up. "You name the terms!" he said. "Thank you! You won't regret this!"

His kissed her cheek and then sprinted off, presumably to radio Walter Simmons the good news.

"I already regret it," Ilene said.

She looked down at Jia.

This is our home, Jia signed. *Ours.*

"Our home is together," Ilene replied. "You and me."

In the distance, Kong grunted, then growled, very low. Agitated.

You have no idea, big guy, Ilene thought. However things turned out, in the immediate future Kong was going to be a very unhappy Titan.

Russell House, Pensacola

Madison's dad showed up late, looking tired and carrying a pizza, which he laid on the table. She acknowledged him with a bare nod. It had been a full day since she had seen him, since their fight at the aid site. She had spent the night with her aunt, but had received a text to return home after school. The pizza said he might be trying to make amends, but she wasn't sure she was ready to play along.

"Look, Madison," her dad said. "I'm sorry. Just when you showed up, things were—you saw. And you're down a letter grade in three subjects."

Right, she thought. *This isn't about Godzilla at all. It's about homework.*

"Two," she said. "I took the make-up quiz in Chemistry."

"You shouldn't be down in any of them." He sighed and pulled some plates from the cabinet. "You know that," he said. "I don't have to tell you."

"Then don't," she replied, and was immediately sorry she'd said it. "I shouldn't have bugged you the other day," she said.

"I get it," he said. "After last time. But I just... If I could have kept you away from all of that, I would have. And maybe I could have, if I had been around. I wasn't. But I'm here, now, Maddie. I don't want to see you pulled into this mess."

"I just know I can help," she said. "I have as much experience as anyone with these things. I learned a lot from Mom. I know you may not want to hear that..."

"Maddie, I loved your mom. I still love her. But that situation—with Jonah and his men, all of those murders, Ghidorah ... you shouldn't have been involved with any of that. You were a kid. And as much as you may hate to hear it, you still are."

"Dad—"

He bent his head down. "For me, Maddie," he said. "I can't ... the idea of you getting hurt, or worse. I can't take it. So please."

That sounded suspiciously like he was leading up to something.

"What's going on?" she asked.

"They want me at command and control," he said. "I'm supposed to fly up there in the next couple of days."

"Great," she said. "I'll go pack."

He shook his head. "You're staying here. Cassidy is going to sleep here and keep an eye on you."

Madison stared at her plate for a moment, torn, angry, and at the same time on the edge of tears.

"It's not fair," she said.

"You need to keep up with school," he said.

"No, not that," she said. "You're blackmailing me. With

your fear. I'm supposed to cower at home for the rest of my life because you're afraid something might happen to me? It's not fair."

"Maddie…"

"No," she said. "That's fine. You go to command and control. Save the world. I'll stay here and … go to school. But you're going to owe me." She forced a smile.

Her dad nodded. "Are we through fighting?" he asked.

"Truce, for now," she said. "Pizza and a movie."

"That sounds good," he said.

But secretly, she was already making plans. No more asking permission. She would just have to count on forgiveness.

Skull Island

The goal was to put Kong on a ship and sail him to Antarctica. Finding a ship that could carry him and restraints that could hold him turned out to be the easiest part of that equation. Getting him on that ship and *in* those restraints—that was the quandary.

Nathan grew increasingly nervous about the huge task as the day approached.

"We learned a lot from the disaster of 2019," Araya said, studying the feed from Kong's enclosure. "We had a one-size-fits-all approach to Titans, and put far too much trust in our containment fields."

Araya was the head engineer on site. He had read her profile; she had a list of degrees and accomplishments as long as Nathan's arm. She almost as tall as he was, powerfully built. Her eyes were a remarkable shade of brown, almost gold.

"You were in Brazil, with Behemoth, right?" Nathan said. "One of the few survivors."

"Yes," she said.

"But that was sabotage," Nathan pointed out. "Not a fault in the technology."

"Of course," she replied. "But that goes to the trust issue. What can be turned on can be turned off. Even the best door only works if it is closed. But it wasn't just containing them I'm talking about; it was the conceit that we could control them, kill them if we wanted. *Meu Deus*, the hubris. Understand, we found most of the Titans quiescent to begin with. We just built containments around the places they had already chosen to sleep. In several cases, the termination protocols were applied when they started to wake—and failed, anyway. Titans have an ability to sort of … ramp up when they need to. Exceed what we calculated about their resilience from their resting capacity."

"And how is Kong different?" Nathan asked.

"He isn't," Araya replied. "But we've had a long time to study him, and since Ghidorah, we've learned a little humility. How do you think we got him into his enclosure in the first place?"

"I hadn't thought about that," Nathan said. "I guess I figured you built it around him."

Araya shook her head. "Back in 1973, a lieutenant colonel named Packard tried to take Kong down with napalm. He almost succeeded. Of course, Kong was still relatively young then, about a third of the size he is now. What dropped him wasn't the fire but the fact that the napalm sucked up all of the oxygen from the immediate atmosphere. Kong needs a *lot* of oxygen to function. His lungs are bigger in proportion to his size than ours are, but that doesn't matter if there isn't anything to put in them, right? But what Packard didn't realize—if he even understood what happened—was that it also takes time for the oxygen reserve in Kong's blood to completely deplete especially if he's active and angry. Because there is also a *lot* of blood. You ever hyperventilate before diving underwater?"

"Yes," he said. "My brother and I used to see who could stay under longer."

"Right. You enrich your blood with oxygen before holding your breath. When Kong is active, his blood is always enriched."

"I assume you didn't napalm him to get him into the enclosure?"

"No. We sequenced his DNA, and we built models on how to subdue him with an odorless chemical that is both a gas and water-soluble. It bonds with his blood like oxygen does, but it isn't oxygen. That's combined with a general soporific to keep him down after his oxygen levels return to normal. We introduced it when he was already naturally asleep. The first three times we tried it, it failed anyway. No one was killed but … it was close. The fourth time we got the dosage right. Then we used choppers to move him into the biodome and sealed it up while he was still snoozing. So we've done this before. We've got this."

"And it won't hurt him, depriving him of oxygen?"

"There's enough oxygen left that there's no risk of brain damage," she said. "Believe me, nobody here wants to hurt him."

"That's commendable."

"Yes," Ayara said. "Also, if we hurt him, there is a spectacularly good chance he will kill us all. The lieutenant colonel I told you about? Packard? Kong crushed him like a bug."

* * *

Pacific Ocean

Ilene experienced the whole thing like a nightmare she couldn't—or rather, was unwilling—to wake from. When they doused Kong with the gas, he woke, briefly, feebly pawing at his face before succumbing. Techs swarmed over Kong as if he were Gulliver, and they Lilliputians, building a harness around him for the helicopters to fasten to.

Then they opened the biodome with shaped charges, and the rain came in, pounding the last remaining fragment of the Skull Island ecosystem mercilessly, lashing it with lightning, tearing limbs from the trees. She cried, then; Skull Island was a place of great beauty and bloody horror, and it was like nowhere else in the world—and now it was gone, all of it. It sank into her how irrevocable her decision had been; there was no going back now—not for Kong, not for Jia—not for her. Skull Island was as lost to the world as the age of dinosaurs.

For the first time since she had known the girl, Jia wept, pulling into herself and refusing Ilene's attempt to comfort her. If her heart had not already been broken, that would have done it.

The ship was a modified bulk cargo vessel equipped to handle close to 100,000 tons of Titan on its broad deck. The scaffolding had been stripped away and replaced by huge reels to spool on the chains needed to hold the Titan down.

There was nothing to see of the island as the ship pulled away; just the storm, reaching high into the heavens. But as the ship started moving, the giant storm dwindled with surprising speed, until there was nothing to see in any direction except ocean and ships.

Though the expedition's route took them through the Southern Pacific and its inhabited islands, they didn't pass within sight of any of them. This was by design, as they were trying not to draw attention. On the surface, given the size of the fleet accompanying them, that seemed ridiculous. But in practice, the South Pacific and the Antarctic Ocean they were bound for were so vast, four times as many ships wouldn't draw attention unless someone knew where and when to look.

Jia came out of her shell after the first few days. She stayed on deck. When she wasn't looking at the bound form of Kong, she stared out at what for her must have been impossibly distant horizons. Even before the storm came ashore, there had been near-constant tempests surrounding the island. In ten years, Ilene could only remember about four when the ocean horizon was visible, and then usually not for long. She had spent one of those days observing Kong, who had done little but stare at that unusually clear sky and far horizon with what she believed to be intense curiosity. She had watched a rather spectacular sunset with him before the black clouds closed back in. But Jia's people didn't live on the coast. She may have never seen such a distant skyline.

The world is so big, Jia said. *Is this all of it?*

No, Ilene told her. *Not even close. There is a lot more.*

Is it all water? That's all I see.

No, *there's plenty of land,* Ilene assured her. *You will see it one day.*

Jia shrugged her ambivalence, then pointed at Kong with her lips.

He doesn't understand, she said.

I know, Ilene replied.

TEN

"*So you gotta ask yourself, loyal listeners. What is it about Pensacola that attracted not only a Monarch watchpost but also an Apex Cybernetics facility? If you ask that question, they'll tell you it's because of the Naval Air Station. That Monarch and Apex both like having the infrastructure of a military base around. And you know, that makes sense for Monarch. But Apex? Why do they need military protection? Because more than half of their income comes from the military–industrial complex? Or because they do contract work with Monarch? If there was only some way to know who came here first. Oh, wait, listeners, there is. Public records. The NAS had been here since 1913. Monarch is trickier, because they were covert for so long, but I have it on good authority they put in a station here in the 1970s. Apex? They built their plant seven years ago. A.G. After Godzilla.*

"*It goes in a pattern, people. Show me an Apex*

*facility and I will show you a Monarch base nearby.
The question is … why?"*
Mad Truth, *Titan Truth Podcast* #212

The South Pacific

Let me go to him, Jia signed, for perhaps the hundredth time.
Ilene sighed and put her hand on the girl's shoulder.
It's not a good idea, she replied. *He's angry, confused…*
Sleepy, Jia said. *Sad.*
*They gave him something so he wouldn't struggle. But
that's also making him confused. He might not know who
you are. You stay here, with me.*

She and Jia stood on the ship's bridge, looking through
glass at the heart-wrenching sight of Kong stretched out,
manacled at his ankles, wrists, and neck by chains whose
links were larger than most trucks. He was conscious,
barely, his glassy eyes shifting now and then in their
sockets. Beyond the transport, an armada of ships, both
military and civilian, cruised the South Pacific, the largest
navel expedition since the fight with Ghidorah and the
Titans under its control.

Nathan approached from behind them, timidly, as if
fearful Kong would not only tear loose at any moment but
would know who to blame for this degradation and where
to find him.

"Whoo," Nathan said, as he came onto the bridge. "I
can smell him from up here."

Outside, she heard the clanking of chains, and saw
Kong was dragging himself to a sitting position and
looking up toward the bridge.

"He can smell you, too," Ilene replied. "Still not a
fan, huh?"

Coward, Jia signed.

Nathan noticed. "What's she saying?" he asked.

"It's just an Iwi expression," Ilene replied. "It means you're very brave."

Nathan smiled at the girl. "Oh," he said. Then he looked back out at Kong. He glanced at the control panel. The display indicated Kong's level of sedation, which she knew to be over eighty percent. "Use a light touch on the sedatives," Nathan said. "He's our escort. We can't have him comatose when we reach Hollow Earth."

"What happens if Kong won't go down willingly?" Ilene asked. "What do we do then?"

He shied away from her gaze, seemed to be searching for words.

The intercom saved him from having to voice his uncertainty.

"Dr. Lind, please report to the forward deck, Dr. Lind."

"Excuse me," Nathan said. "New arrivals."

Coward, Ilene signed as he walked away. Jia smiled.

The woman from the helicopter carried a titanium briefcase and a lot of attitude. She had straight, glossy black hair; he guessed her to be in her late twenties. If she was impressed by the sight of a zillion tons of ape strapped to a freighter— or anything else for that matter—it did not show. Nathan felt dismissed the instant she laid her gaze on him, but he was determined not to get off on the wrong foot.

"Welcome—" he began.

"Wow," she interrupted, taking off her sunglasses, staring at Kong. "Who's the idiot who came up with this idea?" Then she looked at him, implying she certainly knew the answer to her question. Her eyes were so brown as to be nearly black.

Wrong foot achieved, he thought.

"I'm Maia Simmons," she said. "My father sent me. I run point for Apex."

"I'm Nathan Lind," he replied, stretching out his hand. "Mission chief."

She took his hand and gave it a perfunctory shake.

"Don't worry," she said. "I'm just here to babysit."

She was already moving past him. Nathan followed her, confused and embarrassed, as the well-armed mercenaries she'd brought with her trailed behind him.

"The Hollow Earth vehicles are on their way to Antarctica as we speak," Simmons said. "I know you people are cutting edge, but these prototypes we're loaning you will make what you've been flying look like used compact cars."

"I love compact cars," Nathan said.

She plowed on as if he hadn't spoken. "Forget about the price tag, which is obscene, of course. The anti-gravity engines alone produce enough charge to light up Las Vegas for a week." She glanced over at him. "Feel free to be impressed."

"Wow," Nathan obliged. He had never been to Vegas, but he figured that translated to a lot. He had seen the blueprints, and he *was* impressed—but also uneasy. Why did Walter Simmons think he needed babysitting?

Night fell, and squalls blew in. The sky groaned with thunder. Curiously, Nathan's spirits picked up; the darkness and the rain made the world feel smaller, as if he was holed up in his house on a stormy day, talking to friends instead of lecturing people he hardly knew. Gloomy days were sort of his element.

He presented them his map of Hollow Earth and then got into the details. Maia Simmons was there, along with Admiral Wilcox, commander of the fleet. He was a stoic-looking man in his fifties with high, pronounced cheekbones.

"We'll be at the Antarctic entry in forty-eight hours," Nathan told them. "This path will get us into Hollow Earth. Once we're inside, Kong should lead us to the energy source."

"Is that all we have?" the Admiral asked. "The imaging drones didn't survive the trip?"

Nathan shook his head. "Something down there pulverized them."

"Hence the monkey muscle?" Simmons said.

"Only if we get there in the first place," Nathan said. "The gravitational inversion is like nothing we've ever encountered. Our best guess is on entry it'll feel like bungee jumping—just with the cord tied to your lower intestine. But if your helicopters are as good as you say—"

"HEAVs," Simmons corrected.

"*HEAVs* are as good as you say, I believe we can do this."

"They'll do their job," Simmons said. "You just gotta do yours."

"Excellent," Nathan said.

With that, she left the bridge, leaving Nathan with the Admiral. Wilcox ran his hand through his closely cropped black hair. Then his gaze rested intently on Nathan.

"Yes, Admiral?" Nathan asked.

"Do you have a military background, Dr. Lind?" Wilcox asked.

"Um, no," he said. "I pretty much went from being a nerd in high school to a geek in adulthood. I never did the whole—no, I wasn't in the military."

"It isn't for everyone," Wilcox said. "Not even for everyone in it, if you take my meaning. I have been in the Navy most of my life, Dr. Lind. Just a sailor to begin with, you know. My parents immigrated from Nigeria when I was young. They had big plans for me. Doctor, or lawyer. But I wanted to serve, and that's what I've done."

"I admire that," Nathan said. "I really do. I just don't think I ever had the stuff for it."

"You never know what 'stuff' you have until you're tested."

"Sure," Nathan said. "That makes sense. I—"

"I see you as untested, Dr. Lind."

"Oh," Nathan said, now realizing where this was going. "I—ah—I have been tested, Admiral. It did not go that well."

"People died under your command."

"Well, technically, my brother was in charge so—" He stopped, cowed by the Admiral's unwavering stare.

"Yes," he said. "They did what I told them to do and they died."

The Admiral nodded. "All those ships out there. You see them?"

"Yes."

"Every man and woman on each of those ships, they look to me. They expect me to tell them what to do. They expect me to get them through this alive, if it is at all possible. I am sure you understand this is a great responsibility, Dr. Lind— one I do not take lightly."

"I'm sure you don't," Nathan said.

"I, on the other hand, look to *you*," Wilcox said. "You're the civilian in charge of this expedition. I take my orders from you. But that isn't all there is to it, Dr. Lind. That … Titan out there. And the others. These are far more your realm of expertise than mine. I rely on you. I am counting on you as these people under my command are counting on me. Does this make sense to you, Dr. Lind?"

Nathan regarded the other man for a moment, feeling that weight settle on his shoulders.

"I'll do my best," he finally said.

Wilcox shook his head. "You must do better than that, Dr. Lind. Much better. I expect it of you."

* * *

Ilene stood on the bridge, looking past Kong, through the rain to the lights of the other ships and the dark interstices between them, looking for ... nothing, she hoped. And so far, so good.

Admiral Wilcox, who had finished chatting with Nathan, joined her.

"Dr. Andrews," he said. "We're avoiding Godzilla's known territorial waters, according to your guidelines."

"Good," Ilene said. Although it wasn't. Godzilla's patterns had changed in the past, usually in response to the presence of another alpha. His most recent activity was a bit puzzling, as his attack on Pensacola hadn't been driven by the presence of another Titan, at least not in an obvious way. But that just pointed out what a volatile creature he was. How Godzilla could know Kong had left Skull Island, she didn't know. But she was willing to bet he did. Avoiding his mapped patrol routes was the very minimum—and probably the only—thing they *could* do. She was keeping up with Monarch telemetry, of course, but as he often did, Godzilla had managed to drop off the map again.

The Admiral must have read something in her response, or perhaps her expression.

"Do I need to be concerned?" he asked.

"Yes," she told him. "They have a way of sensing threats. And we believe that they had an ancient rivalry. The myths say they fought each other in a great war."

The Admiral nodded knowingly.

"So if they meet again, who bows to who—is that it?"

"I spent ten years on that island," she said. "Studying him. I know this for sure ... Kong bows to no one."

* * *

The ship lurched, snapping Ilene out of what had been an involuntary nap. She was wide awake now, wondering what could cause such a huge ship to jump like a canoe on whitewater. She was on the small bridge, along with Nathan and Maia Simmons.

"Should she be out there?" Simmons asked.

At first, Ilene wasn't sure who the executive was talking about—or to, for that matter. Simmons was gazing through the window of the bridge, out toward Kong. It was night and pouring rain. She remembered the Admiral saying something about a squall on the radar, and apparently, they were now squarely in it. Kong had pulled himself into a sitting position against the platform at the bow and was yanking on the chains and manacles that held him. The chains were wound into winches, so that his movements would not translate directly to the ship, but the effect was still bone-jarring.

She, Simmons had said.

Then Ilene saw the tiny form of Jia, padding along the deck toward Kong. Her stride was unhurried, her back straight; nothing in her carriage suggested fear.

Swearing under her breath, Ilene bolted toward the hatch and down the stairs leading to the deck. From there, she saw Jia, now very close to Kong, who still venting his anger and frustration. But as Jia drew up to him, he saw her, and calmed.

Jia reached out her little arm toward the Titan. Kong leaned over, gently extending his hand toward the girl. She reached up and touched his finger—a tiny point of contact for Kong, like a person touching the foreleg of a gnat.

But the effect was undeniable. Kong was no longer struggling. He didn't seem angry anymore so much as … melancholy.

Ilene closed the gap between her and the girl, shivering

in the rain. However calm Kong seemed at the moment, she still flinched involuntarily when she got close.

"Come on," she told Jia. "Come on."

Jia ignored her, and she realized she was so flustered she had spoken aloud.

It's not safe out here, she signed.

Jia turned toward her and started moving her hands.

Kong is sad. And angry.

Join the club, Ilene thought. She flicked her eyes toward the mountain of muscle and bone stooping over them. It didn't matter if he was chained; from here he could crush them both without trying.

That's because he doesn't understand, she told Jia. *We want to help him.*

He doesn't believe that, Jia signed.

It was the way she put it that jarred her. The Iwi and Jia in particular did not tend to project their own feelings into words. She was blunt and literal when she said something. If she was speaking for Kong, she was either guessing at his thoughts, or—she *knew* them.

How do you know? Ilene asked.

He told me, Jia replied. Ilene looked up at Kong as Jia's words began to sink in. *He told me.*

Rain cascaded down Kong, flowing around his thick brow ridges. Rivulets coursed through his fur. Southern Pacific or not, the rain was cold. Her breath caught in her chest as Kong lifted his hand, brought it up to his face. His hand formed a shape.

A sign.

Home, he said.

Ilene gaped in amazement. There was no mistake. But as if to prove it, he lowered his hand and raised it again, and again.

Home. Home.

She didn't notice the rain anymore, and her fear dropped away, replaced by awe.

I knew it, she thought. But to see it made real, to know for a fact was quite … overwhelming. She was watching the dawn of a new world.

Nathan stood next to Maia Simmons on the bridge, watching the strange tableau, the little girl and the immense Titan.

"Did the monkey just talk?" Simmons asked.

Nathan was too awestruck to answer.

Russell House, Pensacola

Madison closed the door of her room behind her and locked it. Then she gazed around her office, her sanctum, her war room. Newspaper clippings, Post-it notes, photographs and magazine articles were pinned all over the walls, along with a big map of the world with all purported sightings of the Titans for the last three years marked on them. She studied it for a moment, and then placed a Post-it note next to Pensacola.

Apex, it said. *Why?*

She sat on the bed and looked over at the alligator skull she'd found by the creek in the woods behind the house.

Why? And why wouldn't Dad listen to her? Or better yet, why had she even gone to him?

Fighting with Dad—or Mom, for that matter, back when that was possible—had never gotten Madison anywhere, and that was now truer than ever. Her father did not trust her. He didn't trust her opinions, her feelings, or her capabilities. Maybe it stemmed from the trust issues he'd had with her mother—he might have just shifted those onto her after Mom died. Or perhaps it went even deeper than that. All that she knew was that she had proven in the past that her instincts were good, and he had somehow convinced himself of the opposite. He'd said it himself: he only saw her through the lens of what *he* wanted in his life right now. Someone who would just do what he said. Someone he wouldn't lose.

But if life had taught her anything so far, it was that losing people was part of life. Everybody died. And some people died way too young, for no reason. And maybe some people who should die survived. The universe didn't weigh you in the balance before deciding to kill you or spare you, it just did what it did. If you worried too much about that, you would never achieve anything at all.

But even so, she did not make the decision to act on her own right away. If Dad wouldn't listen to her, she reasoned, *someone* would. She had some credibility, didn't she? So she had taken to emailing or DMing everyone she could think of—she still had contacts in Monarch—and anyone who might have some sort of pull, laying out her case.

But she should have known better. They were all nice, and encouraging, and told her they would take her input into consideration and meanwhile she should keep safe and do her schoolwork.

Keep safe? From Titans? The only way to do that was get ahead of them, take the initiative. Act.

But how? There was no ORCA to steal this time, no obvious course of action for her to follow as there had been before.

Or maybe there was.

Apex was obviously at the heart of this, and there just so happened to be a mostly ruined Apex complex right down the road. That was the place to start, if she knew what she was looking for, but she didn't. What she needed was a guide.

And that … she might be able to find.

She listened to Mad Truth's latest podcast, and when that didn't give her a starting place, she pored back through his archives.

"Okay, class, listen up. There's dozens of Apex facilities up and down the coast. Why'd Godzilla target Pensacola? Wanna know my theory? It's all about patterns and variables."

So, on many levels Mad Truth was pretty far out there, she thought, as she went back through the earlier stuff about crop circles and chemtrails, alien visitors, and the works. But when he talked about the Titans, and Apex, he mostly made sense.

Mostly, she thought, as she scrolled past one entry, "Mothra Pregnant?"

She'd been present when Mothra was born—or at least when she went from egg to pupa—and his speculations on the details of a Mothra pregnancy were ill-informed at best. But his inside information about Apex seemed pretty solid and fit with a lot of what she knew or suspected.

"Stick with me, I'm gonna take you back to grade school with this. Godzilla only attacks when provoked, that's the pattern. Pensacola is the only Apex coastal hub with an advanced robotics lab, and that's the variable, and add them up and your answer is? That Apex cybernetics is at the heart of the problem."

Right, she thought. Exactly what she had been thinking. Godzilla only attacked when triggered by something, or when there was another Titan looking to be the alpha. You could add to that at least one case in which he had attacked humans who were trying to capture a Titan. There had been no other Titan in evidence at Apex. But that didn't mean there wasn't one. What if Apex had a captive Titan, and Godzilla had been trying to free it?

But that didn't wash either, because if that were the

case, why *hadn't* he freed it? The handful of jets firing on him would never have stopped him. It was pretty clear that whatever Godzilla was looking for, he hadn't found it, and then he'd just left.

Then it hit her. What if Apex had figured out how to build an ORCA?

The ORCA was a bioacoustic device her mom and dad had invented together to try to communicate with cetaceans. When they tried to use it, it had been a horror show; a pod of killer whales had beached themselves. They had decided to abandon the whole project—or at least, Dad thought they had. Later on Mom started tinkering with it again to try to deal with Titans that were hunting Godzilla and just generally wreaking havoc. Later, after her mother and father split up and she was living with Mom, she had perfected the device as a way of communicating with Titans. And if you tuned the thing to sound like an Apex Titan, it tended to control the lesser ones and attract the alphas—like Godzilla and Ghidorah.

Her father had shelved the device after Ghidorah was dead and the threat was over. He and Monarch had deemed the technology too dangerous to fool around with. But a lot of people knew about it, knew what it could do, and there were plenty of recordings floating around on the internet of the ORCA working; after all, she had played it over the broadcast system at the ball park to disrupt Ghidorah's hold over the other Titans. Enough clues for a genius like Walter Simmons to reverse engineer the device, right?

Why? She didn't know. Simmons seemed to have a real hatred for Godzilla. Maybe he had *lured* him to trash his Pensacola facility to frame the Titan. Or maybe he had a deeper, more devious plan.

Or none of that. She didn't have enough information.

But she knew someone who might.

Mad Truth. She had to find him. In person.

And she might know how.

She called Josh.

"Hey," she said. "I'm gonna need a favor, okay?"

"Yeah, of course," he said.

She told him the favor.

"I meant of course *not*," he said. "You know you can ask me anything—except maybe that. Yeah, definitely not that."

"Uh-huh," she replied. "Make it work. In about an hour, okay? Before my aunt gets back."

She hung up on his objections, then went back to her computer. She found her Mad Truth files, clicked on "episode transcripts" and began parsing through them. As she listened to the latest installment, she thought she remembered something, about bleach…

"*Okay, class, listen up. In the midst of Godzilla's attack on Apex Pensacola, I found some crazy tech with no official classification. What I saw didn't match any of the engineering specs I've ever seen, so what are they working on in such a black-ops secrecy room? This could be the thread that finally unravels the Apex sweater of conspiracy. You better believe I'm gonna keep tugging. For now I'm secure, anonymous and hiding in plain sight…*"

It took a while, but she found it. The thing about the bleach, and Chinese grocery stores…

She jerked at the loud bang outside of her window, her reflexes immediately pulling her back in time, to the gunfire in the Monarch facility in China, the bodies everywhere, people she knew, alive one minute, gone the next. And then later, in Antarctica, all of those people…

She jumped up and ran to the window, heart thumping, but there were no guns, just a van backfiring. An ugly, dirty, beat-to-pieces van. Music blared from within; her friend Josh sat in the driver's seat.

She smiled. She had known he would come through.

She grabbed her things and ran down to the curb. Josh had stepped out, meeting her halfway to her door. As usual, his mop of dark hair was in disarray, and he looked put-upon. He was here, obviously, but he wasn't happy about it.

"Just to be clear," Josh said, scowling at her through his black-rimmed glasses, "my brother can never know."

"To be clear," Madison retorted, nodding at the junked-up van, "even if we got into an accident, I don't think he could tell."

Josh started for the driver's seat, but Madison beat him to it.

"No, no, no," he said. "My brother would never let you drive."

"My mission," Madison said. "My wheel."

He reluctantly walked around to the passenger window, but he stopped, a conflicted expression on his face, one that she had come to know quite well.

"I just don't think it's the best idea to go looking for some secret weirdo off the internet," he opined. "We had a school assembly about literally exactly this."

"He's not a weirdo," Madison said, putting her hair up in a ponytail. "He's a covert investigator, the *only* one looking for the truth about Godzilla and Apex."

"So let *him* look," Josh said. "Why do we have to help him?"

"Because if we don't, *nobody else will*."

She caught his gaze and held it. "So you coming or not?"

Josh sighed. "Obviously I'm coming," he said. He reached for the door handle and pulled. Nothing happened.

"It's stuck," he said.

As she hit the gas and started to peel out, he yanked open the sliding door in the back and scrambled in, hollering the whole time.

ELEVEN

"Talk! Converse! Do not moan or wail. Talk, each of you to your kind, within your type," they were told—the deer, the birds, the pumas, the jaguars, the serpents. "Say our names. Revere us, we who are your mother and your father. Speak, and say: 'Huracan, New Thunderbolt, and Brutal Thunderbolt, Heart of Sky and Heart of Earth, Creators, Formers, Bearer of Children.' Speak! Pray to us! Venerate us!" they were told. But they could not speak like people. Instead they screeched, chattered, bellowed. Their language was not understood because each one made a different noise. When the Creators, the Formers heard this, they said, "This has not turned out well. They cannot speak. They are not able to name us. We made them. This is not good." The animals were therefore told: "You will be changed, replaced, because you could not speak."

From *Popol Vuh: Sacred Book of the Quiché Maya*

Pensacola

Josh reached over from the back to turn off the radio, but he slipped and his hand hit the wheel. Madison beat him back.

"We've been listening to this dude for hours," Josh complained.

"Knock it off," Madison snapped. "This is the part I was telling you about."

"*...because one or two gallons won't cut it, I need my bleach in bulk ya'll because spy dust is real. Soviet-designed pollination technique, invisible to the naked eye, need special UV to know you been marked and I'm taking exactly zero chances here.*"

Madison switched it off.

"That's how we find him," she said. "The bleach."

"Bleach?" Josh said.

"He consumes tons of bleach," Madison clarified.

"He drinks it?"

"Showers with it," Madison said.

"Oh, yeah," Josh said. "Wait, what?"

"Prevention against organic tracking technology," she said. "See? Tradecraft."

"Drinking would have made more sense," Josh muttered.

There were a lot more places near the plant that sold bleach than Madison would have thought, but they were able to narrow things down; Mad Truth liked Asian grocery stores. He had done a whole podcast on why, but it was not one of the more coherent or memorable ones. It seemed to have something to do with wherever he had lived before moving to Pensacola.

"Really?" Josh sighed, as they piled out of the van in front of yet another grocery store.

"Yes," Madison said. "Just one more place."

"It's just, it's getting old," Josh said. But he followed her in.

It was an everything-sort-of store. Outside, they passed huge bags of various kinds of rice and open produce boxes full of ginger, bok choy, empty-heart vegetable, taro, chiles, and twenty other assorted vegetables. In the front were a few tables, and a string of red paper lanterns, and in the back a guy tossing something in a wok. But there were also shelves full of colorfully packaged foodstuffs, cooking gear, bowls, plates, flip-flops, postcards, tanks full of live fish, canned goods ... a real general store. Madison made straight for the guy at the register.

"Hey," she said. "You sell bleach?"

The man looked at her suspiciously. "Is this another one of those internet challenge things?" he asked. "Because when I sold those kids all those detergent pods, I had no idea they were gonna eat them. I'm still dealing with the lawsuits."

"I told you this wouldn't work," Josh said.

"Look," Madison told them man, "we're looking for a guy who works for Apex industries and buys a lot of bleach. Like every night."

"Probably paranoid," Josh added, "high strung, doesn't really like daylight, lots of leftover crumbs in his beard, if he has a beard..."

"Look," the man said. "You kids want some candy? Because I can help you with candy."

Madison felt her fuse starting to shorten. "Look at me in the eye, okay," she said. "I need information—"

Josh slapped a ten-dollar bill on the counter.

"We want *lots* of candy," Josh said.

"Josh," Madison began, "What are you—"

"Oh!" the guy said. "You mean *Bernie*. Yeah, I know that guy. Buys like a ton of bleach."

Madison and Josh exchanged a surprised look.

"I know where he is, too," the fellow went on. "If you buy a live fish, I'll give you his address."

* * *

A few minutes later they were at the address the man had given them. Madison knocked on the door. Nothing happened, and she was about to knock again when there was a sudden loud crashing sound from inside, as if someone had thrown a kitchen's worth of pots and pans on the floor.

"Bernie!" Madison shouted.

There was a light pause.

"Mister Bernie not at home," someone finally responded, in a weird accent that dithered between being Spanish or Russian or something else entirely.

"That was definitely Mister Bernie," Josh whispered.

"Listen," Madison said. "We want to talk about Apex … and Godzilla."

A sudden buzzing drew her attention to a camera on the wall.

"No! Ah, no! I've got your faces!" the Spanish Russian said. "I contact the authorities!"

"For what?" Josh said. "Knocking on your door?"

"Bernie, you don't trust the authorities," Madison said. "Bernie—please. My name is Madison Russell. My father works for Monarch. My mother was—"

The door flew open. Standing there was a man wearing welding goggles and holding what looked like a modified Taser gun. He lifted the goggles, staring at her with wide eyes.

"Emma Russell," he said. "Right?"

"That's right," she said.

He looked dubiously at Josh.

"And this guy?"

"He's all right."

Bernie glanced behind him into his house, then seemed to think better of it.

"Wait here," he said. "I know a place we can go."

* * *

The "place" was a Chinese restaurant, lit almost entirely by red neon. Madison was surprised at how hungry she was and realized she hadn't had breakfast, or anything since. The three of them ate, mostly in silence, with Bernie eying them furtively from time to time. But when they were done, Bernie pulled out a notebook and leafed through it. From what she could see, it was filled with rambling notes and clippings. He stopped on a page labeled "Emma Russell."

"Before we go any further," Bernie said, "I've got one question—tap or no tap?"

That was an easy one, if you had listened to any of his podcasts.

"No tap," Madison said.

"Excuse me?" Josh said. "What is tap?"

"Water," Bernie said. "They put fluoride in it. Learned it from the Nazis."

"The theory is it makes you docile," Madison said. "Easy to manipulate."

"I drink tap water," Josh admitted.

"Yeah," Bernie said, "I kinda figured that. But she does the thinking for both of you, so it should be all right."

"Thanks?" Josh said.

"Okay," Bernie said, turning his attention back to Madison. "Whatya got?"

"I believe Godzilla's most recent attacks haven't been just random," she said. "I think he targeted Apex."

Bernie looked her over. He seemed to like what he heard, but he also seemed … well, paranoid. Of course, if half of the stuff he laid out in his podcasts was true, he had a right to be.

"I'm of the same opinion," he finally said.

"But why?" Madison asked. "What is Apex up to that's provoking him?"

She didn't want to bring up her own suspicions just yet; she wanted to hear what *he* had to say before giving up that much.

Bernie lowered his voice further. "You know," he said, "for five years I've embedded myself inside this company. Trying to figure out what their game was. I started at a plant in Port Huron making ELF transmitters. Not like the elfs from the North Pole, which is something they tried to cover up for years…"

"Got it," Madison said. She had heard the North Pole stuff. Bernie had done three podcasts about it. Mad Truth—Bernie—could get really derailed by the North Pole stuff.

"Okay," Bernie said. He looked like he was trying to focus. "Then one day the design changed—they wanted us to create a circuit that conducted bone. *Bone!* Did some snooping, found out those transmitters were being sent *here*, to the Pensacola factory. So I asked for a transfer."

He produced a thumb drive, holding it like it was the most valuable thing on Earth.

"Then last week I stole this—a manifest of heavy cargo sent from here to Apex headquarters in Hong Kong, which makes no sense because we are not equipped for heavy shipping."

He smiled slightly and leaned back in the booth. Like the case was closed.

"And then what?" Josh asked.

"And then, *boom*, Godzilla shows up. Caved in half of the facility, but gave me a quick look at some suspicious tech inside a secret bunker—some pretty suspicious tech."

Bernie had been leaning closer to Josh as he spoke; Madison saw Josh's eyes flick down and widen.

"Yeah, but, uh … what is that?" Josh asked.

Madison saw it too—a concealed gun holster.

Bernie reached into his jacket and drew out a flask.

"This?" he said. "Katzunari single malt whisky."

"Yeah," Josh said. "But it's in a gun holster."

Bernie looked at him blankly for a moment.

"It was a gift from my Sara," he finally said.

"You have a Sara?" Josh said.

"Had," Bernie said. "She was my wife. She passed on."

He flipped through his notebook until he came to a picture. He held it so they could see. It was the two of them together. She looked happy and sweet, and the smile on her face could have lit up ten rooms at least.

"Lost her in a car accident," he said. "Happened a week after she left her job … at Apex Industries." He let that hang for a second, his eyes on the picture. Then he looked back up at them. "She was my rock. My true love. I'll tell you something," he said, indicating the whisky. "The day this is empty, that's the day you'll know I've given up."

Bernie stared back at the picture of Sara, and Madison knew that look. It was what she probably looked like when she saw the old family pictures, the ones with Andrew and Mom. Still alive, still smiling.

She had read a book once that said that every time a person died an entire universe was lost, a universe with planets and stars and infinite space and unlike any other universe that had ever or ever would exist. That was how she felt when she thought about Mom and Andrew. And she could see that was how Bernie felt about Sara. He had lost a universe; they had that in common. But what Madison had trouble imagining was how lonely Bernie must feel; because no matter how screwed up things got for her, she'd always had someone. Yeah, her dad was dismissing her right now. But he was *there*. And even though school in general was awful, she did have Josh.

Bernie didn't have anyone but an audience. He needed a partner in crime. And she needed that, too. And loss was not the only thing they had in common. There was also Godzilla.

"Bernie," she said, "I think we can help each other."

"Okay," Josh said, a little nervously. "I guess, now we're a team, I feel like we should have a plan."

To Madison, that part was obvious. And she knew Bernie was on the same page just as surely as if she could read his mind.

"We're breaking into Apex," she told Josh.

"Wait, what?" Josh said, as Madison got up and headed toward the door.

"You heard her, Tap Water," Bernie said.

"Well … shit," Josh said.

Tasman Sea

Ilene watched as Kong tucked into the several metric tons of fish one of the trawlers accompanying them deposited on the deck. They had packed away a ship's worth or two of concentrated protein rations in case they had a few bad catches, but so far, the sea had provided well, and Kong seemed to enjoy the catch well enough. She had been trying to engage him in conversation, but since demonstrating he could sign, Kong hadn't been inclined to do so. Not with her, anyway. She had hoped he would, now that the secret was out. It would be better if Jia wasn't the only one who communicated with him. She hadn't been getting anywhere, but once the food arrived, she knew it was hopeless. So instead she went to see the other half of the equation. Jia.

She paused at the door to her quarters. Jia was there, drawing, her Kong doll near at hand. For an instant she might have been any little girl, anywhere. But she wasn't, was she? She had suffered unimaginable loss. Ilene had believed she could fill part of that void, and perhaps she had. But until now, she hadn't realized to what extent Kong and the girl had a hold on each other. She knew that Jia was emotionally connected to Kong, but she had never realized that the relationship went both ways, or how strong it was. Strong enough for Jia to lie to her—or at least to omit the truth.

She sat on the bed.

Why didn't you tell me? she signed. *You know I've been trying to communicate with him. To understand.*

He didn't want you to know, the girl replied. *He was afraid.*

Afraid of what? Ilene wondered. But now she knew; Kong did not trust her. And after what had been done to him—what she had allowed to happen to him—he probably never would.

"Now everyone knows," Ilene said.

Jia nodded, continuing to draw.

If he had talked to me, maybe things would be different, Ilene said. *Does he understand that?*

I told him that, Jia said. *He didn't believe me. Now I'm not sure either.*

What do you mean? All I want to do is protect him.

Jia paused for a moment. Her face was without expression, which Ilene took to be a bad sign. The Iwi expressed so much meaning in their facial and body language that when they chose to be neutral, it could be interpreted as an active sign of distrust.

You have him tied up, Jia said. *It is not the first time. He doesn't know how you make him sleep, but he doesn't like it. It makes him helpless. He is helpless now. Are you stronger than a Skullcrawler? If one comes to get him, could you stop it?*

There are no Skullcrawlers here, Ilene replied.

No, Jia signed. *Worse. Godzilla is out here. You say what you are doing is best, but if Godzilla comes, you cannot protect him.*

You saw all of these ships, Ilene said. *All of the flying machines. They can protect him.*

Do you really believe that? Jia said. *Kong knows what is best for Kong. No one else should get to say. That is why he doesn't trust you.*

And you? Ilene asked. *Do you trust me?*

You do what you think is best, she replied. *But you are not Kong. And you are not…* She stopped signing and went back to her drawing.

Ilene felt her breath catch in her throat.

I'm not Jia, she signed. *I'm not you. Is that what you meant to say?*

Jia didn't answer, but she turned the picture around.

It was a drawing of Kong, lying down. He was surrounded by human figures bearing spears, maybe twenty of them, but most of them didn't have legs. From what Ilene knew of Iwi iconography, that meant they were ghosts, or ancestors. Only two of the figures had legs; one was smaller than the other. At the edge of the picture Jia had colored a dark cloud, and in it a pair of evil-looking eyes. It appeared to be entering the frame, coming down on the helpless Kong. The human figures had their spears pointed up toward the cloud.

This is you? she asked, pointing at the smaller figure.

Jia nodded.

Ilene pointed at the second figure with legs, which was holding a spear but did not have it raised in defense.

And this?

You, Jia said. And still she showed no expression.

Ilene nodded. *Stay in here,* she said. *I'll be back.*

In the ship's commissary, Nathan tuned out the clatter of cooks and other crew. He turned his little spaceman between his fingers a few times, laid it down, and then took out the picture of him and his big brother Dave. The last picture of them together, in fact, and the last time he had seen him, preparing to enter his modified aircraft.

Unto the breach.

Over time, the irony of the phrase had grown on Nathan. It came from Shakespeare's *Henry V*, spoken when the king was rallying his men to renew their attack on the French Army despite seemingly hopeless odds. Although Dave had never meant it that way, in retrospect it suggested that entering Hollow Earth was an act of war. If so, the first victory went to Hollow Earth. But the phrase had acquired another meaning over time: *try again.*

We'll get there, Dave, he thought. *Just wish we could do it together.*

He noticed Ilene coming toward him with two coffee cups. He tucked the picture away.

"Here," she said, handing him one of the cups.

"Thank you," he said. "How's Jia?"

"Calm," Ilene said. "So calm it's scary."

He pictured Kong's hand again, forming the sign.

"That was extraordinary," he said.

"I had been signing the alphabet," she said. "Basic commands. But he never…"

"Do you have any idea how long they've been communicating?" he asked.

She didn't answer right away.

"No," she said. "I mean, I knew that they had a bond. He trusts her. Without her, he'd be tearing this ship apart. You know … Jia's parents were killed on the island. When the storm took over the island, it wiped out the native people. But Kong saved her. She had nowhere to go. So, I made a promise, then and there, to protect her. I think that, in some way, he did the same."

"Do you think he'd take directions from her?"

"No," Ilene said. "No way."

But he heard something in her voice. She was protective of the girl, obviously. She felt responsible for her. When it came to Jia, he couldn't necessarily trust Ilene to tell the truth.

"If we have someone who can keep the reins on Kong..." he said, attempting to persuade her.

"No one can keep the reins on Kong," she said. "And she's a child."

Monarch Office, Pensacola

"I'm sorry," Mark said. "Can you repeat that?"

"It's why I wanted you to come here," Director Guillerman told him. "There's a lot going on, and frankly, I need an experienced man at my side."

"Sure," Mark said. "But just go over that bit again, will you. About moving Kong."

"We're moving Kong to Antarctica," the director said. "It's part of a new initiative to enter Hollow Earth. Apex has discovered a power source down there; they think it's the same energy Godzilla draws on. It may be our key to defeating him."

"Apex," Mark said, slowly. "As in the company that owns the facility in Pensacola that Godzilla attacked."

"Exactly."

"And you think this is a coincidence?"

Even as he said it, he realized he was echoing Madison, who was doubtless channeling her favorite conspiracy theorist. And yet it was now beginning to sound less crazy. Simmons had publicly declared war on Godzilla after his plant was attacked, but if he had this new information about some energy source in Hollow Earth, he must have been working on this way before that even happened. How long had Simmons and Apex been interested in Godzilla— and Kong—and why?

"Doubtless it isn't," Guillerman said. "We've worked with Apex in the past, mostly contract projects. But Walter Simmons has shown interest in the Titans since Godzilla first appeared in 2014. That's hardly surprising, when you think about it."

"Sure," Mark said. "It makes sense for someone who made their fortune in tech to be interested in the Titans. Any one of those things is a walking source of potential technology. The question is, when and why did Godzilla become interested in Walter Simmons?"

"Agreed," Guillerman said. "We're looking into that."

"And how did Apex end up running a Monarch expedition?" Mark pressed.

"They aren't," the director replied. "They're supplying the tech, but Dr. Lind is heading up the project."

"Dr. Lind. You mean Nathan Lind?"

"I believe you know each other."

"Sure, but I mean—his track record with Hollow Earth isn't exactly, ah, stellar."

"We've seen his plan," Guillerman said. "With these new Apex vehicles, he should be able to overcome the technical problems of the last expedition."

"And they need Kong because?"

"Hollow Earth is huge. Dr. Lind believes Kong will lead us to the power source."

"Oh my God," Mark said, sitting down. "Again."

"We have every chance of success this time," Guillerman said. "The Apex vehicles can withstand the strain of the gravity reversal."

"That's not what I meant," Mark said. "Again we're rushing into a situation we don't understand. Dealing with power we have only the faintest comprehension of. Have you asked Walter Simmons what he plans to do with that 'energy source' once he gets it?"

"He claims he will be able to control Godzilla," the director said. "Take him out, if necessary."

"Take him out," Mark said. "How? With what? What were they building in that factory?"

Guillerman nodded. "As I said, we're looking into it. If you have any thoughts on the matter, I would love to hear them."

Mark sighed. "I know," he said. "Answers are hard, and questions are cheap. But that's all I have right now."

"You and me both, Dr. Russell," Guillerman said. "I know I had big shoes to fill when I stepped in to take over where Serizawa left off, but—"

"You inherited a mess," Mark said. "A mess I had a part in making. I'm trying to come up to speed, too."

"We'd better both come up to speed, fast," Guillerman said. "If we don't, I'm afraid there might be hell to pay."

"Been there," Mark said. "I've got the ticket stub and the receipt."

TWELVE

From the notes of Dr. Brooks

And through the two of them heat took hold on the dark-blue sea, through the thunder and lightning, and through the fire from the monster, and the scorching winds and blazing thunderbolt. The whole earth seethed, and sky and sea: and the long waves raged along the beaches round and about, at the rush of the deathless gods: and there arose an endless shaking. Hades trembled where he rules over the dead below, and the Titans under Tartarus who live with Cronos, because of the unending clamour and the fearful strife.

Hesiod *Works and Days*, circa 700 BCE, trans.
Hugh G. Evelyn-White, 1914

Tasman Sea

Playing with her Kong totem, Jia could feel the Titan's heartbeat through the metal skin and bones of the ship.

It was smoother now, more even than it had been earlier, but she knew he was still angry, confused. More than that, he felt *lost*.

He had felt that way back in the fake jungle, too. He had known things weren't right, that the island that had been the home to their kind for so long was no more. But at least the rocks had still been there, just as the bones of his parents had remained to remind him that they had once been real. Now even that was gone, and all that remained of the island was the two of them, Kong and Jia. The last members of their people.

She felt the loss, too, but she also had a mother. She knew Ilene wasn't her real mother, of course, the one who had given birth to her. But with the Iwi, all women were mothers, whether they had given birth or not. Men, too for that matter, although that was sometimes difficult to explain to outsiders. Anyone who looked after you was a mother, and Ilene looked after her.

And in that same sense, Jia was a mother of Kong, and he of her.

Right now, he could not look after her. So she had to look after him.

She wondered exactly what others felt when someone's mouth moved, when language came from the tongue and lips—from the wind passing through them—instead of the hands, the face, the body. It would be useful, at times, to know what someone was saying when you weren't looking at them. On the other hand, she could feel things that they did not. Like Kong's heartbeat.

And … something else. *What was that?* Kong's heartbeat was picking up; he was more alert. More than alert, worried. More so than when he had first awakened, tied down. And his heart continued to beat faster.

But Jia felt something else. Something that wasn't

coming from Kong, but which he also was aware of. The thing that was making him anxious.

She put her hands against the metal wall, and felt it more strongly, tremoring through the water and into the skin of the ship. She had never experienced the pulsation before, or anything like it, but she knew what it was. Because *he* knew what it was. Kong had heard this back on the island, when he stood and pounded his chest. He had told her about it, but it was too faint for her to feel back then. Or maybe she just hadn't been ready to feel it. But now she did. A heartbeat, like Kong's, but different. And there was another vibration, high, then sharp.

As if he had a star inside of him.

And he was close, almost here, strong, getting stronger. And Kong, even with the stuff they had given him to subdue him—was becoming frantic. He knew what was happening. The old war had come for him, the war her people once told of. And Kong was helpless.

Understanding, Jia didn't hesitate any longer, but sprinted out of the room, searching for Ilene-Mother.

She ran into one of the many people on the ship; she signed, asking him where Mother was. He looked at her as if he didn't or couldn't understand.

Useless. She ran on, searching.

"I know Jia is only a child," Nathan said. "But she's the only one he'll communicate with. And we need Kong to find that power source. The world needs him."

Ilene was forming an answer when red lights began flashing and the ship's alarms blared. She turned and saw Jia standing in the doorway, signing like crazy. One of the signs was a new one—fingers held up, spread wide. Ilene had no doubt what it meant. She suddenly felt heavier, as if every molecule in her body had doubled in mass.

"What's she saying?" Nathan asked.

"Godzilla," Ilene replied.

When they reached the bridge, the crew was working frantically. Something—something big—had appeared in sonar, only to vanish in radiation interference as it got closer.

"Radiation readings are off the chart," someone said.

"Did we change course?" Ilene asked the Admiral.

"No," Wilcox said. "We're nowhere near the areas you flagged."

Nathan was staring at the monitors. "Well, it looks like he's coming for us anyway."

"He's not coming for us," Ilene said.

"What?" Simmons said, looking at Kong. "Him? Then dump him! Dump the monkey."

"Why don't we throw you off instead?" Ilene snapped.

Set Kong free! Jia signed frantically.

Kong seemed to agree. He was testing his chains again, but he also kept casting his vision out to the waves.

Ilene knew Jia was right. Their plan had depended upon getting Kong to Antarctica without Godzilla noticing he'd left Skull Island. It was now clear that they had failed. She did not know if Kong could survive a confrontation with the other Titan under the best of conditions, but he certainly had no chance tied up like he was, all prepped for vivisection.

"We need to release him," she told the others. "We have to let him go."

"See?" Simmons said. "I knew you'd come around."

"Not *dump* him," Ilene said. "Set him free."

"If we lose Kong the mission is over!" Nathan said.

"He's a sitting duck out there," Ilene said. "If Godzilla kills him, if he destroys this fleet, the mission is over. We have to let him protect himself. And us."

Nathan looked down, then away.

"It's your mission," Admiral Wilcox told him. "Call it."

But Nathan still didn't say anything; he just pursed his lips and seemed to be looking at something that wasn't there. The Admiral's expression shifted; Ilene thought it looked like disgust.

"Do something, Nathan!" Ilene shouted.

An explosion shattered the air; out on the water, a destroyer went up in a fireball. Black smoke boiled toward the sky.

The Admiral turned away from Nathan, disdain now written clearly on his face. "Scramble fighters!" he commanded. "All stations, acquire target lock and fire at will, *fire at will!*"

Nathan watched, paralyzed, as missiles and shells fired from every part of the fleet converged on a distant, still unseen target. They ruptured in the ocean, hurling up plumes of water and smoke, sending a shock across the ocean and in the air. It seemed impossible any living being could withstand such power. But then he saw Godzilla's fins appear as the monster cruised out of the smoke.

On deck, Kong was thrashing ever more desperately, trying to break his shackles, and for a terrible instant the Titan looked straight up at the bridge, directly, it seemed, at Nathan, both puzzled and angry at his helpless state in the face of his enemy. And there was something else in that look. Ilene believed the Iwi and perhaps other humans had gone to war with Kong in the past, and there was evidence that Godzilla, too, might have once had human followers. Did Kong feel ... betrayed?

Or did Nathan just feel like a betrayer?

He glanced at the Admiral, who was no longer paying attention to him. Why should he? Nathan had shown what he was made of, again.

He should have known better than to let Dave bully him into continuing the Hollow Earth mission. He had known in his bones that something was wrong, that he didn't have enough data, that his calculations were somehow off. He had let it happen anyway. He could not make the wrong decision again. He couldn't. Not with so much at stake. And yet the choice he had to make was impossible. There was no workable solution.

He watched in helpless horror as Godzilla cut a destroyer in half with his dorsal fins. Bombs tracked along his back; the unstoppable Titan kept coming, still swimming with his head down and his back out of the water, like an alligator. A pair of jets dropped down low over him and pounded him with missiles, which erupted in impressive columns of flame. Before they could reach safety, Godzilla's tail lifted from the water, curling as high as a skyscraper, swatting one of the jets from the air as if it were an insect. Then he brought the tail back down, bisecting a pair of warships, sending their crews running toward the rails as flames roared up from their fuel and munitions.

And on he drove toward them, toward Kong.

To make matters even weirder, one half of the destroyer the Titan had just annihilated suddenly jerked in the water and then began racing behind Godzilla, reminding Nathan of a fishing bobber after a big fish hit the hook.

Must have caught the anchor chain, he thought numbly, watching as the Titan came on, dragging half a freaking battleship behind it. Surreal didn't even begin to cover it; part of him wondered if it had finally happened and he was experiencing a psychotic episode.

He saw Ilene grab Jia and pull her toward the bridge

elevator. Where was she going? Kong? What did she think she could do?

Then Godzilla went under, and a moment later, so did what was left of the destroyer.

Kong, meanwhile, was slamming the deck, desperately trying to tear free of his restraints. Nathan glanced at the controls that would set him free, but he was still paralyzed with indecision. Was Ilene right? Was setting Kong free the only solution? Surely not. Surely with all of the firepower the fleet commanded, they could drive Godzilla away. Maybe he was already gone; it seemed like a long time since he vanished beneath the surface.

Then Godzilla came out of the ocean like a killer whale breaching, smashing into Kong and the deck he was chained to. Nathan watched, aghast, as the entire ship tipped over. It took him an instant to realize that this wasn't just something he was watching, that it was the ship he was *on*, that it wasn't just the deck tilting but the bridge, too. And him. And everyone else.

As he fell and slid across the swiftly tilting deck, he smelled seawater, and then everything whited out.

Ilene pulled Jia into the elevator and sealed the hatch behind her. She was acting on instinct now, trying to put one more barrier between Jia and the monster outside. As much as she had studied Godzilla, as much as she thought her experience with Kong had prepared her for other Titans, the reality was terrifying. In a handful of minutes, Godzilla had shrugged off everything the fleet could throw at him, destroyed three battleships, obliterated a fighter plane, and capsized a vessel large enough to carry Kong. Now they were upside down, and water was pouring into her chosen hiding place—and into the bridge even faster.

She gaped, horrified, at the sight of Kong, underwater, still in chains, fighting a losing battle for his survival. All of Monarch's planning, all of their military might swept aside with no more effort than someone on a picnic brushing their blanket clean of ants.

They had to release Kong. It was the only chance any of them had. But the pressure outside was too great, preventing her from opening the hatch. She began banging, trying to get Nathan's attention before the bridge filled completely with water and he drowned.

When Nathan came to, he was floating; water was gushing into the bridge, and everything was upside down. He heard muffled screaming and pounding from the elevator and saw Jia and Ilene were in it. They were above water, but like the bridge, the elevator was quickly filling. He couldn't tell what Ilene was saying, but he followed her frantic gestures. Through the bridge window, he saw Kong, underwater, still bound and still flailing, continuing to pull the ship over.

The ship should right itself, he thought, in a weird moment of clarity. *But it can't now with Kong pulling it down.* He was floating, with his head pointed at what had once been the floor. He looked down, toward the former ceiling, the controls, and the lever that would release Kong's manacles.

He shucked off his down vest and struggled toward the controls, as spiderweb cracks formed in the glass. When that shattered, the bridge would finish filling in an implosion, and it would be too late to do anything.

He steadied himself. *You can do this.*

But he ran out of breath and came up short.

Gasping, he dove again, swimming back down to the lever. Outside Kong had managed to rip off one of his manacles, but it was going to be too late if he didn't …

He felt his muscles hit their limit and knew he didn't have it in him. His lungs ached, and he remembered his talk with Ayara, about how he and his brother used to see who could stay under longest.

It had always been Dave who won. *He* was the failure, and always had been.

But then he remembered something else.

You can do it, little brother. Dave had said, as he breathed, preparing himself. *Another ten seconds this time. Don't worry about anybody else. This time you'll do your best.*

Goddammit, Dave, he thought.

And he squeezed everything he had left in him into reaching the lever. His finger touched it. Now it was in his grip, and he was still afraid of failing.

But he pulled it anyway.

Then the universe tossed him aside as Kong finally freed himself. Gravity reversed again as the huge vessel righted itself and water began to drain away; as if in a nightmare, he saw the colossal forms of Godzilla and Kong grappling beneath the surface. As the reptile snapped at Kong's face, the ape managed to kick Godzilla down into the depths, reaching for the ship.

Nathan felt the burn of saltwater in his throat and sinuses as Kong hauled himself out of the water and back onto the now righted, if listing ship. The Titan was gasping, too. But his eyes were tracking Godzilla, whose fins could be seen moving in a wide circle around the fleet. Kong pulled himself up to his full height. He reached up and broke the metal band around his neck, and roared, beating his chest.

Behind him, the elevator door opened, pouring out Ilene and Jia. The Admiral and bridge crew were recovering, but the controls were all dead.

Oh, Nathan thought as Kong continued to follow Godzilla's path. *Kong isn't going to wait for Godzilla to come back for him, is he?*

No, he thought, as the gigantic ape took a very short run across the deck and leapt. He bounced off a frigate as if it were a stepping-stone in a creek and landed squarely on the flight deck of an aircraft carrier. The whole ship lurched but Kong steadied himself, roaring a challenge at the other Titan swimming toward him. He grabbed one of the jets from the carrier deck and flung it at the oncoming Titan; Nathan saw the pilot eject an instant before the craft slammed into Godzilla's back.

It didn't slow the monster down. Tail pumping furiously, he broke from the water and slapped down on the deck, destroying several planes as he pulled his entire weight from the sea and gathered his hind legs beneath him.

But by that time Kong was ready. He threw a punch that would have made any street-brawler proud, connecting with Godzilla's snout and knocking him back on his taloned heels—but not far enough. Godzilla recovered and returned with an open-clawed slap that overbalanced Kong, tumbling him back. Godzilla stooped over him, but then a fusillade of missiles blasted into his back, stunning him for the few seconds it took for Kong to come up swinging, this time punching Godzilla over the side of the carrier. The reptilian Titan vanished beneath the waves.

For a moment, nothing happened; Kong stared down at the sea, his huge brows knit in concentration, searching for his vanished foe. Then he suddenly leapt aside as a blue bolt of energy shot up from below, blasting through the ship and narrowly missing the huge ape. Cut in half, the carrier began to sink, as Kong plunged into the water after Godzilla.

* * *

Free of the elevator, Ilene came alongside Nathan in time to see Kong dive.

Kong had never been shy of the rivers and lakes of Skull Island. He bathed in them, hunted in them, especially for mire squids and the enormous amounts of protein they contained.

But while he liked to look out over the ocean, especially in the rare days when the storm parted, he had always avoided getting into it, probably because he didn't like the idea of water deeper than he was tall. Whether he knew that from experimentation when he was younger, of from instinct, she did not know. Did Kong know how to swim? She couldn't remember if other apes swam or not. It seemed unlikely. But then again, Kong was not like other apes.

Whatever the case, Godzilla spent *most* of his time in the water.

"Kong could hold his own on solid ground," she told Nathan. "But this isn't his terrain. He needs our help."

But once again, Nathan was frozen with indecision, as if his effort in freeing Kong had drained him of all initiative.

"We're running out of time, Doctor!" the Admiral said.

The emergency power kicked in, and suddenly the controls and monitors of the bridge were alive again.

"Depth charges," Ilene said. "Depth charges. Maybe we can confuse Godzilla."

Lacking any input from Nathan, Wilcox seized on her suggestion.

"All ships, set submersibles for cyclical expansion. Multiple sources. Multiple sources!"

The enemy pulled Kong down.

Kong had sensed him before, many times. Sometimes it had been like an itch, but deep inside where he could not reach to scratch it. He had never seen him until now, yet there were no surprises when he did; like when he saw the bones of his parents, he knew what they were, although he did not really remember them. The shape of the enemy was like nothing he had ever seen, much less fought; but just the scent of the creature made him angry, and everything about it fit into a hollow spot inside of him, as if something had been taken out long ago and left empty until now.

He would have let it be. He had no interest in it; it did not threaten his island and those he protected. Why should he care about it or what it did?

But it had come for him, come when he was helpless. And for that, he wanted to break it, tear off its limbs, suck the meat from its bones.

But it was bigger, stronger than anything he had ever known. It made him feel things he did not understand and did not want to understand.

He had known the instant he was in the water that he'd made a mistake. He had fought things like this, the giant scaly predators that lurked in the waters of his island, that pulled smaller beasts beneath the surface and kept them there until they died. The largest of them had tried to kill him, but he always managed to plant his feet on the bottom of the river and snap them in half.

There was no bottom to this water, and the only thing to plant himself on was the enemy. While the water was also Kong's adversary, the enemy was friends with it. Rather than trying to go back up, where he could breath, the enemy only wanted to go down, deeper, where Kong could not.

If Kong let that happen, he knew the darkness in the middle of him, the ache for air, would eventually spread out into his arms and legs and the place where light came into his head. And then the enemy would triumph.

He had to break away, find his way back up to the air.

But as he thought this, the enemy only dragged him deeper with sweeps of its powerful tail. Parts of the metal things the small ones made went drifting by him. The things that floated on water, the flying-dead things like leafwings but faster. All falling in this pool that had no bottom. Like him.

Then the water slapped him, his ears rang from a sound like the booming the sky made, but closer to the booming made by the small ones with their flying-dead things. It hurt, but the enemy jerked in his grip. More booms came, and for the barest instant, the enemy lost his grip. Another sound happened just behind the enemy's head. Kong tore his arms loose and swung.

The water made his arm too slow, but his clenched fingers still connected. It was like punching a mountain, but even a mountain could give way if you hit it hard enough.

He pulled his legs up, put both of them against the enemy's chest, and pushed, even as everything seemed to be getting darker, like when the brighter circle light went into the water and the clouds blotted out the little dim ones. The middle of him hurt more than ever, aching for air. He pushed harder, broke free, but then the huge tail hit him, and all of the air came out of him in huge silver bubbles, and water rushed in to take its place.

The ocean's surface boiled from underwater explosions, and then an immense column of water geysered up. Ilene braced herself for what would come next, but it was … calm. The water went still.

That was bad. Godzilla was completely at home in the depths. If only he came up, it probably meant he had prevailed. If neither came up, it probably meant the same thing. The only way this turned out well was if…

Her thoughts were interrupted when Kong's hand shot out of the water and slammed onto the deck. Slowly, painfully, the Titan pulled himself onto the ship, coughing up tons of water and marine life. Then he collapsed, exhausted.

Relief flooded through her. He had survived. But had he won? She doubted it. If Godzilla came back for another try, it would all be over. Kong looked as if he could scarcely raise a fist.

Nathan could not focus. He was supposed to be in charge, why? Because he had such a great track record? All he wanted was out.

On one hand, he was aware that he was consumed with panic, and on the other hand, the nature of panic was that it would not let you think.

In the distance, Godzilla's fins were briefly visible through the flame and smoke of the ruined fleet.

"He's circling back," he said.

"This won't end until one of them submits," Ilene said.

I know that! He screamed in his mind. *Don't you think I know that?*

As long as the threat remained…

Wait. The threat. He remembered something, something Mark Russell had told him once over a beer in a hotel in Denver. About Godzilla, and Castle Bravo…

"Shut it down," he told Admiral Wilcox. "All of it. Guns. Engines. Shut it down. Now!"

"If we do that, we're dead," Wilcox retorted.

"No," Nathan said. "We're *playing* dead."

For a heartbeat or two, no one answered. But Ilene got it.

"Make him think he's won," she said.

The Admiral looked at Nathan, and his face changed. Nathan wasn't quite sure how to read it, because he hadn't seen the expression from him before. But it looked like ... approval.

"Cut all engines," the Admiral commanded. "Cut all power. Cease fire. No radio. Kill anything that makes noise." He glanced out to sea. "This had better work."

Everything went quiet, so quiet it was surreal. Nathan hadn't realized just how much ambient noise there was even without the explosions until it was gone.

Come on, he thought. It had to look real enough; most of the ships really were gone. Smoke and fumes obscured vision; the water was full of their wreckage, of burning fuel and flotsam. And ... bodies. Nathan had no sense of the casualty count yet. He prayed that it was small.

For a stretch of time, nothing happened. Then, in the distance, the water rippled as Godzilla's head rose from it, just a little, like an alligator having a surreptitious look around.

Kong was still laid out on the main deck, exhausted, one eye wearily tracking for danger, his chest rising and falling slightly but the rest of him as still as a corpse.

Please let this work, Nathan silently pleaded. No more fighting, no more death. He had promised Ilene Kong would be okay. He had promised Jia.

Served him right for promising things not in his power to deliver. If Godzilla didn't fall for this, everything was lost.

The reptilian head glided through the water, rotating here and there, surveying the wreckage, the flames, the silent remains of the armada.

Then Godzilla abruptly rose out of the water, slamming his tail into the waves and screeching a long nightmarish howl of victory, before plunging once more into the depths.

At first, Nathan feared it was just another ruse, that the Titan would surface again, right beneath their feet and savage what little was left of their expedition. But after several very long minutes, it seemed the ruse had worked.

Jia went to the window; Nathan saw Kong had lifted his head and was staring at her. The girl signed something. Then Kong slumped to the deck. His eyes closed, but he could still see the Titan's chest moving.

THIRTEEN

"So, loyal listeners—class—I'm going to give you an assignment. Dr. Strangelove. It is a movie. And yeah, it's in black-and-white—get over it. Get a little culture. You need to see it. Not because it's funny—oh, it's really funny. But because it's the blueprint. It's got the stuff in it. The whole truth about the military–industrial complex, the government, everything. And they got away with it because they were playin' it for laughs. Laugh all you want, but pay attention. Tap water, the privileged conspiracy for the 'select persons' to survive a nuclear war, the power elite—all there. Watch it. Take notes. Then we'll circle around back to this."

Mad Truth, *Titan Truth Podcast* #98

Tasman Sea

Ilene watched Jia sign to Kong.

Thank you, friend, was how she would translate in English. But the Iwi concept of "friend" was deeper in every way than its English counterpart. Kong seemed to acknowledge that before he passed out.

She regarded the devastation around them. Godzilla had wrecked their seemingly indomitable fleet in minutes.

Wilcox was in conference with his aides. When he was done, he approached them.

"This vessel is no longer seaworthy," he told them. "We might limp a little closer, but we'll never make it to Outpost 32."

"Can we use another ship?" Nathan asked.

The Admiral shook his head. "Anything we might have had capable of handling Kong is at the bottom of the sea or on its way there. We might make the Antarctic coast, but not all the way around to the outpost. We would founder somewhere east of there. Or we could try to make it to Australia or South Africa. Either way, I don't like our odds. I'm looking for a supertanker or something that might be able to meet us at sea, but so far everything is too far away. We're really in the middle of nowhere here."

"As soon as we move," Ilene said, "he'll be back. So how are we going to get the rest of the way?"

But Nathan had an idea.

"How is Kong with heights?" he asked.

"You're absolutely certain we need him? The monkey?" Maia Simmons asked. She crossed her arms and looked at Kong. "The HEAVs will make it to Hollow Earth, I promise you."

"Sure," Nathan said. "But once we get there, then what?

Your father's satellite imaging shows there is a power source down there. But to use it, we have to locate it."

"How hard can that be?"

Nathan put up his hands as if holding a globe.

"If I'm right," he said, "Hollow Earth is huge, a whole world unto itself. Think about it—if the Titans came from there—"

"Then it's big, yes," Simmons said. "I get that. But if we can literally see this power source from orbit, we should be able to triangulate it once we're down there."

"Maybe," he conceded. "Eventually. But there is a *lot* going on between here and there—there's the membrane, polarity reversal, all kinds of weird magnetic phenomena. Imagine we are going into a huge mansion, and we want to find an electrical socket to plug something into. There are wires everywhere; if we have the right equipment, we can even trace the electrical wires in the wall. But there are lots of wires, right? And in this whole three-story mansion, there's only one socket, and we don't know where that is."

"And the monkey does?" Simmons said, gesturing toward the Titan with one hand. "I thought he'd never been down there."

"Genetic memory," Nathan said. "I think he has a map of this place built into him, whether he knows it or not. Look—when loggerhead sea turtles are born on a beach in Florida, they take an eight-*thousand*-mile trip around the Atlantic basin. With no one to guide them, right? The mothers lay the eggs and leave. But these little turtles, they know where to go, and they steer using variations in the Earth's magnetic field, until they—the females, anyway—end up back up on the same beach where they hatched to lay *their* eggs. This isn't learned behavior. It's hardwired. Having the biological equipment to sense the magnetic fields isn't enough: they have to *know* when to turn.

Where their mothers turned, and their mothers, on back for thousands, maybe millions of years. Like recognizing a landmark you've never actually seen before—"

"Okay," Simmons said, pushing one palm toward him. "You don't have to beat it to death. I get it. You think Kong is tuned to this energy the way sea turtles are to magnetic fields. And even if it's been a few generations since his kind came up here, he should still be able to recognize these 'landmarks.'"

"Yes," Nathan said. "That's it exactly. I discussed this with your father. I thought he might have mentioned it."

She raised her eyebrows.

"You think so?" she said. "But that would be too easy. My father thinks a lot of me. He trusts my intelligence. He trusts it *so* much he is always testing it. He told me where to bring the HEAVs and gave me instructions about the power source. He failed to mention our primate friend would be involved. Probably his little joke. I'm sure he knew that I would either figure it out or you would tell me. That's my dad. Always thinking of my betterment."

"Okay," Nathan said. "I'm sorry he—"

"Oh, get over it," she said, rolling her eyes. "I have. One day I'll inherit a multi-billion-dollar empire. I can deal with a few head games for that, even if it does give me daddy issues." She nodded, as if to herself. "So," she continued, "you've got a plan to get the monkey…" He made a little face. "Fine," she muttered. "I know he's not a monkey, you know. To get *Kong* the rest of the way?"

"Yes," Nathan said.

"Great," she said. "The HEAVs should be in Antarctica by now. Sounds like we're still on."

"We're still on," Nathan agreed.

* * *

As Ilene zipped herself into the dark blue flight suit, Jia continued to stare at the one provided for her.

See, Ilene signed. *It's just clothes.*

Looks strange, the girl replied. *Tight.*

We need to wear them, Ilene said. *So we can stay with Kong.*

Jia frowned. *I like my clothes,* she said. *My maiden shawl…*

Ilene knelt down in front of her. *You can keep that on,* she said, taking the red shawl and settling it over the girl's head. *It can be your hood, okay? And you can keep your necklace and circlet on, too.*

She held up the little suit. *It looks tight, but it's okay. It will help protect you.*

Jia took it from her, held it gingerly. Then she nodded.

For Kong, she signed.

Apex Facility, Pensacola

The Apex facility wasn't so hard to break into now that most of it lay in rubble. Madison, Josh and Bernie had to evade a few security guards half-heartedly patrolling around the wreckage and cross some yellow tape. After that, most the obstacles were rubble related.

"So what's the plan?" Madison asked.

"We find out what's on sub-level 33," Bernie said.

They turned on their flashlights and followed Bernie across a fissure in the concrete.

"I don't have the right shoes for this," Josh complained.

"Keep it moving, Tap Water!" Bernie said.

A moment later, they stood at the mouth of a dark tunnel that had collapsed so as to slope downward.

"All right, Mad Hatter," Bernie said. It wasn't clear to Madison if he was talking to her or to himself. "Down

191

the rabbit hole." He and Madison shared a complicated fist-bump before they sat on the incline and he slid down to the next floor.

"Are you sure we can trust him?" Josh whispered to Madison, as she prepared to follow.

"Yeah," she replied. "Why?"

"I don't know," Josh said. "Well, maybe because he mostly says crazy shit all the time and carries a bottle of whisky from his dead wife like a gun?"

"I think it's romantic," Madison said. Then she slid down after Bernie.

"I really don't understand women," Josh said, behind her.

"This all looks really different than it did before it was smashed up," Bernie said, as they made their way through darkened, debris-strewn corridors. "I mean, I used to work here. I used to use that bathroom right down there."

"I feel some of these details aren't needed," Josh said.

"Thing is," Bernie said, "I like it better this way. Quiet and destroyed. Oh, man did I hate this place. I've never been so happy to be unemployed."

"Are you sure you're unemployed?" Madison asked. "I mean, on the news they were saying they would find jobs for everyone."

"Yeah," Bernie said. "Everyone alive. With any luck, they think I'm dead."

"You faked your death?" Josh said.

"I didn't report in," Bernie said. "Last time I checked I was on the missing list."

"Won't that worry somebody?" Josh said. "Your mom, or dad, or ... somebody?"

Bernie stopped for a second. He looked down at the floor. Then, after a breath or two, he continued on.

"Anyone ever tell you you talk too much, Tap Water?" he said.

"Honestly," Josh said. "All the time."

They came to a security door; Bernie used a screwdriver on the control panel to jimmy it open. They entered a long hall, collapsed in most places.

"This whole place came down," Bernie said, looking around. "And there was this … eye." He shone his torch through a broken wall; inside was a great hollow space, with lots of severed wires and conduits. As if something had been hastily pulled out.

"What are we looking for?" Josh asked.

"No, no, no," Bernie muttered. "It was right here. I swear to God, it was right there!"

Madison was noticing something else.

"Hey guys," she said, motioning to an elevator. "Anyone know where this leads to?"

She stepped in. Whatever the condition of the rest of the building, the elevator looked like it still had power.

Bernie and Josh followed her in.

"You believe me, right?" Bernie said to Josh. "'Cause I know there was something there."

"Sub-level 33," Josh said, as Madison pushed the button. "How deep does this thing go, Bernie?"

"Hell," Bernie muttered. "It goes to hell."

When the elevator door opened, they were no longer looking at a ruined facility, but a highly functional one. Sub-level 33 was obviously way below the damage Godzilla had caused; the Titan had scraped off the top of an anthill, but most of the nest was underground. They must also be far below sea level, Madison figured. That made her a little nervous, but the dozens of people going about their tasks were the obvious, more immediate worry. No one seemed to have noticed them arrive, though, or at least didn't give them a second glance if they did. Unauthorized personnel on this level were probably unheard of. If you got off the elevator, you belonged. And Bernie, at least, had on the right outfit.

Still, they moved away from the elevator immediately.

The space itself was enormous; in the distance she saw techs at control panels, but most of the area immediately in front of them was occupied by lozenge-shaped transportation pods with blue LED lighting tracing their contours. A crane had just lifted one of the pods and was conducting it toward a large pair of doors set above the level of the floor. As she watched, the doors opened, revealing a tunnel. The crane placed the pod in the tunnel and the doors closed.

"What is all of this?" she asked.

"Breakaway civilization," Bernie said. "I mean, c'mon. This is page one in the Apex-playing-God handbook. Huh? I mean, the Illuminati running a shadow economy all to fund a hidden colony for the elite in case any of these governments or mega-corporations accidentally hit the doomsday button." He looked at Josh, walking away from him. "Makes a lot of sense, if you think about it," he insisted.

"Ah," Josh said, dubiously. "Yeah."

Madison took that in. Monarch had bunkers all over the world designed for civilization to hide out in in case thing went really badly, and they had in fact been used three years ago. She had been in the one near Boston. But this didn't look like a bunker. The voice on the loudspeaker kept calling out destinations—Mexico was the one she caught—and times so that it was more like a train station.

"Maglev," Bernie muttered.

"What?"

"The manifest. Said something about maglev. That must be what these things are."

"Yeah," she said, slowly. "I think you're right."

Madison had seen prototypes and working models of advanced magnetic levitation trains while hanging around Monarch, and she had ridden the maglev train in Shanghai, one of the few already in use. This looked a lot like a next— or maybe next-next—generation version of that. When in operation, the pods would be suspended above a track using one set of magnets and propelled by another set. As a result, there was no friction between train and track to slow it down. Accelerated like a metal slug in a railgun, the only thing limiting its speed was the amount of energy put into the acceleration, the drag of gravity, and air resistance— and she was willing to bet that further down that tunnel the atmosphere would be pumped out, creating a near vacuum where the upper velocity could be faster than a supersonic jet.

Bernie had his notebook out and was scribbling like mad.

Madison understood the train. But the rest of it, what was actually going on here...

She heard footsteps approaching.

"Someone's coming," she said.

They were close to one of the maglev cars now; the three of them ducked in to hide.

When the footsteps faded, Madison peered out the train window opposite to the door they had come in. Outside, Apex workers with flashlights were loading something into another train from huge pallets; giant egg-shaped objects with fetus-like shadows floating inside.

"Oh, my God," Madison said. Because she knew what they were. She had never seen one in person, but in her time with her mother she'd learned plenty about them.

"They look like eggs," Josh said.

"Skullcrawlers," she said. Massive semi-reptilian monsters

from Skull Island, these were the chief antagonists of the island's alpha, Kong. Nasty, terrible things by all accounts. "What's Apex doing with Skullcrawlers?"

"Um … Madison?" Josh said.

She turned to find out what he wanted, and then she saw. The car they were in was already packed with Skullcrawler eggs.

"Oh, crap," she said.

"Yes," Bernie said. "I think maybe it's time we leave. I've got a podcast to record, and—"

He was cut short by the metallic sound of the door they had come though gliding shut.

"What was that?" Bernie asked.

The whole car jolted and then started to lift up.

"Uh, guys?" Josh said. "I think we're moving."

"No kidding," Madison said.

They were being lifted up by a crane, in fact. But as far as she could tell, looking down, still no one had noticed them. They had just become unwitting additions to a shipment of Titan eggs headed—someplace.

Josh and Bernie were using brute force trying to get the door to open but having no luck. Josh did finally manage to pop a panel open that had a screen inside with routing information.

"Oh," he said.

"What?"

"It says we're heading to Apex headquarters—Hong Kong."

Bernie seemed to relax. He even smiled. "Hong Kong," he said. "That means we're going to get some answers."

The doors opened, revealing the tunnel again. The crane settled them in, and they bumped forward until the doors closed behind them. The car began to rise up into the air. Madison flicked her eyes nervously around the Skullcrawler eggs that took up most of their space. She felt as if the walls of the pod had shrunk to fit her skin, making it hard to breathe. What if the eggs sensed food and hatched early?

"I hope that these guys don't mind that we're tagging along," she said.

"What happens if they hatch? Do they, you know, get on your face?"

Madison shook her head. "Hatchlings are fully independent at birth. Just smaller versions of the adults."

"Okay," Josh sighed.

"They're born starving," Madison said. "They will just straight-up eat us."

Josh stared at the nearest egg. "No, please," he said.

A few yards down the tunnel, the car took off like a rocket. She glanced back at Josh, at the fear on his face, and she wanted to tell him that it was okay, she was scared, too. But knowing Josh, that would have the wrong effect, give him license to panic. As long as he thought she was okay, he would try to hold it together, if for no other reason so she couldn't make fun of him later.

Instead, Madison tried to piece together exactly what was happening. Hong Kong? That meant the tunnel they were in ran all the way beneath southern North America and then the entirety of the Pacific Ocean. That was one hell of a tunnel. And Apex had built it all without anyone knowing about it, with maglev technology? And if there was one tunnel like this, how many more were there? How many places could Apex ship massive cargoes of Titan eggs or whatever without the risk of being noticed?

Even some of Bernie's crazier conspiracy theories were starting to sound more reasonable. This was going to be some ride.

"Here we go," she said.

Antarctica

"Yeah, whatever," Sergeant "Class" Zivkovic said, flipping off the handset.

"What's up, Sarge?" Ryan asked, wiping frost off his gloves.

"Just Eskibel out on the point, yanking our chains again," Class said.

"What this time?" Ryan wanted to know. "Another man-eating penguin?"

"Something like that." He looked past Ryan at Martin, who was clicking his rosary beads again.

"Martin," he said. "You okay?"

"I don't like this place, Sarge," Martin said. "All those people, just straight up murdered at the outpost. You know they laid out there almost a year before anybody ever came and got 'em?"

"It's a deep freeze here, Martin," Class said. "I'm sure the bodies kept just fine."

"Yeah, their bodies," Martin said. "But…" He trailed off.

"You think there are ghosts here, Martin?"

Martin looked stricken. "Sarge, you know I do," he said. "People have souls. When we die, sometimes they go on. Sometimes they don't get far at all. I feel like some of these are hanging around, y'know?"

Class sighed and nodded.

Personally, he didn't believe in ghosts, but it had been a bad business, the massacre at Monarch Outpost 32. A bunch of mercenaries lead by an ecoterrorist and a rogue Monarch scientist had engineered it and blasted the frozen Titan Ghidorah out of its icy tomb. After that, of course, all hell had broken loose. The old base had been mostly destroyed by the explosion and the ensuing fight between Ghidorah and Godzilla. But the Monarch guys and the government had found something else to merit their attention out here on this godforsaken frozen continent. The Vile Vortex. They were a few miles from the old outpost, but they had done recon there earlier, and it had left some of the men shaken—Martin in particular. And the new site about three klicks south of them—well, it had its own weirdness.

Why exactly he and his men were here hadn't been explained to him, only that they should report in if they saw anything other than birds.

"Yeah," Martin said, suddenly, apparently not done with whatever it was he felt he needed to say. "I know you all think I'm crazy, but yeah. I mean they've got the freakin' gateway to hell right up there, and things—bad things are hanging around."

"That's not what it is," Class said.

"Yeah? The 'Vile Vortex,' then. You know what happened to the last poor souls who tried to go in one of those."

"Soldier, get a grip," Class said. "Nobody is asking you to go in, are they?"

"No, sir," Martin said. But after a moment he went back to his rosary.

"So what was it, Sarge?" Ryan asked.

"What?"

"Eskibel. What was he yanking your chain about?"

"Oh," Class rolled his eyes. "Monkeys. Eskibel said to keep an eye peeled for flying monkeys."

"Yeah," Ryan said. "Okay, then. And maybe a wicked witch or two."

Class was just calling in another report when they heard the thuttering in the distance. The sound was unmistakably helicopters, and a lot of them. Dozens, maybe.

"Choppers," Ryan said.

"Yeah," Class replied. "Must be our flying monkeys."

"You know what's going on, Sarge?" Ryan asked.

"That's above my pay-grade, soldier," Class said, as the sound drew nearer.

He strained his eyes to see through the fog. Well, it wasn't fog really, but instead a fine mist of snow and ice particles suspended in the Antarctic air, but the effect was the same.

He saw them then, heavy-lift choppers, flying in formation.

Then he looked lower, at the immense shadow below them, something lying in a bowl-shaped mesh net bigger than a football field.

"Oh, shit," Ryan said. "It *is* a flying monkey."

Sure, Class thought. If a monkey was the size of the freaking Chrysler Building. But he was aware his jaw was hanging open and shut it deliberately.

He tracked the huge ape as it passed over them, suspended by cables from the helicopters above.

"Well," he said. "There's something you don't see … ever."

Behind him, Martin's prayer grew a little louder.

"*Piki ába ish binili ma. Chi hohchifo hát…*"

"Martin?"

Martin broke off. "Sarge?"

"Go ahead and pray," Class told him. "And uh, you can include the rest us, if you want."

"Sure," Martin said, and started again, in English this time. "Our Father, who art in heaven…"

FOURTEEN

There is only one untouched reservoir of raw
materials left in the world, and that's in the region
known as Antarctica. An area larger than the
combined area of the United States and Europe. The
American government is sending a naval expedition
to that region. The purpose is to train our navy in
polar operations so that it may better perform its
function of preserving the peace upon the seven seas
of the world. Beyond that, the American government
is seeking to do its share in the discovery and release
to the world of the unknown treasures of Antarctica
in the interest of all mankind.

James V. Forrestal,
United States Secretary of Defense,
in the documentary
The Secret Land, 1948

Antarctica

They'd had to tranquilize Kong again, of course. His fight with Godzilla had left him exhausted, but they couldn't take chances. They had dosed him while he slept and strapped him into the same harness they had used to transport him onto the ship in the first place. The ship had lasted long enough to get them within around two hundred miles of their objective before she could no longer support Kong's weight.

From there it had been a long, slow flight carrying the Titan by helicopter. Wilcox had used what resources they still had to set up an in-flight refueling schedule, since there was no place to set down. They had cast a wide net, alert for Godzilla, but fortunately, the big lizard didn't catch on to what they were doing. Either that, or he no longer cared.

Nathan rode in the back of one of the helicopters, along with Maia, Ilene and Jia. They had all donned their flight suits, so as to be ready to board the HEAVs as soon as it became necessary. He noticed Jia still had on her red shawl, now configured to serve as a hood. The girl watched with fascination as the sea became spangled with broken sheets of ice and eventually merged into the ice pack of the frozen continent.

He noticed Jia signing to Ilene.

"What's she asking?" Nathan asked.

"Why everything is white," Ilene responded.

"Yeah," he said. "I guess she's never seen snow before."

"There's a lot of things she's never seen before," Ilene said. "There are a lot of things I'm not at all eager for her to see."

"I'm sorry," he said.

She shook her head. "It's not your fault. Well, some of it is. But really it has just been a chain of events that started with Monarch first finding Skull Island in '73. We should

202

have left it alone, once we knew what was there. That *he* was there. But we didn't. And I was a part of it, too. I could have studied anywhere, but it had to be Skull Island."

"You didn't cause any of this," he said.

"I didn't stop it," she said. "When they started talking about setting charges in the Skull Island Vortex, to open it up for exploration, I knew it was a bad idea. I knew it in my bones. And I did nothing. So now Kong and Jia have no home. Unless you're right. Unless it's down there."

"You don't think it is?" he asked. "It's your theory."

"It's still my theory," she said. "But to paraphrase Thomas Wolfe—who was, by the way, paraphrasing Ella Winter—sometimes you can't go home again."

Nathan nodded, not so much because he was agreeing with her, but because it felt like the conversation had run its course. Everyone had regrets, and everyone had fears for the future. He had let that petrify him on the ship. He couldn't afford that kind of indecision anymore. Hindsight was easy. Looking forward was hard.

He watched the frozen terrain of Antarctica go by beneath him.

"We're getting close," he said.

Ilene nodded, but didn't say anything. Jia's young face was creased with concern.

The moment of truth was coming. He had been thinking of Kong as a walking compass needle, a guide with no agenda of his own. That was why it had been easy to watch him anesthetized, loaded onto a ship, strapped down, made helpless against his foe. But now Nathan knew better. Jia and Ilene had always known better, had been trying to tell him all along. Finally he had to face the fact that the Titan not only had agency but was accustomed to exercising it. Used to being in charge of his own fate. And while Nathan could drag the proverbial horse halfway around the world, he could not make him drink. A captive Kong couldn't lead them anywhere; it was entirely possible at this point that a freed Kong wouldn't either. In this moment it all hinged on the Titan—and the tiny girl who had bonded with him.

They approached a vast, snow-covered canyon, far too symmetrical to have been made by nature. The immense, squared-off trench ended in a gigantic metal valve that was opening as they arrived. The canyon walls were covered in catwalks and entrances to interior space, like a city had been built into the vertical walls. The new, improved, slightly relocated Monarch Outpost 32.

The helicopter Nathan and the others were in settled on a helipad dug down into one end of the canyon, which formed a semi-protected hangar, as the other choppers landed Kong into the snow below. He was still sedated, of course. If he had awakened in flight, Nathan shuddered to think what would have happened.

"Where are the HEAVs?" he asked Simmons.

"Downstairs," she said. "Warming up."

He nodded, feeling the heaviness of the moment. Despite his pretensions to the contrary, deep down Nathan knew they were about to truly venture into the unknown. Walter Simmons and his daughter insisted these new vehicles could make the trip, survive the gravity inversion that had killed Dave and his team. And while Nathan believed he understood the physics of how the HEAVs operated, he was a geologist, not an engineer. And whatever trials the Apex scientists had put these things through, they had not yet encountered the only test that actually mattered. The Vortex itself.

"That's it, isn't it?" Ilene said.

He followed her gaze to the enormous circular opening that had been bored in the ice-covered cliff and braced with a metal frame. He knew that the hole was usually closed by a dilating door, but that had already been withdrawn into the surrounding mechanism, leaving the way to Hollow Earth wide open. He nodded.

"I've only seen it in pictures," he replied. "Back when we were trying to decide on an entry. It's bigger than I thought. And they've … uh, done a lot with it."

"This is where they found Monster Zero," she said.

"Near here," he said. "In fact, I didn't even know about Ghidorah back in the day. That was above my security classification. I thought Outpost 32 was all about *that*." He nodded at the opening below them.

"It seems like more than coincidence," she said. "That Ghidorah should be frozen in the ice so near an entrance to Hollow Earth."

Nathan nodded. "Lots of theories there," he said. "Was Ghidorah going into the Vortex, or had it just come out of it? Or neither? The ice all around here is more than thirty million years old. The ice around Ghidorah was younger, based on the samples they took when they found it. And the structure of the ice is different; it clearly melted quickly and re-froze quickly. How did that happen? There isn't enough evidence to land on a good explanation."

Ilene was staring down, off to their left, at the entrance to the rift.

"It's bigger than the one on Skull Island," she said. "Why didn't you use this one before?"

"Bigger means less stable," he said. "Wait until you see it inside. The opening is comparatively small. You've seen those little burrows sand crabs dig in the beach? Just an inch or less in diameter? Those are pretty stable. Now imagine trying to dig a burrow ten feet in diameter in the same sand."

"It wouldn't hold," she said.

"Right. The structural integrity of the sand doesn't scale up. And it's more than just that; I speculated that a larger opening also increases the intensity of the membrane. The acceleration will be even greater than in the Skull Island Vortex. Back then, math said nothing we could build would make it through. I thought at Skull Island we had a shot, but even there I miscalculated. But the HEAVs change everything."

"You hope," she said.

"That's right," he replied. "Look, it might be best if you and Jia—"

"If Kong goes, we go," she said.

And there, of course, was the billion-dollar question. Would Kong go?

He noticed Jia signing something to Ilene.

"What?" he asked.

"Kong's waking up," she replied.

The cables snapped explosively from the net, and the helicopters turned and started to fly away.

Nathan looked down and saw the ape's gargantuan eyelids fluttering open. Kong watched the helicopters leave, probably wondering what the hell was going on. Then he spotted them, looking down on him from their balcony.

Nathan realized he was holding his breath. If Kong bolted now, it was all over. They might be able to capture him again, but that would further lower their chance of obtaining his cooperation. If they couldn't, it was debatable whether the Titan would starve or freeze to death first.

This had to work. They could enter Hollow Earth without Kong, but it might take years to find what they were looking for. And with Godzilla gone mad, they did not have years. Or even weeks.

Kong scooped up some snow in his palm, looking puzzled, then angry. He roared as he sifted it through his fingers; he clearly did not approve of the frozen precipitation or his surroundings in general. How could he? He had spent all of his life on Skull Island, near the equator, where even the tallest mountain peaks had never known the kiss of snow or ice. There were no trees here, no underbrush, no waterfalls, and there had not been for tens of millions of years. It was difficult to imagine what Kong was thinking right now, what he believed was going on. How he would react.

It was easier to imagine, Nathan thought, as Kong clambered to his feet, who the Titan would blame for the situation. He had seen the intelligence in those eyes, the accusation. Kong knew who had done this to him.

Time to face the music, he thought.

Kong rose up from the frozen field below until his head was level with their perch. He stared right at them, anger evident on his features, so humanlike and so alien at the same time. His gaze switched between the three of them, as if weighing them somehow. Deciding something.

Then he huffed, reached down and scooped up more snow. He presented it to Jia, his brow furrowed. Nathan wasn't an expert on Kong's nonverbal communication, but it didn't take a degree in ethology to figure this one out.

What's going on? he was asking.

Kong was looking to Jia for the answer. That was a good sign. But Jia was no easier to control than Kong, was she?

Jia looked at Ilene, then back at Kong. The moment stretched out. Then, making her decision, Jia pointed to the Vortex.

Home, she signed.

That's right, Nathan thought.

But when Kong looked at the rift, he seemed anything but convinced. Jia held up her little Kong doll, pointed to it, then back to the Vortex.

Nathan realized he was still holding his breath, and he was starting to get dizzy. He let it out and drew in the clean, cold air. But it did not make him feel more confident.

"It's not working," he said.

"Wait," Ilene said. "Just wait."

But that wasn't good enough. All of those people who had died at sea, trying to get them here. And for what? It rested on a little girl being able to convince her god to do something he didn't want to do. Kong had been told he was going "home" before, on the ship. Now he was in a strange, cold place—clearly not "home"—and now Jia was pointing him toward the only place around that looked even worse than where he already was.

"What…" Nathan said, thinking out loud. "What if she tells him that there are more down there? Like him?"

"We don't know that," Ilene said.

"Then what are we supposed to do?" Nathan demanded. "He's not moving! We lost our entire fleet getting here. There's no way back for him. And he can't survive here. This is your theory. Hollow Earth is his home."

As Kong's options dwindled, for days Ilene had kept the despair at bay by trying to imagine alternatives. There were islands in the Pacific no one lived on. They were small, to be sure, but some were bigger than Kong's containment had been. The ecosystem of Skull Island was destroyed, but before that destruction was complete, a team had collected seeds, spores, cell tissue, and even eggs from many of the doomed species. Why not populate some nowhere island with Skull Island flora and fauna, build a containment around it, and start again? It wouldn't even have to be an island—they could build a preserve in some remote corner of the Congo or the Amazon Basin.

It was a nice thought. An alternative to the unknown. But now that they were actually here, on the precipice, the fantasy evaporated like morning dew in the desert. Even if she could get the funding and the staff to build such a place, it would still be cage, a zoo, a test tube. Kong would never be free, never in control of his own destiny. The next time somebody like Nathan came up with some "use" for Kong, he would be just as vulnerable—and the next person might not be as well-intentioned as Nathan.

Anyway, if Kong was anywhere in the known world other than in containment on Skull Island, odds were good that Godzilla would come for him again. On dry land, Kong might fare better in a rematch, might even beat Godzilla, although that was now hard for her to imagine— but it would also mean a return to the days of Titans fighting in human territory, and all of the destruction that meant. Even if he won, Kong would never be able to rest.

Down there, where she believed his species had originated—maybe he could. It was a chance, at least. And if Nathan was right, and the energy down there could also stop Godzilla—that was bonus points.

The way down was dangerous. Kong would not be in a HEAV. But the evidence was that Titans had been making the transition from the surface to Hollow Earth for millions—maybe hundreds of millions—of years. Their size and biological make-up must be adapted to the dangers posed by the Vile Vortex.

Kong's species had come from Hollow Earth, of that she had no doubt. So there might be more of his kind down there. It wasn't a lie to tell him so. To give him hope. He had been the only one of his kind since moments after his birth. On some level, he must long to meet others.

"All right," she said, turning to Jia. *All right. Tell him there could be more like him. Inside.*

Family? Jia signed.

She didn't want to lie to Jia. *I don't know,* she said. *I hope so.*

Jia considered her for a moment, then turned back to Kong.

Your family might be down there, she signed.

Kong looked toward the entrance to the Vortex again, then back at Jia, who nodded incrementally. Kong held her gaze for a moment. He finally vented a loud *huff*.

Then he turned and strode toward the entrance.

Nathan stared after him, looking a little stunned. Then, as if suddenly remembering there was more to all of this, he sprang into action, grabbing the radio transmitter.

"He's going right now!" he announced. "Prepare to launch! Everyone to your stations, we need to go *now*!"

And then everyone started moving at once.

Techs led them downstairs to the hangar where the HEAVs were waiting. Nathan had seen photographs of them, but this was the first time he'd seen them in person. They were compact, blunt-nosed craft, a bit on the boxy side. Not nearly as aerodynamic or sleek as a jet.

"Where are the wings?" Ilene asked.

"Oh," Nathan said. "No, they don't have those."

Instead of wings they each had four stubby projections that resembled ramjets, one forward and one aft on each side. When the craft were at rest, the cylinders were vertical, and would act as hover jets to lift the craft from the ground. Once they achieved airspeed, they would rotate back to act as thrusters. Despite appearances, however, the engines were not ramjets, or jets of any kind, but were instead drives that manipulated gravity to create propulsion.

"Don't worry," he said. "I'll vouch for them. You and Jia ride in that one. Simmons and I will take this one. See you down there."

"Kong's got such a big head start," she said.

"We'll catch him," Nathan said, fervently hoping he was right. He had not expected Kong to just *bolt* like that. It seemed that when the Titan made a decision, he didn't hesitate.

Maybe he could learn a thing or two from Kong.

After she helped Jia strap into the HEAV and secured herself, Ilene nervously listened as the pilots went through their checklists. Jia alternated between watching the pilots flip switches and looking off after Kong, or rather, where he had gone, for he was now nowhere in sight.

The three HEAVs kicked off in unison, turning to enter the rift.

Ilene had studied diagrams of the Antarctic entrance on the ship coming over and had been trying to get its measure when they had touched down, but there really wasn't much to see beyond a hole in the ice. As they entered it, though, it looked pretty much like a tunnel, reinforced with some sort of bands. It looked as regular and symmetrical as a subway tube, and for a moment that was reassuring. Then she understood why: the tunnel had been drilled through the ice pack to reach the caves beyond, which—as they drew within sight—she saw were much more unruly. In an instant the regular, predictable shaft was behind them, and they entered a sprawling natural cavern far wider than it was tall, branching off in all sort of directions. Steel I-beams had been placed into the stone like braces in an old-fashioned mine, presumably to increase the stability of the caverns. She remembered Nathan's tunnel-in-the-sand analogy and was not reassured.

The HEAVs flew through this nightmare at a ridiculous clip, and studying the craft in front of hers Ilene could now see a pearlescent energy wrapped around what she presumed were the engines, spinning like mad on the side projections and emerging as something like exhaust from the rear jets. It did not look like any form of combustion, and she half remembered Maia jabbering on about a gravity drive or something and wished she had paid more attention.

Not that it really mattered. The engines were clearly working, and right now the how of it didn't matter.

"There he is," she heard Simmons say, over the intercom connecting the three craft.

And indeed, there was Kong, up ahead of them, brachiating, swinging from one steel brace to the other as if the whole thing was a set of monkey bars built to the scale of a god. She thought once again about Nathan's analogy of a tunnel through sand and suppressed a shudder. Kong weighed … a lot. What if the tunnel couldn't withstand the force he was subjecting it to? They were right behind him, moving far too quickly to slow down, much less stop if the passage collapsed.

She noticed the tunnel was tending decidedly downward now, growing steeper and steeper as they went.

Nathan glanced at the diagram, showing the tunnel cutting through the Earth's mantle into the hollow core.

"You're sure he'll survive this?" Simmons asked. He looked back over his shoulder to the back seat where Maia was strapped in.

"You mean the monkey?" he said. "The one you wanted to dump?"

"Hey, if we need him, we need him," she said. "Is he going to make it to the bottom in one piece?"

"Oh," Nathan assured her, "he'll be fine. It's us I'd worry about. We're about to be launched a thousand miles in two seconds."

He cracked an antacid tablet from its packet and

plunked it into his water bottle. "Until gravity inverts itself and spits us into free fall." He tipped the water bottle so she could see the pill fizzing and bubbling like crazy. "It'll be the most amazing thing you've ever seen." He handed Simmons the paper bag tucked in front of his seat.

"Here," he said. "For the vomit."

"What?" she said.

Ahead, Nathan saw Kong lose control as a steel beam snapped under the force of his swing. He landed on his backside on the bottom of the tunnel and began to flail about, slipping on his butt as if going down the largest waterslide on the planet. As the slide became a cliff, the Titan managed to turn over and claw at the cliff to no avail—there was absolutely nothing to afford purchase for something of his mass.

As they, too tipped over the edge, Nathan saw Kong below, limbs outstretched, in free fall. Below him the pulsing, swirling energy membrane they called the Vile Vortex spanned the entirety of the rift. This was where things were going to get *fun*.

Kong hit the membrane; it seemed to stretch with his weight and then close behind him as he vanished.

And here we go, Nathan thought.

The membrane appeared to elongate as they hit it, to cling to them, like they were trying to punch through a sheet of rubber. Time slowed, somehow, even as they went faster and faster and acceleration pressed them back into their seats. The world went very strange. Color saturated everything; bizarre cavescapes that lived for an instant and then vanished into memory came and went at incredible speed. The HEAV shook, then shuddered and yawed, rattling as if it was on the verge of simply coming apart around them, and he felt like his ribs were trying to flatten against the back of his seat.

They could sell tickets, he remembered Dave saying. He was having trouble breathing.

It's coming it's coming it's coming...

The moment. That last moment. Dave's final instant of life. Maybe his as well.

It came, as they were thrown out with brutal force and incredible speed into ... another world.

Below them, above them—for the moment up and down had no meaning. It was the world Nathan knew, turned inside out.

There was no sky; or rather, there was, but it was sandwiched between two different downs. "Below" them, from the direction they had come, he could see vast forests, mountains, rivers, stretching out in every direction. But ahead of them, through a veil of clouds, was another landscape, equally beautiful and rugged, with tree-covered mountains hanging like stalagmites. And those clouds between them centered on a storm, incandescing with interior lightning, illuminating the whole weird scene almost like daylight.

Which way was actually up? His inner ear was terribly confused. Behind him he heard Simmons making use of the bag he had given her.

At least he hoped she was.

The HEAV lurched toward the cloud. Kong had come out behind them, due to his greater inertia, but now he flew past them for the same reason. But the Titan suddenly came to a stop, reversed direction, and came hurtling back toward the HEAVs. At the same time, all sorts of noises started up in the cabin, some from alarms, some from the pilot.

Engine failure. It was all pretty surreal, because all he could think was, this was how it had ended for Dave, this is how it ended for him. So much for Apex and their miracle craft.

Simmons screamed, and Nathan saw Kong hurtling

past, missing them by a matter of feet, staring right through the window at them. Maybe he was starting to form his own bond with Kong, because it seemed clear what the giant was thinking.

What the hell, man?

Then they hit the wall, the next gravity inversion point, and the "sky" became the "ground."

Again, that should have been it. In the first gravity inversion—right when they came out of the Vortex—they should have been shredded by deceleration. Simmons's miracle machines had saved them from that; the HEAVs had done their job, absorbing and dissipating their inertia into the gravitic anomaly. But it seemed to have been too much for the engines, because now they were caught in the interior gravity of the planet—they had, it seemed, chosen one of the competing *downs*, and they were now hurtling toward the forest floor with exactly the same acceleration as a fall from thousands of feet from the surface. Sure, the fall wouldn't kill them, but the sudden stop at the end would. Unless they started flying again.

"All Delta," Nathan said. "Reverse gravity propulsion now!"

In front of him the pilot flipped switches and pulled back, but they continued their tailspin as the system refused to reboot. He watched, unable to even scream as the alien topography seemed to rise to meet them. It felt to him as if Hollow Earth was a living, sentient thing, mocking him.

You thought you could do better than Dave? You stupid ass.

Then the G's kicked in, and all of the blood drained out of his head, and brilliant light washed everything out like an over-exposed photograph. He clung to consciousness through the white-out—barely. Distinction came back first, then color. They were alive, and the ship was leveling out.

He watched as Kong dropped down and hit a mountainside, clawed at it, alternately falling and sliding until he crashed into a lush, misty rainforest like none Nathan had ever seen. Flights of aerial creatures of some sort teemed up from around the Titan, and as the terror drained away, Nathan found himself smiling.

They had made it. Alive. Holy crap.

And it was unreal. Or rather, it was very real, and more amazing than he had ever imagined.

Ladies and gentlemen, he thought, *I give you Hollow Earth.*

FIFTEEN

In Xanadu did Kubla Khan
A stately pleasure-dome decree
Where Alph, the sacred river, ran
Through caverns measureless to man
Down to a sunless sea

"Kubla Khan" by Samuel Taylor Coleridge, 1816

Hollow Earth

Kong came to ground like thunder, and with no hesitation whatsoever went down onto all fours and began to run, following a canyon that cut down the side of the mountain into a realm of complete amazement. Even from high in the air and behind him, Ilene felt that she could see the same feeling mirrored on the Titan's face. This place was utterly strange, like no place on Earth—except Skull Island. She saw a flight of creatures that could easily be relatives of leafwings, or maybe they were more like pterosaurs—at this distance she couldn't quite decipher the details. Waterfalls cascaded from soaring peaks, above them and below them. If there was a Kong paradise, surely this was it.

"It's beautiful," she murmured.

"*This is HEAV 3*," the comm cut in. Nathan glanced at the radar, clocked its position just in front of him. Jia and Ilene were in HEAV 2; he didn't know anyone on HEAV 3. There hadn't been time to get acquainted.

"*We're getting some weird radar activity*," the HEAV 3 pilot said. "*We're going to circle back—*"

The pilot was abruptly cut off as something came tearing from out of Nathan's right field of vision and snatched HEAV 3 out of the air. The craft exploded, blinding him for a moment, buffeting his HEAV so hard he feared the pilot would lose control, but their flight quickly smoothed out, and now he could see what had just obliterated HEAV 3.

At first glance, its wings reminded him of those of a butterfly, both in shape and because they were bright orange in color. It had a long, sinuous, snake-like tail, but the front of it, where the wings were, widened considerably. It was turning, obviously not particularly fazed by its crash with the HEAV, and he could not quite see the head, although it gave a brutal, blunt impression. He watched it turning, trying to get behind them, and saw the deceptively beautiful wings were supported by boney spines, extensions of the rib cage, maybe. No modified arms, like a bird or bat or pterosaur, not like any true flying vertebrate on Earth, although there was a species of lizard that had similar rib-wings used only for downward gliding. But this thing was not gliding; it was as agile a flier as any he had seen, especially given its size.

The pilot yelped, and Nathan whipped around, then

screamed as he saw another one, coming straight for their windscreen, its mouth open, full of ragged teeth. And then—suddenly—it was receding. Kong had snatched it by the tail and was yanking it back toward him.

He watched, panting, as the Titan heaved the monster in an arc over his head and slammed it hard into the stony ground.

The first creature was coming back, bearing down on Kong, but he still held the tail of the one he'd grabbed. He swung it like a bat, smacking the oncoming beast away before flinging the other in the opposite direction.

The monster he had hit crashed into a cliffside, but quickly recovered, rising up like a cobra as Kong pounded his chest. Nathan could now see its head was more like a lizard or an alligator than a snake, although it looked closer to a dragon than anything else.

It struck like a snake, though, latching its toothy mouth into Kong's arm. Once it had purchase, it quickly wrapped around the Titan like a constrictor, pinning his arms to his sides, and then folded those enormous, beautiful wings around Kong, covering his face and smothering the giant.

"All ships!" Nathan snapped. "Prepare to attack!"

An instant after his command, both HEAVs launched missiles. He watched them streak toward their target, exploding all across the monster's wing. That must have caused it to loosen its hold, because when the smoke cleared, Kong had it by the throat, and was pulling it off of him. He crushed it against the ground, snapping the spines that supported its wings, and then picked it up again, slamming it back and forth like he was beating a rug. Not quite content with that, he then pounded it to a pulp with both of his fists.

Then the Titan turned his attention to the HEAVs. Nathan swallowed, but then he saw Kong didn't seem to be displaying his usual annoyance. He was looking at him,

Nathan, and held the contact for a moment.

You're welcome, Nathan thought silently. But he couldn't help feeling an unexpected swell of satisfaction. He had done good, and Kong had acknowledged it, or at least that he had not screwed up again.

So he would take it.

Kong ripped off the monster's head and began sucking the green gunk out of it.

"That is so gross," Simmons said, as Kong devoured the reptile.

"He's a big, active boy," Nathan said. "He needs his protein."

He took a breath and found the plastic spaceman in his pocket. He gave it a squeeze.

We made it, Dave, he thought. He wished he'd thought to bring along some of the awful whisky his brother had liked.

Finished with his meal, Kong oriented himself and then started off. Ilene thought she saw a certain eagerness in his manner.

Looking for family, Jia said. *Hope it's true.*

What about you? Ilene asked. *Does this feel like home to you?*

Jia shrugged. *Home is wherever we are,* she signed. *You and me.*

I think so too, Ilene replied.

And Kong, Jia added.

Ilene realized the HEAVs weren't moving.

"Kong's on the move," Ilene said. "We gotta go."

They chased Kong across a vast, flat plain of stone and scrubby vegetation. Ilene watched in delight as the Titan loped through what looked like a field of boulders, except that as he passed through them, some of the "boulders" scrambled away on crab-like legs. This turned out to be a bad idea for the crab-creatures; several large lizard-like monsters converged on them, now that they had given up their cover.

Across the plain, at first dim with distance but increasingly coming into sharper relief, was a mountain, jutting up from the flat landscape—and another mountain hanging down from the "sky" nearly touching it, like a stalagmite and stalactite on the verge of fusing into a pillar.

"He seems to know where he's going," Nathan said.

"He certainly can move," Ilene said, feeling a swell of pride.

When Kong reached the slopes of the peak, he immediately began to climb it.

"Do you see that?" Nathan asked.

"Yes," Ilene replied.

The stone of the mountains was seamed in blue; not blue stone, but an azure glow that seemed to be seeping from beneath the mountain. She noticed a flicker of the strange light here and there on the lower slopes, but the higher they climbed, the more pronounced it became.

"That's the energy we're looking for?" Maia Simmons asked.

"I'm sure it is," Nathan replied.

"Then why not stop here?" she asked. "We can get our sample and be done with this."

"You remember my analogy of the house wiring?"

"Of course," she said. "You're saying this isn't the wall socket."

"That's right," Nathan replied. "But I think it means we're on the right track. Kong is going for the source."

They continued following Kong as he clambered up the increasingly radiant peak, and until they reached the summit and the sheer cliff hidden behind it. Here, gravity began to invert once more. In the threshold between the two mountains boulders large and small floated in midair, caught between the two gravitational fields. Kong studied them curiously, then poked at one, pushing it toward the peak of the other mountain hanging just above them. His improvised missile struck a second boulder.

Knocked from their gravitational purgatory, the boulders crossed the inversion point and began to fall "upward" toward the opposite mountain. As they did so, they clipped a rock formation that looked suspiciously like a giant hand, partly opened, as if reaching toward Kong.

For a moment the Titan stood there, grappling with what he had just seen.

Then he pushed off with his feet, floating gently toward the stone hand. He crossed the inversion point, and then began to pick up speed. He reached for the stone hand, brushed it, and used the friction to turn and land feet first on the mountaintop.

SIXTEEN

It was the secrets of heaven and earth that I desired
to learn; and whether it was the outward substance
of things, or the inner spirit of nature and the
mysterious soul of man that occupied me, still my
inquiries were directed to the metaphysical, or, in its
highest sense, the physical secrets of the world.

From *Frankenstein*, Mary Shelley, 1818

Somewhere under the Pacific Ocean

It seemed to Madison that the Skullcrawler eggs were pulsing,
and more than once the shadows inside their translucent
shells shifted. Josh yelped the first time he saw it.

"What the hell?" he said.

"It's cute," Madison said. "The baby is kicking." She
reached over and smoothed her hand against the shell. As
she suspected, it was leathery and slightly pliable—like a

reptile or monotreme egg, not the hard, brittle shell of a bird's egg.

"You and these things," Josh said.

"Skullcrawlers?" she said. "I've never seen a live one before."

"I mean Titans in general," he said. "The whole time I've known you. It's like you're friends with them or something."

Madison studied Josh. He was scared, she could tell. And maybe a little mad that she had gotten him into this. Josh was a great guy, and she liked him a lot, but he wasn't exactly the rugged adventurer type. That was actually part of what she liked about him.

Right now, though, he seemed like he was on the verge of being an ass.

"To start with," she said, "the Titans aren't all the same, any more than all animals are the same. They're different. Some of them are pretty awful. Others—others I think really are our friends."

"Like Godzilla," Josh said. "The 'friend' who just trashed half of my town."

"He's reacting to something," Bernie interrupted. "Like maybe *these* things. Skullcrawlers in Florida? That's not okay. The big guy knows that. Even though I think there's also something else going on. Something bigger than Skullcrawler eggs."

"Like what?" Madison asked.

"I told you about the circuits meant to conduct through bone," he said. "Well, what do Skullcrawlers have in abundance?"

"Skulls?" Josh said.

"Which are made of bone," Bernie said, tapping his head with his finger. "What if Simmons is trying to put remote controls in Skullcrawlers? Imagine an army of these things, all under the command of Apex."

"Hang on," Josh said. "Remote control? You mean like, telling the monsters what to do with a game controller?"

"Something like that. You know, but on a more industrial scale."

"Like a *really* big game controller," Josh said.

"That makes a horrible sort of sense," Madison admitted. "If that's true, a lot of other things fall into place."

"Hang on," Josh said. "What about your big, giant eye?"

Bernie shrugged. "Maybe part of the control system," he said. "Maybe a whole other thing. Apex probably doesn't put all of its eggs in one basket. Not even if they are Skullcrawler eggs." He nodded in their direction of travel. "Anyway, our answers are up there. Hong Kong. It's a little further than I had planned to travel this time around, but you know. Anything for the truth."

"By the way," Madison said. "The pregnant Mothra thing—you weren't right about that one. I know from experience."

"Sure," Bernie said. "In this business you have to try every road. Some of them are dead ends. But you've gotta look at everything to see anything."

"Like bathing in bleach?" Josh said. "That seems like something you should have looked at twice."

"Shut it, Tap Water," Bernie said.

"Tap water is clean, inexpensive, and disease-free!" Josh said. "There are people all over the world who would give anything for that luxury!"

"Sure," Bernie said. "That's the idea. Then, *bam*. Docile pets."

"I'm not a docile pet," Josh grumbled.

"What's that?" Bernie said. "What's that, Tap Water?"

"Never mind," Josh said.

Bernie glared at him for a moment, then turned his attention back to Madison.

"So you've been up close and personal with Godzilla," he said. "Tell me about that."

Madison told him, and then they knocked around the Skullcrawler theory a little longer. She had to admit, given the evidence, it now made more sense than her ORCA theory.

She checked her phone.

"You won't have reception here," Josh said.

"I know," she replied. "I'm checking the time. That readout over there gives our speed, so I'm trying to calculate the mileage. It might be useful for Monarch to have that information."

"You don't think Monarch knows about this?" Bernie asked. "You don't think they're in on it? C'mon."

"No," Madison said. "I don't think they know anything about this."

"Not everyone," Bernie said. "Not your dad, I'm sure. But at the top. Monarch has used Apex as a contractor plenty of times. I mean, did you never wonder why Monarch put a base in Pensacola, of all places? And like, years later Apex built a base? You think that's coincidence? You want me to name all of the cities where Monarch and Apex both have facilities?"

"Bernie—"

"Hong Kong, for instance?"

"Monarch and Apex may have some of the same interests," Madison said. "But they're not the same."

"They both do shady, covert things with Titans," Bernie said. "But I see this is bothering you. I'll stop. I just ask questions. It's what I do."

"I get that," Madison said. "But I'm not so interested in questions right now. I want answers. If you have any, please stop hinting around and just *say* them, okay? Do you have any actual evidence of what you're suggesting? And don't answer my question with another question."

Bernie drew back a little. "Touché," he said. "No proof, no. I get it, I get it. A hundred questions don't add up to a single answer. You think I don't know that by now? You think if I really had the answers…" He broke off and put his hand on the flask in his holster.

"Okay," he finally said. "But I'm trying to get them. I am. I'm tired of questions too." He nodded at her phone. "What time is it?"

"I don't know," Madison said. "It's not working."

"Is it out of charge?" Josh asked.

"No," she said. "It's on. It's just not working."

"Electromagnetic fields," Bernie said. "From the train— more likely the tunnel. Oh, man. We'll probably all have brain cancer in a week."

"Yeah," Josh said. "I'm sure they didn't think of that when they built this."

"You see any other people get on, Tap Water?" Bernie asked, caustically.

"Oh," Josh said, frowning. A few minutes later Madison noticed him pressing on his head with his fingertips.

Apex Facility, Hong Kong

Madison knew they were approaching their destination by the incremental deceleration of the train. Josh felt it too, enough to wake him from his nap.

Bernie, studying his notes, looked ahead, down the tunnel.

"Okay," he said, as their deceleration intensified. "Okay, slowing down."

They came to a stop in front of a door identical to the one at the Pensacola end. It slid open, and another crane picked them up and lowered them toward the floor.

"*Attention*," loudspeakers blared. "*Shipping pods arriving*." Then the message repeated in Cantonese.

Yeah, Madison thought. *But with some unexpected cargo.*

After they were settled to the floor, the doors opened. The three of them peered out. A ramp rose to meet the car, leading down into yet another gigantic chamber, although the light was so low it was difficult to see exactly how big it was. Behind them the wall seemed to be stone, but everything in front of them was metal, and the place had a distinctly industrial feel. But there didn't seem to be anything *in* it except the maglev cars that had just arrived.

"Going in?" Bernie asked.

"Yup," Madison replied.

They stepped out, and almost immediately the car doors slid shut behind them.

"No!" Josh said. "I swear, every time. Doors hate us."

"Oh, yeah," Bernie said, staring out into the shadowed space.

Madison continued to examine the chamber, or hangar, or whatever it was.

Bernie suddenly shouted; echoes came back as if he had yelled into the Grand Canyon.

"Oh, my God!" Madison said. What the hell was he doing? The point was not to get noticed here, right?

"It's so massive. It's stupid," Bernie said, as if that explained something.

"What is this place?" Madison wondered.

"If there's a corporate-friendly term for sacrifice pit," Bernie said, "I'd say we are in it." He waved his hand at something on the floor.

She had been wrong; there *was* something else in the room, lying just a few feet away. It looked like an eyeball the size of a cantaloupe that had been ripped out of its socket, along with about a yard of optic nerve.

"Oh, God," Madison said. "That smells." She knelt

down to look at it, realizing as she did that the stink was far too pervasive to be just the whatever-it-was. The air was heavy with the sickly-sweet metallic scent of blood she was all too familiar with.

"Smells like an abattoir," Bernie said.

"A what?" Josh asked.

"A slaughterhouse," Bernie said, pulling his finger across his throat. "Look."

Madison saw it, too. In the dim light you could miss it if the place didn't stink so much.

Bloodstains, and lots of them.

Loudspeakers suddenly came on, belling out an alarm, the kind that made Madison think of heavy equipment operating or a warning to get the hell away from whatever was making that sound.

"That's not good," Madison said. "Bernie—"

"I already hate this place," Bernie said, walking forward. Red warning lights were now flashing everywhere—and then brighter lights snapped on.

"*Warning,*" a woman's voice came over the loudspeaker. "*Project M demonstration will commence on floor A in one minute. All personnel are to stay clear of the arena area.*"

In the brighter light, Madison saw there were a number of large metal doors set in the walls, each numbered in large white letters. Higher above, observation windows. Higher still, in the ceiling, a panel was opening, revealing an industrial fan. Not too far away, a little bunker was sunken into the floor with glass observation ports all around.

Arena, the voice had said. Somebody was about to watch something happening here, but what? Sports were played in arenas, but somehow, she felt there was not about to be a pick-up game of indoor soccer starting up. Fights? Fights happened in arenas. Boxing matches, wrestling, mixed-martial arts. Who—or what—was fighting here?

Her eyes returned to the bloodstains on the floor. There was a *lot* of blood. Not just buckets, but dump trucks full.

She thought about the maglev cars, and their cargo of Skullcrawler eggs, and did not like the picture that was emerging.

First she felt a hum and then an aggressive vibration in the floor beneath her feet, and then a huge circular hatchway opened, near enough to them that they had to stumble back. And from below that cavernous opening, a platform began to rise. With something on it.

It was big, but Madison couldn't make out what it was through all of the steam surrounding it. What she *could* see was sort of a mound, with strange squared-off bristles or projections sticking up from it. Like a metal hedgehog, rolled in on itself.

Vents opened and began sucking up the steam; the air began to clear. And whatever it was started to unfold from its crouched position. It began to stand and become decidedly un-hedgehog-like.

From inside of the control room, Ren Serizawa watched as the machine that was far more than a machine rose into view on the screen. His gaze flitted around the command center, but it came to rest on the focus of everything: the skull.

He climbed inside, where a Titan's brain had once been, imagining the massive nerves that must have depended on it, witnessed by the size of the stem opening in its base. The organics were long gone, rotted away, but they had been replaced by wires, conduits, fiber-optic cable and strands of superconductor. Some tracked in from supercomputers outside; others were grounded in the skull itself. But all of it snaked itself to the equipment at the crux of it all. The control helmet.

He ran his fingers across the interior of the skull. It had been love at first sight when Simmons showed it to him, but his affections had further deepened as he studied its structure, the fine lacework of rare metals and minerals that ran through it. And even before he began experimenting with it, he felt the power sleeping in that mysterious bone. The fierce sentience that had once burned behind those empty sockets was gone, but some of what had enabled it remained. The skull had not just been a case for the brain inside, but an integral part of the creature's sentience. And while the neurons and nerves had decayed, what remained in the skull itself was still potent; a natural set of hardware waiting for the right hand to bring it back to life, to harness the essence of it.

And best of all, there had been not a single cranium, but two. Together, the skulls had allowed him to create a radical new technology in a few short years that might have otherwise taken him decades to perfect.

Simmons was over in the observation room, waiting. He thought this was his moment. But it had been he, Ren, who had made this possible. Simmons was good at what he did, but this—this was beyond him. Simmons's true genius lay more in his vision, and in knowing who to bring in to get the job done than on original invention. And of course, he was quite good at taking credit for the work of others.

Ren was clear-eyed about that, and he didn't care. The only person he might have cared to impress had abandoned him.

Would you be proud of me, Father? he wondered. To his father, the Titans had been gods to be trusted—served, even. Ichiro Serizawa had never understood the true potential of the beasts he spent his life studying.

Humanity had always been beset by animals stronger, more deadly than its feeble primate members. Tigers were faster and had sharp claws and teeth. A rhinoceros or a bull aurochs could break any man in one charge. A tiny virus or bacteria could wipe out entire populations.

But humanity had risen above all of them. They had fashioned spears longer and sharper than the claws of any predator. Rhinoceroses had been hunted to the brink of extinction for their horns. Aurochs had been tamed into cattle to furnish meat and leather. Bacteria and viruses were still worthy enemies, but for the most part the worst infectious diseases had been eradicated, and many of these organisms had been repurposed for genetic engineering. All this done by the physically weakest of all of the great apes, creatures possessing no natural weapon other than their brains.

The Titans, for all of their size and power, they were just more of the same. The only question was whether they would be driven into extinction or repurposed for human ends. They were not gods; they were not worthy of worship—or of sacrifice. They were animals to be mastered, nothing more.

His father could never have understood that. *Let them fight,* he had famously said. Only a man who did not care about human beings could say such a thing; only such a man could brush aside the untold casualties that "letting them fight" always led to. When he heard those words—in the media, of course, not from the man's own lips—he had not been surprised. A man who could neglect his own family so thoroughly was not likely to care about the human race as a whole.

His mother—his father's *wife*—had been dead for a week before his father even knew of it. He had been off on some expedition, out of touch with them. He had shown up two days after the funeral—a funeral Ren had been forced to organize himself. At the age of eighteen.

"She understood," was all his father said to him when he finally came home.

Maybe he was right. Maybe his mother *had* understood. But that was irrelevant to him, because *he* had not. Where before there had been a divide, afterward was a chasm. And his father had never supplied so much as a plank to try to bridge it.

Ren took a breath, realizing he had allowed himself to become upset, when he should be celebrating. He took up the helmet and placed it on his head.

Outside, he saw, Simmons was almost in rapture. Of course. But with Simmons it was all about his ego; he didn't see this moment as the culmination of human potential, but of his own success. Not content to be the master of a corporate empire, he sought to control it all. Ren did not care about that, either. The god-kings of Babylon and Egypt and Tenochtitlan had come and gone, as had countless conquerors and dictators. All were dust now. But the human race itself always moved on, growing in knowledge, in power, in mastery of its world, and someday soon, other worlds. Let Simmons have his moment. Ren's achievements would outlive him. Whether anyone knew that or not, he did not care.

He sat in the reclining chair and considered the control helmet, with its dozens of connections snaking off into the surrounding machinery.

Ren settled the psionic helmet on his head. It ran through the colors of the rainbow and back again; he felt the colors in his brain and smiled a little. The control helmet was not only his invention, but also his new favorite toy. Each time he put it on, he felt it had expanded him in some way. At first, he had used it merely to manipulate shapes on a screen, but eventually he had developed to moving the fingers of a mechanical hand; and he had *felt* the hand. But it was interfacing through the skull that was truly amazing. The granular control; the insights into his own psyche—unsought, but incredibly valuable. In these last several months he felt like he had finally truly become the man he was meant to be.

"*Commence uplink,*" Simmons said, over the comm.

"Engaging uplink," Ren confirmed.

And as energy began to course through the hardware and the skull, it all poured into him. He reached out with invisible senses toward the other bone in the machine. They touched, united, and in an instant the senses of his own body dropped away.

At first Madison thought she was looking at a machine—wires and gears, metal and synthetics. But there was something organic about it; in places Madison thought she saw muscle and sinew, nerves instead of wiring. And up there, on the head, a robotic eye, whirring, dilating—the thing, she realized, that Bernie had described seeing in the lab in Pensacola. The missing object.

Now found.

Of what it was supposed to be, there could be no doubt. The squared off-fins clicked into place as Madison watched, forming a ridge down the middle of the back of the construct, following down to a long, armored tail. Standing on colossal legs, waving far smaller arms, the thing was almost a parody of Godzilla, a child's attempt to make a Titan from an erector set.

But when the eyes began to glow, it didn't look silly in the slightest. It looked incredibly dangerous.

"It's like a … robo-godzilla…" Bernie said.

"No," Josh said, slowly. "That's Mechagodzilla."

So I guess they aren't building a Skullcrawler army,

Madison thought. *Then why all the eggs?*

The machinery supporting the construct retracted; then the giant robot—cyborg?—began running through a series of motions; lifting its arms, opening and closing its claws, and so forth, like a series of check-ups, Madison realized. If the "eye" Bernie saw just got here, that probably meant this monstrosity had just been completed. They wanted to see if it worked.

And they were in an arena with it. Her bad feeling about this situation was just getting worse and worse.

SEVENTEEN

From the notes of Dr. Chen:

The cuneiform texts unearthed at Ras Shamra tell of a battle between Yahm-Nahar, whose names mean "sea" and "river," with Baal, whose name means "Lord." Yahm's palace is in the Abyss, where he lords cruelly over the other gods. Baal travels to confront him. He is beset by various sea-monsters and is in danger of defeat, but then Kothar-wa-Khasis, Craftsman of the Gods, steps in:

Thereupon answers Kothar-wa-Khasis: "As I have been telling you, and as I tell you again, Cloud Rider. You must annihilate your foes. Then you shall reign as king forever.

Then Kothar brings down two weapons and names them: "Your name is Yagarush, Banisher. Yagarush, banish Yahm, banish Yahm from his throne, Nahar from the seat of his authority. Spring from the hand of Baal, like a bird of prey from his fingers. Strike Prince Yahm between the shoulder blades, between the shoulders of Judge Nahar.

The club springs from the hand of Baal, like a bird of prey from his fingers. It strikes Yahm between the shoulder blades, between the shoulders of Nahar. But Yahm is strong; he is not beaten, his joints do not quiver, he does not fall.

Kothar brings down two weapons and names them. "Your name is Ayamar, Driver. Drive Yahm from his throne, Nahar from his seat of power. Fly from the hand of Baal, from his fingers like a raptor. Strike on the skull of Prince Yahm, between the eyes of Judge Nahar. Let Yahm collapse and fall to earth."

The weapon flies from the hand of Baal, like a raptor from his fingers. It strikes the skull of Prince Yahm, between the eyes of Judge Nahar. Yahm collapses, he falls to the earth. His joints tremble. His spine shakes. Then Baal drags him out to finish him.

The Baal Cycle, from clay tablets written circa 1500 BCE

Apex Facility, Hong Kong

Ren felt his connection with the Mecha strengthen, but for the first time since wearing the control helmet there was almost a sense of resistance, a slight pushing-back. He knew the biomechanical body was there, felt his control of it, but lacked the ultimate tactile sense that it was *his*. He could not close his eyes and feel where his feet were. Perhaps it was because this was his first time with the entire machine; the last components had only recently arrived and been incorporated. Naturally the whole was more difficult to control that the parts.

But then, like a piece snapping into place, he felt …

completion. Fire surged in his veins, but they were not veins, there was no blood, only *connection* and power. He opened the eyes he was not born with and saw in colors no human being had ever seen before. Joy like he had never known swelled in him, a sheer delight in this new existence, his mind finally being fulfilled in a body worthy of it.

"Release Number Ten!" he heard Simmons say, as if from another universe.

Well, then. They were about to see, Ren thought, still giddy. This … this was going to be awesome.

Somewhere in the Pacific Ocean

He moved through his territory; his territory moved in him. He knew his domain by its voices, sounds, scents. By cycles larger than epochs and smaller than heartbeats. He knew it by its thirsts and hungers. By what it needed. Territory was not a place, not an area with boundaries. It was a compulsion.

He had defeated the ancient three-headed foe. He had accepted the obeisance of the others. He had rested, and then heard the song, the strange voice of another. He had followed the call and been met with the sting and fire of the small ones, but the prey had eluded him. He could not find it. Not in the deeps, where no sunlight reached, not in the shallows, in the reefs bustling with life, not in the currents where the great swimmers travelled. His territory seemed safe again. But as his anger subsided, as he sank toward his place of rest, his territory was invaded. Not by the hidden one, but by the Other, another ancient enemy, older than the three-headed one, a rivalry written into his very blood and bone.

So he sought him, and they fought, and again the small ones attacked him with their stings and smoke, and he knew that something was changing. Those who once fought with him had turned against him.

The world had changed before; it was always changing, mostly slowly, sometimes quickly.

What never changed was his territory.

Victorious over the ancient enemy and its small allies, he had gone, once again thinking of rest, but the waters still stank, the winds that blew from the core of the world still carried the shadow of the nemesis, and he thought perhaps the ancient adversary was not dead after all. He had not seen the corpse. He had been lulled by quiet, but quiet did not always mean victory. So he renewed his patrol. He sensed something in the direction of the cold place, where the three-headed one had once slept. So he turned there, following the falling current, the cold flow from the end of the planet.

But then, like a blow, he felt the hidden one, hidden no longer. A weak, thin voice no more. An intruder, an illness, a blight in the midst of his territory. With a bright shriek of rage, he turned that way, and he swam. He followed the dark paths that cut through the crust. And even when the distant cry faded, it was still burned in his memory. He knew it would wake again, that it was waiting for him.

He would not make it wait long.

Apex Facility, Hong Kong

Another set of warning buzzers went off, and these sounded a lot more … serious. Madison heard a grinding behind them and turned to see that one of the huge, numbered hangar doors—this one was labeled with a large number ten—was lowering behind them. She heard a scratching, and then another hideous shriek as claws jammed through the opening, and a long wicked snout pushed through.

Skullcrawler, she realized. A big one.

Bernie and Josh screamed like they were being disemboweled. She was vaguely aware that they were also running like hell, but all she could do was stare at the nightmare coming through the door. It was like something in the back of her brain was commanding her to be still, that maybe it would not see her, that it would go after the *moving* prey. It was exactly like she was back in Boston, with Ghidorah staring through the window at her. Like she had never really escaped…

"Madison!" Bernie yelled. "Get to the hatch!"

She didn't know what he was talking about, but the shout snapped her out of it. She turned and started pumping her legs as hard as she could, following Bernie and Josh. She heard the Skullcrawler coming behind her, fast, like the biggest set of nails scrabbling across a chalkboard the size of Boston Common.

She saw what the other two were running toward now, the little octagonal bunker set down into the floor. Probably for observing stuff like this up close and personal…

Then she felt its hot breath on her back, choked on the charnel stench of it. She saw Josh and Bernie climbing into the top of the little bunker, but she was still yards away. She did the only thing she could; she threw herself flat, hoping it would just run right over her.

She did not think it would work. *This is over,* she thought.

And yet, the claws and teeth didn't sink into her; the hideous pain she anticipated did not arrive. Instead, she only felt a whoosh of air.

As Number Ten came out of his cage and ran across the floor, Ren allowed himself a grin.

He loved Skullcrawlers. They were so extreme; it was

literally impossible for them to eat enough to sate their hunger. They were always starving; they had no patience at all for stalking or hiding; evolution had designed them to kill, eat, repeat. It was surprising they ever found time to mate, and that they did not eat each other while they were doing so. Although some studies suggested that males did not always fare well in such amorous encounters.

He admired their purity, and he absolutely had no compunction about killing them. As they were made to prey on everything else, he had been built to end *them*. He was the alpha now, the apex predator.

Any other animal might have known it was dead when he picked it up in his powerful hands, already squeezing the life out of it. But not a Skullcrawler. It still somehow saw a meal in front of it, a fight it could win.

He felt the smile grow inside of him as the energy built up in the infernal engines contained in this body. Everything was becoming *more*. He senses were sharpening, his strength building. Instincts buried deep in the ancient, reptilian part of his brain broke through the barriers his primate mind had built around them, freeing him to be everything his kind had ever been since crawling from the ocean. He had claws, not nails; sharp teeth, not dull leaf-grinders. And he had the lightning and fire of heaven and hell coursing up his dorsal fins.

He opened his mouth, and red energy surged forth. It pierced the Skullcrawler through its gaping maw. He dragged the beam down to disembowel it, cut it completely in half. He felt a shudder of ecstasy as it died, writhing in his grip. This was what it was like to be a god, he knew.

Madison scrambled back to her feet and saw that the Mechagodzilla had snatched the Skullcrawler up. She ran toward the open hatch of the bunker, where Bernie and Josh were frantically gesturing her on.

As she reached it, she saw a red beam shoot out from the mechanical Titan, a horrible, distorted version of Godzilla's ultimate weapon. Then she reached the bunker, jumped in, yanked down the hatch, and turned the metal valve that secured it.

Through the windows ringing their shelter, Madison was able to crane her neck and see the red beam split the Skullcrawler in half. Then, quite suddenly, the mechanical monster dropped the corpse. She flinched back as the thing hit their hiding place, drenching it in yellow goo.

Every inch of Ren trembled as the Skullcrawler disintegrated in the red energy of his breath. He had fantasized what such power might be like, but his imaginings were pale compared to the reality. He pulled the monster apart as it split down the seams, enjoying every second.

Then it was all fading, gone; the claws, the legs, the fins, were no longer his. The Skullcrawler in his grip vanished like a mirage. The power dropped away—not gradually, but like a fuse blowing, a stroke, a catastrophic failure that cascaded through the Mecha's systems. It almost felt like his own body was failing too, as if his heart had stopped and his lungs were empty, with no more air to draw into them. Every nerve ached and then he lost sensation in his limbs, his back, finally everywhere. All of his senses switched off; his sight was the last to go, and then he was in an absolute void. For that moment, he thought he had died, that the connection had been so intense that when the tech failed, his real body had shut down, too. But then his mind adjusted; he was once again small, and flesh, staring at the warning that his on-board battery was depleted.

"System only reached forty percent power," he reported to Simmons, when he could talk again. Depression washed in, a cold, black tide—familiar, but never welcome.

"As expected," Simmons replied. "Don't worry, once the Hollow Earth signal is uploaded, our power troubles will be over."

"If they can find the energy source," Ren said. He tried to rein in his pessimism, the disappointment. He had been so close! To be shut down like that was … hard to take. He needed more power. He craved it. Only then could the Mecha be what he had designed it to be. Only then could *he* be what he was meant to be.

"I have faith in Maia," Simmons replied. "I have faith in our creation. And humanity will once again be the apex species. And once I destroy Godzilla, the world will bow to me."

"Our" creation, Ren thought, caustically. *Just give me this energy source, you chattering baboon.*

But he said nothing. He needed Simmons. For now.

Aboard the *Argo*
En Route to Hong Kong

Mark watched their flight path, a long arc over the pole bending toward Hong Kong. He remembered his last trip there with Emma. She had been a few weeks' pregnant with Madison at the time, and they were both still innocent to how much that simple fact would change their lives. He remembered street food and the waterfront, hiking through the mountains that stuck right up out of the metropolis, a long day on the beach. There had been a conference, too, and they had both given papers, but he would be hard pressed to remember what either of them had been about. He remembered it as one of the last times the two of them had been alone. When Andrew came it had been wonderful, and he had fallen in love again in a way he had never imagined he could, with both his son and his wife. But it had all been different, more complicated. He wouldn't have done anything different, at least not up until the point, years later, when Andrew was killed. But if he could go back to that day on the beach at Big Wave Bay with Emma one more time, he would.

He doubted he would see the beach this time, at least not up close, not with Godzilla's latest activities. The Titan had appeared to attack the convoy escorting Kong to Antarctica. Mark had seen the briefing, watched grimly as the Titan leveled a fleet of ships and beat Kong nearly to death. Lind had managed to salvage the situation, sort of, but the loss of life and property was appalling.

Godzilla might have been their ally once against a common threat. But it seemed clear that that no longer held true. The Titan's need to be the alpha had become toxic.

Of course, he'd vanished after the attack, only to surface again near the Philippines. He had bypassed those islands, though, and all of the models predicted an arrival in Hong Kong. And Godzilla was hauling ass, even for Godzilla.

And so the director had called him in.

And apparently wanted a conference call now. Mark logged on to his laptop computer and entered the video call. The background showed the inside of the command center, with displays and techs behind the director.

"I'm on my way," he said.

"So I see," Guillerman replied. "Thank you for responding so quickly. I'm looking forward to your arrival. But events are developing quickly here."

"I understand," Mark said.

Guillerman had been brought in a few years before to replace Ishiro Serizawa. Those were big shoes to fill, and Mark had his share of qualms about the guy, but on the whole, he was probably doing a good job. Cleaning up after a disaster as large as Monarch—and the world— had experienced was a thankless job. Serizawa had died a hero, so some of his questionable decisions were forgotten. A living, breathing administrator was not in the same position.

"There's very little doubt he's coming here," the director said. "And so far, he hasn't caused any trouble on the way."

"And idea what's drawing him there?" Mark asked.

"There's no evidence of any other Titans," Guillerman said. "But—have a look at this."

He tapped a keyboard, and a window appeared on Mark's screen, displaying a signal.

"As you can see, the signal is weak," Guillerman said. "And we don't know quite what to make of it."

Mark studied the signal for a moment.

"It looks like a Titan," he said. "A little. In fact, this segment of it seems familiar, although if I'm remembering right that doesn't make any sense."

"Could it be a manufactured call?" the director asked. "Like the sort of signal the ORCA put out?"

"If I had to guess," Mark said, "I would say that's exactly what this is. It almost looks like an attempt to synthesize Ghidorah's call, although it's wrong in some key ways. What's the point of origin?"

"Here," the director said. "Hong Kong. But we're not sure from where in the city."

Mark frowned as the signal repeated itself on a loop.

"Isn't that where Apex headquarters is?" he asked.

"Yes."

"I think you should focus your efforts on them," Mark said. "Monitor any signal coming out of there. Walter Simmons has sworn to destroy Godzilla. He did it on international television. Nathan—Dr. Lind—he's off on some Hollow Earth boondoggle for Simmons as we speak, something about a power source he says can control or destroy Godzilla, right? None of this seems like a coincidence. Maybe Simmons is trying to lure Godzilla here for some reason. Maybe he's set a trap, and Pensacola was practice for it."

"Lure Godzilla to a city of eight million?" Guillerman said. "He'd have to be insane."

"Simmons wouldn't be the first person to have an insane reaction to Godzilla," Mark said. "Hell, I've been there myself. No telling who Simmons lost back in 2014 or 2019. Or maybe it's something else. Maybe he has a plan to stop him before he gets to the city. But we'd better be ready for anything."

"I'll start an evacuation as quietly as I can," Guillerman said. "And we'll see what we can dig up on Apex. I will see you soon."

Mark nodded as the screen went blank. He was starting to feel like he owed Madison an apology, not to mention telling her he was significantly more out of town then he'd thought he would be.

He checked his phone and found Madison still hadn't answered any of the four texts he has already sent her. He tried to call her, but she didn't pick up.

"Damn it, Madison," he murmured under his breath.

He knew he had disappointed her, but he also knew he was doing the right thing. He had lost a son and a wife to these monsters. Madison was all he had left, and he did not intend to put her in harm's way. If that meant she sulked for a while and ignored his texts, he could deal with that. It was far better than the alternative.

Checking again, he saw he *had* missed a text from his sister. Several, in fact.

He read through them as they grew increasingly more panicked. Maddie hadn't been home when Cassidy had dropped by to pick her up, and she hadn't called or texted. Eventually she'd learned that Maddie's friend Josh was also missing, along with his older brother's van.

"What the hell are you up to, Madison?" he muttered. He should have known this would happen. Should have seen the signs. This was Madison backward and forward, off to try to save the world again. And poor Josh, it was easy to imagine her bullying him into this. But where were they going?

His laptop made a noise. Guillerman again.

"We just got eyes on Godzilla," he said. "He's under a hundred klicks out now, headed straight for us. I've scrambled jets, for as much good as it will do. Maybe we can distract him while we evacuate."

Mark nodded, finding it difficult to concentrate, knowing Madison was running around—in a van, no less.

But Godzilla was in Hong Kong, not Pensacola, and there was no way for Madison to reach Hong Kong by van. How much danger could she be in? His sister was doing what could be done to find her in Pensacola. And the fact was, as much as he hated to admit it—and even more hated to rely on it—Madison could handle herself. She had run off on her own because he hadn't believed her, and he hadn't trusted her. That wasn't an excuse, but it was a reason. And it was something they were going to have to talk about. Perhaps while she was grounded for the next year or so.

That would be fun. Right now he only had an angry Godzilla to deal with.

Hollow Earth

The HEAVs followed Kong down the now right-side-up mountain, across a rocky, rather lifeless landscape. But as on the mountain, the blue energy was bleeding through everywhere. Kong's course seemed more certain with every bounding step.

Their destination appeared to be a mountain with a single large peak in the middle flanked by smaller ones one either side. The steepness of the mountain and the symmetrical proportions suggested to Ilene that it wasn't a natural formation—or at least not entirely natural. It reminded her of the structures in Angkor Wat, in Cambodia.

Directly above the central peak, a lightning storm flashed and fumed, but it wasn't moving, as though it was created by the mountains, which had more of the blue phosphorescence than anything they had seen thus far. But along with the blue light, there was a red glow as well.

Look at that! Ilene signed to Jia.

House, Jia signed. *Big house.*

"That has to be it," Nathan said.

As they drew closer, the red-gold glow became more pronounced.

"Is that … magma?" she asked.

"It's not a volcano," Nathan said. "At least, not like any I've ever seen. But yeah, I think you're right. If I had to guess, I would say that there is so much of the life-force energy here, it's causing the rock to heat up and glow."

"Do you think it's dangerous?" she asked.

"Absolutely," Nathan replied.

Even closer, Ilene saw that she'd been right, or at least partly so. The mountain itself was probably natural originally, but it had clearly been modified. What at first had appeared to be a hornlike split at the top of the central peak was actually a facade carved to suggest columns flanking what was an arched stone temple door, defined with a carved double-arch around it.

The myths and legends, the cave paintings, the hieroglyphs. They all pointed to this. The ancestors of the Iwi and Kong *were* from here, and Kong knew it. Felt it in his bones.

Ishiro Serizawa had proven that Godzilla—or others like his kind—had human followers, that they had built a great civilization, and a temple dedicated to him. She had long believed the same was true of Kong, and here was the proof. The ancestors of Jia's people must have lived here, built this holy place for their gods, Kong's ancestors.

She realized that she was tearing up as she watched Kong approach the structure with what appeared to be something akin to … reverence.

Then he approached the gates. The doors themselves were plain—except for a single, very large, red handprint on one of them. Ilene had seen prints like that before, found all over the world in the caves and rock shelters of her own prehistoric ancestors. They were markers, signs—I was here. *We* were here.

Kong roared, but it was not like any sound she'd ever heard issue from his throat. It was … a question. He tilted his head—as if listening for a response—then repeated the sound—then listened again.

When no answer came, Kong placed his hand on the print. It was almost, but not quite, a perfect match. She saw it on his face as he understood what that meant. A different member of his species had made this. He was not the only one.

Kong studied the gate for a little longer. Then he pushed it, then pushed harder—and the doors swung open.

The HEAVs followed him but kept their distance. Ilene couldn't tear her eyes away.

Inside was huge, mysterious. It reminded her a little of a

cathedral, for it had a row of arches enclosing a vast circular space and stone columns reaching high into darkness. There was an immense central pillar, although it looked like a natural formation that had been minimally carved. The upper reaches of the temple—for that's what it was— looked entirely natural, with stalactites hanging down. More of the red handprints were visible in the deep recesses of the place, and what were almost certainly paintings.

The glowing blue seams in the stone were everywhere here, and the stone of the floor glowed here and there with reddish hotspots, like magma was pooled just below the surface. Scatterings of huge bones were visible in that dim light; in the brighter HEAV floodlights they were recognizable as those of Titans. And one, still largely articulated, seemed especially familiar. She had seen pictures of such skeletons, from the Philippines, and elsewhere. She'd seen bones like this covered in muscle and scale. It was a species that resembled Godzilla.

Kong noticed the remains. He stared at them at first without comprehension, but then she saw fury dawn on his features. He stood over the skeleton for a moment and then, with great deliberation he bent toward the reptilian neck. She saw something was lodged there, and as she watched he took hold of it, pulled, and then yanked it free and held it aloft, beating his chest. It looked for all the world like some sort of outlandish scepter, sized for Kong.

"Congratulations," Nathan said. "You were right."

She nodded. "He's home."

And as if he also recognized that fact, Kong approached the central pillar, holding his prize, and sat down upon a seat carved into the base of it. And now he was complete; the throne, the scepter, the king.

He roared once again, and something changed in the set of his shoulders. In his expression. Even though there were no other living members of his species here, he knew he was part of something bigger and older than himself. That ancestors of his had sat on this same throne, in this place.

Like her, Jia had just been taking everything in, but now she began signing.

Kong's family, she signed.

Yes, she replied. *This was their place. Built for him by your people.*

Jia looked at her, puzzled, then shook her head.

The Iwi lived here with Kong's family, yes, she signed. *But this was built by Kong's family.*

What do you mean? Ilene asked. *How do you know?*

I remember the story now, Jia said. *Look, nothing small here. Nothing the size of Iwi. This was built by Kongs.*

And in a sudden flash, Ilene realized that had to be true. Humans *could* have built this place, given time, and numbers, and basic machines like block-and-tackle. But they hadn't. Now that she looked more closely, with different eyes, it didn't look like human architecture, and not just because of the scale.

The HEAVs settled down and quietly, cautiously, Ilene and the others climbed out and entered the cavernous temple. Standing on the floor in front of Kong, she felt as tiny as an insect, just as the Iwi must have felt, gathered around him. Kong watched them for a moment, but quickly lost interest—he seemed absorbed in his own thoughts.

Jia tugged at her hand, pulling Ilene toward something. At first it just looked like a series of incisions in the floor, forming a circle around the column the throne was carved into. But as they walked the circle, the details became clearer. The depiction looked like it could be Godzilla, albeit stylized, looking more like a serpent biting its tail. The most peculiar thing about it was that one of its dorsal fins seemed to be missing—where it ought to be was only a hollow space...

EIGHTEEN

Behold now behemoth, which I made with thee.

Job 40:15

Apex Facility, Hong Kong

Shortly after the shower of Skullcrawler guts covered their hideout, the arena shut down and the lights went out. Mechagodzilla, however, did not withdraw into the floor, but remained where it was, inert now, slumped over, all the fire gone out of its eyes.

"This is why Godzilla attacked the Apex facility," Madison said. "They're trying to replace him."

"Yes," Bernie said. "Yes. The eye I saw. That's it up there, on the robo-Godzilla."

"Mechagodzilla," Josh corrected him.

"Really?" Bernie said.

"Bernie," Madison said, "I think you have to let that one

go. And I need you to focus. What now?"

"Now?" Bernie said. "Now?"

"I think it's time to go," Madison said.

"Yes," Bernie said. "Yes, I think that's entirely appropriate."

Madison turned the valves, cracked the hatch slightly, and looked out.

"Coast is clear," she said. "Come on."

"Yeah, let's get out of here," Bernie said.

Madison glanced up at the observation balconies overlooking the arena. Whoever had been controlling the mechanical Titan must be up there someplace, along with an explanation. It wasn't enough to know that Godzilla hadn't just gone rogue for no reason; she needed to be able to prove it.

They climbed out of the bunker, trying to avoid the Skullcrawler guts as best they could.

"That's probably an exit down there," Madison said. "Let's check it out."

"Yeah," Bernie said, stepping over some sort of organ. "I really, really hate this room."

The scale of the place had fooled her; what she thought was an exit looked more like a freight elevator. The door was closed, and the keypad next to it suggested getting on was not going to be easy.

"You're a hacker, right?" Bernie said to Josh. "You think you can open that?"

"Maybe," Josh said. "Or we could take the stairs." He pointed to a smaller door.

Madison pulled on the handle, and it opened easily. Inside, stairs led both up and down.

"Huh," Bernie said. He looked around. "You see another door?" he asked. "Maybe one that just says 'out'?"

"What are you talking about?" Madison said. "It's here. It's all here, like you said. All of the answers."

"Yeah?" Bernie said. "Stealing memos and shipping manifests is one thing. All *this*…" He pointed at the resting Mechagodzilla. "That's another. Look, you may be used to almost being eaten by these things. I am not. I am a journalist, a truth seeker. I am *not* a Titan entrée."

"Not an entrée," Josh said. "Not even an appetizer, really. More an amuse bouche."

He shrank back a little as Bernie leaned over him.

"What?" Josh said. "I like food television."

"Do what you want," Madison said. "I'm going this way." She hesitated for just a moment. Did they want to go down? That's where the big mechanical Titan had come up from. But while it might have been built down there, her strong feeling was that whoever was controlling it was *up*.

The first five landings with doors didn't look promising, just darkened access corridors that seemed to service the building's infrastructure. Eventually, though, they did come to a more promising exit. She was just starting to push the door open when she heard footfalls outside. She eased the door shut and they all flattened against the walls as the steps grew closer and then began to recede. She pressed the door open and peered out just in time to see a pair of armed guards turn a corner.

"Okay," she said. She slipped through the door with Josh and Bernie behind her, padding down the corridor, glancing through the doorways as they passed them. She felt as if she was going the right way—toward the viewing areas above the arena—but she couldn't be sure. The place was like a maze, and they might have gotten turned around.

They reached a dead end, but there was another door and more stairs. They went up them to the next level, where they entered another corridor.

Madison looked up and down it and started to the left.

"Hang on," Bernie said. "I think—"

He was cut off by more footfalls, and a couple of voices chattering in the distance. Madison pushed open the nearest door and they all ducked in, waiting for the guards to pass. When they finally did, Madison breathed a sigh of relief and cracked the door.

Bernie got ahead of her. "Hey guys," he said. "The exit is this way."

"Madison!" Josh said, from behind them.

She turned to look and so did Bernie.

They hadn't stepped into just any room. They had stepped into a really *weird* room.

To begin with it was a sort of technological nightmare, a mad scientist's playground. A mass of computers and machinery connected by freeways of electricity, complete with blinking lights and glowing components and a generally neon feel. But in the center of it all was something decidedly non-technological, at least on the surface; an immense horned skull, suspended by wires and fiber-optics and tubes of some kind of goo and who knew what else.

Even without the scales and skin, Madison had no doubt what it was. She had been too up close and personal with its former owner to ever forget.

"Oh my God," she said.

"What?" Bernie gasped.

"A Titan skull?" Josh said.

"No, no," Bernie said. "Not just any Titan skull. That's Monster Zero."

"Ghidorah," Madison said.

Bernie seemed to have forgotten he was trying to flee the scene. He approached the skull almost reverently. "They hardwired its DNA," Bernie said. "Self-generating neuro-pathways capable of intuitive learning..."

"Uh," Josh said. "So, like—I'm smart, but I'm in high school?"

"It's a living supercomputer," Bernie clarified.

Bernie drew even nearer and ran his fingers over the skull, the wire embedded in it like filigree.

"It had three heads," Bernie said. "Its necks were so long that it communicated telepathically. There's one here—there's another one inside of that *thing*. It could be a psionic interface."

"Which is?" Josh asked.

"Mind-to-mind connection," Bernie said. "The two skulls are still in contact. I think that's how they control the…" He looked at Josh and sighed. "Mechagodzilla."

With a jolt, Madison realized someone else was in the room. A man, seated in a chair *inside* the skull, wearing a cap with hundreds of wires and cables connected to it, running out into the machines and the skull itself.

"It's the pilot," Madison breathed.

Bernie peered in, then hid once more behind the skull.

"He's in a trance," Bernie said. "Psionic uplink. It follows his will. Oh, Apex, what have you done?"

As if in response, the man shifted a little. Bernie moved back, waving them back, too.

"Hide!" he whispered, as the pilot reached to remove the helmet.

With no time to reach the door, they did the only thing they could; they ducked underneath the skull, scooching toward the middle.

Monarch Command and Control, Hong Kong

"This is the day we feared," the director said, as Mark rushed from the helipad into the command and control. "I've given the order, Doctor. The city is being evacuated."

"Where are Apex's defenses?" Mark asked.

"They're not responding," Guillerman said.

"Maybe we were wrong," Mark said. But he didn't finish. What was there to say? The monster was here.

Mark watched, stone-faced, as Godzilla emerged from the sea. The monitors were full of the evacuation, some of it orderly, much of it characterized by the screams and hysteria that were inevitable when a three-hundred-foot-tall lizard came wading up to your metropolis. Fortunately, Hong Kong, like most major cities, had spent the past three years building secure bunkers just in case something like this were to happen again. Unfortunately, Mark knew that no shelter built by human hands could withstand the full force of Godzilla's attack. Their best hope was that they were right, that Godzilla was headed straight for the Apex building and would ignore everything that wasn't between him and it.

For Mark's part, he felt a sort of grim déjà vu.

He had spent years hating Godzilla, blaming him for the death of his son, the dissolution of his marriage and his family. But in the end, he had come to believe he was wrong, that Godzilla was on the side of humanity, that his hatred and anger were misplaced. And three years ago, he had felt vindicated. Even now it was hard to imagine how Ghidorah could have been defeated without the aid of Godzilla.

But now, maybe because of something Apex was doing or maybe just because, Godzilla had turned on them. That meant they had to do whatever it took to stop him.

Of course, he didn't know what that might be. The only thing that had been able to stop Ghidorah was Godzilla, and Godzilla had proved pretty definitely that there was no other Titan that could challenge him, most recently by making an example of Kong. So what was their plan?

Maybe Simmons had something up his sleeve. If so, Mark hoped whatever it was wouldn't be as destructive as Godzilla already was.

"Landfall," one of the techs said.

Mark nodded, watching the familiar silhouette advance into the city, the monitors capturing him from various angles.

Then, the Titan suddenly stopped, jerking as if something invisible had arrested him. He screeched and then began whirling around, his tail cutting through buildings. The entire city shook, and in the harbor, boats, swamped by miniature tsunamis, began to sink.

What the hell was he doing? Mark wondered. More than anything, it reminded him of a Titan's reaction to the ORCA, or the call of another Titan. If the call was centered on *him*.

He's confused, Mark thought. *But what…?*

Then Godzilla stopped and faced toward the earth. Blue light crept up his dorsal fins, and then a cerulean bolt of energy blasted from his mouth, tearing into the asphalt and concrete at his feet, and then deeper, into the very stone the city was built upon. Mark felt the earth shuddering through the concrete of the bunker and the mountain it was embedded in.

He had seen Godzilla do this before. For seconds, for tens of seconds maybe, and always directed at an enemy.

But now his enemy seemed to be the Earth itself, and he did not stop. He kept going, drilling toward the core of the planet.

Kong Temple

Ilene and Jia wandered around Kong's temple, and found more ancient art lurking in the shadows; like the building itself, Ilene suspected much of the painting and sculpture had been done by the Kongs themselves. Dozens more handprints graced the walls, all huge, but still of different sizes, reflecting different members of the race—different sexes and ages. They also found hundreds of smaller, human-sized prints, virtually invisible until you went looking for them, lost in the cavernous space. Most of the small prints were low, near the floor, but once they started looking for them, they saw some were much higher, and far from any ledge in the stone that might have given a human purchase.

Kongs lifted them up, Jia said. Ilene knew the girl was speculating, but it made sense, especially when she thought about the relationship between Kong and Jia.

They found more images of warfare, too, one fairly spectacular. It depicted a Kong and a Godzilla-like creature grappling. Below the Titans were smaller figures, human. And not just human; she was sure from the depictions, and some she had seen before, that they were Iwi. Jia's people.

Jia had known it before she had. The girl was shaking with emotion, and Ilene gathered her in and held her tightly.

Family, the girl signed. *Family.*

There were more painting and carvings, with the two Titan species clashing in a variety of poses and situations; but in none of them did Ilene see a figure similar to Godzilla missing a dorsal fin. That seemed unique to the floor mosaic, and so she was eventually drawn back to that, wondering what it could mean. Kong continued to sit in his throne, examining his new toy now and then. Although at first Ilene had thought it was ceremonial, she was now starting to wonder if it was actually a tool—and, more specifically, an axe. Chimpanzees made weapons of stones and branches, but the thing Kong held looked like a blade had been hafted to a large bone, the kind of complex weapon only humans were known to make.

Of course, chimps did not build temples for themselves, or work in abstract art. The time for comparing the species that produced Kong to other great apes was probably long past. There was evidence of great intelligence here, of a complex culture. What else had this species created? Were there lost cities scattered through these jungles and wastes? They had only seen one small section of Hollow Earth. If they explored far enough, they might find living members of Kong's species.

When they returned to the mosaic, they found Maia Simmons standing near it, with an odd-looking device in her hand.

"I don't understand," Simmons said. "The energy source is right below our feet."

Ilene glanced up from the carving. The energy source—in her fascination with the temple, she had almost forgotten what they were here for. Considering it, though, she felt somehow that the carving on the floor around the throne was the key. There was something there, she knew, that she did not understand. Something the pictures were trying to tell her. And Simmons and her device were pointed right at it.

They all gathered closer, surrounding the ancient image.

A faint blue glow fell on the mosaic, but Ilene quickly realized it wasn't *coming* from there. When she looked for the source, she saw that Kong's scepter was glowing. Kong looked at it, puzzled at first, then a little angry. He scowled at it.

If it was an axe—and Ilene was increasingly inclined to think it was—it wasn't the whole thing glowing, but just the blade. It was not metal, or stone, but something else, like crystal, but not exactly. The light pulsed inside of it, stronger each second, as did the sense of familiarity, the feeling that she had seen something like this before.

Kong figured it out before she did; she saw the light switch on behind his eyes. Brandishing the axe he rose, took a step, lowering the huge weapon onto the carving encircling the throne, placing the axe blade so that it rested in the hollow where the missing fin should go.

Ilene understood then. Kong's axe was made from the dorsal fin of something like Godzilla. And now it was glowing more brightly, the same light, the same color as the energy that Godzilla exhaled in his most devastating attack.

"It's the axe," Ilene said. "It's drawing radiation from the core like it's charging it. The myths are real."

Even as she said it, the blue energy began spidering outward from the axe, filling first the carving, bringing it to a semblance of life, then spreading on across the floor.

"There was a war," Ilene said. "And they are the last ones standing."

Everything began to shiver, then tremble, as the blue light waxed in brilliance.

Apex Facility, Hong Kong

Walter Simmons watched as Godzilla crushed his way through Hong Kong, toward him. He knew he ought to be worried. His creation was still powered down and, even if it weren't, it would never last long enough to defeat Godzilla. He had other weapons systems online, but zero confidence that any of them would even slow Godzilla's advance, so he disdained to use them. It would seem desperate. He might well be looking at his doom approaching; if that were so, he would meet it with dignity.

But he believed what he had told Serizawa: his daughter would come through in time. There was more at work here than the plan and his genius. Destiny was also on his side; he could feel it. It was time for Godzilla to join the fossils of his ancestors. The time of the Titans was done, and his time was just beginning.

As if on cue, Godzilla suddenly shrieked and jerked to a

halt; he spun as if confused, leveling the buildings around him.

"Whoa," Simmons said. Then he understood. *It's beneath your feet. How long before you figure it out?*

His question was answered a moment later when Godzilla stopped and set his stance. Blue radiation ran up his back.

Then he began blasting a hole into the Earth itself.

Simmons felt the building shake beneath his feet as the Titan drilled through the mountainous foundations of the city. In the distance, on one of the monitors, he saw the Tsing Ma suspension bridge shudder and sway until the huge cables snapped and it crumpled into the Ma Wan Channel.

Fantastic, he thought, taking a sip of his Scotch. *Better than I could have ever imagined.*

He grinned, because it could only mean one thing.

"Godzilla's responding," he crowed. "They found it!" Maia had come through, as expected.

Kong Temple

As her scanning device began beeping close to a steady tone, Maia Simmons gestured to her men. Nathan watched as they lifted something from the cargo area of one of the HEAVs and brought it toward the mosaic. It looked like a spider crossed with a power drill and maybe a three-dimensional printer, and it *walked* across the floor until it was near the axe, settling over a part of the floor effulgent with a pure blue light. Then it locked down and began drilling into the stone. Kong growled, deep in his belly. Nathan was about to ask Maia exactly what she was doing when he was distracted by something in the darkness behind Kong's throne. He had noticed movement on the ceiling earlier; creatures that reminded him of bats. But they had not shown any interest in leaving their dark resting place, at least not after they saw Kong. Maybe it was the weird play of blue light, tricking his eyes, but he thought he saw them moving around up there. Or possibly it was just the general sense of unease he was beginning to feel. Maia's team was acting awfully quickly, with no particular care taken to determine what they were dealing with.

He hesitated, trying to frame his words carefully, but Ilene beat him to it, and with no attempt at diplomacy.

"What are you doing?" Ilene demanded of Simmons.

Simmons nodded at the machine. "Extracting the sample," she said.

"This is power beyond your understanding," Ilene said. "You can't just drill into it."

Maia shrugged, unimpressed with Ilene's outburst.

"My father gets what he wants," Maia said. "That's Apex property now." She looked at the core of glowing stone now inside a little reservoir in the machine. The digital readout began running numbers; it was uploading something.

"We should be able to replicate this now," she said.

Apex Facility, Hong Kong

Ren was running another series of diagnostics when the needle moved on the energy signature. A lot. It was like a nine-volt battery had just been replaced with a nuclear power plant. This was it. This was what they had been waiting for.

"Energy upgrade incoming," he reported.

On another screen, a string of figures indicated DNA code uploading. The system around Ren began to respond immediately, incorporating the data, ramping up. Waiting to *become*.

"Good girl, Maia," Ren heard Simmons say.

Ren turned to the monitor, watching Gojira, sizing him

up. He had watched countless videos of the Titan, read everything he could find, including his father's notes. He had finally seen him for the first time in Pensacola, but then it hadn't felt as if Gojira was coming for him.

But that's what the Titan was doing. Not for him, but for the Mecha he had designed. He had come for it in Pensacola when they first tested some of the components, but by shutting the test down and then shipping out the parts, they had managed to stop him. Gojira had still destroyed half of the factory, but the thing calling him was no longer there, so he had eventually gone on his way. For Simmons, it had actually been a boon, despite the destruction of his facility. It had made Gojira out to be a capricious monster, no better than Ghidorah. People's fear of Gojira had once been tempered by the belief that he was on the side of humanity. No longer. When the Mecha destroyed him, no one would weep. Simmons would have everything he wanted.

So would he. Defeating Gojira and thus surpassing his father was only the beginning.

But staring at the incoming data, he was starting to sense a problem. This time, they knew the cost of testing the Mecha; they knew it would draw the real Gojira. And Simmons believed they were ready for that. He was ready to bet everything on that. Even his own life.

Ren was not so sure, and he was growing even more uncertain as he watched the upgrade and the odd readings that came with it. The system had been designed to make use of the Hollow Earth energy without knowing exactly what that energy *was*. And it would work—there was no doubt the Mecha would reach its full potential as designed.

But it might do more. The new data suggested a whole series of uncertainties from the quantum level up. They had harnessed the telepathic potential of the two Ghidorah skulls without ever *really* understanding how and why they worked. And this new genetic information, so intimately related not just to the energy, but to Gojira and how he metabolized that energy—all of this was introducing a series of X-factors that ought to be explored, quantified, understood. If they kept his creation shut down, if they turned off all of the ancillary systems connected to the skulls—chances were Gojira wouldn't know exactly where to look. In fact, Ren thought, they could probably relay a false signal elsewhere, to draw Gojira away—give them more time to truly perfect his creation.

But he had a sinking feeling that he would never convince Simmons of any of that.

NINETEEN

At a certain time, the Earth opened in the West, where its mouth is. The Earth opened and the Cussitaws came out of its mouth and settled nearby. But the Earth became angry and ate up their children. Therefore, they moved further west. A part of them, however, turned back and came to the same place they had been and settled there. The greater number remained behind, because they thought it best to do so. Their children, nevertheless, were eaten by the Earth, so that, full of dissatisfaction, they journeyed toward the sunrise.

Speech given by Chekilli, Head Chief of the Upper and Lower Creeks in Savannah, in the presence of Governor Oglethorpe and written on a buffalo skin in 1735

Kong Temple

"This is the discovery of the millennium," Ilene told Maia Simmons. "You can't just strip it for parts."

Simmons looked at her for a heartbeat or two. Then she shrugged and signaled to her men.

Instantly they moved up, rifles lifted, pointing at her, at Nathan and Jia. Ilene put up her hands; so did Nathan. But Jia just stared at the barrel of the gun pointing at her.

No, Ilene thought. *They're threatening Jia. Kong's going to lose it.*

He did. Roaring, the Titan stepped forward toward the girl.

Simmons pivoted, fear plain on her face. How she could have expected Kong not to react, Ilene didn't know but...

The distant fluttering in the heights of the cave suddenly came down on them. Whether drawn by the increase in the blue energy or—more likely—spooked by Kong's outburst—the creatures were flying all over the place. Their wings were batlike, but they were hairless, wrinkled, awful-looking things with raptor-beaked heads. They reminded Ilene of griffins designed in hell. Hellhawks would be a good name for them.

They swarmed Kong, who merely swatted at them in annoyance. They were far too small to be of any real threat to him.

But they were two or three times the size of a person.

One of the flying devils snatched up one of Simmons's mercenaries. Simmons started to run, her men along with her, but another of the hellhawks snatched a second one of them.

Everything was shaking now, and it wasn't the monsters, or the machine; it was something coming through the earth itself.

Apex Facility, Hong Kong

Simmons felt giddy as more information poured in. Microscopic cell structures unfolded, looking not so much like animal or plant cells, but more like carbon snowflakes, pulsing with blue energy. Four-letter genetic data became digital instructions. Whatever Maia had found, whatever her machine was analyzing, the results were beyond belief. Everything was falling into place, just as he had known it would. He glanced out at his Godzilla. He had built a jet engine, but thus far he had been running it on rubber bands. But the power of Titans was on the way. Primitive man had feared and worshipped lightning, but even they had learned to steal the fire that storms often left in their wake. Legends told of those who stole the fire of the heavens—Prometheus, Raven, Water-spider—and brought it to mankind. Millennia later, early scientists like Kleist, Musschenbroek, Franklin, Faraday and Ohm had ripped lightning itself from the sky and put it to work in the engines of industry. In the next two centuries, humanity learned to pry energy from the sun, rivers, from the very heart of the atom itself.

The gods of old had been upstaged; mankind now owned all of the power they once had.

Except this, the power at the core of the planet, the life force, the last thing the gods had to give before they were completely eclipsed by the little apes that had once worshipped them. This was not only the culminating achievement of his own life's work, but of every scientist before him who had dared wrestle with the powers of the universe and seized them for themselves—for the human race itself.

"Mr. Serizawa," he said. "Start your engines."

Serizawa didn't reply right away. Simmons cast him a questioning glance.

"The upgrade is untested," Serizawa said, at last. "Once we get online, Gojira will come straight for us."

"He's been coming since our creation first awoke," Simmons said. "We must embrace it."

Serizawa was still hesitant. "We shouldn't rush this," he said. "We have *no* idea how this energy source will affect the AI."

"Get in the goddamn chair," Simmons snapped.

Serizawa nodded curtly, then settled into the control chair. Outside, the mechanical Godzilla came back to life; not like before, barely limping along on rubber bands, but ready to take off on jet fuel. Fully operational.

Kong Temple

Dust and flakes of stone drifted down from above, and as the ground shook harder, the ancient temple began to break apart. Ilene watched it happening with two hearts. One was breaking, as a structure that was probably older than any human civilization was being destroyed; the loss was staggering. The other beat in terror; the very real possibility of being crushed fought for precedence with the fear of being killed by one of the hellhawks.

She, Nathan, Jia and their pilot bolted toward the HEAV as the stones collapsed behind them, but they hadn't made it more than another ten steps when one of the winged monsters came down on the pilot, pinning him to the ground just in front of the vehicle with its nasty, clawed feet. A second landed beside it, and the two began a short spat over the body.

The first drove the intruder off, and then turned to look at them.

* * *

Nathan stepped in front of Ilene and Jia, feeling helpless. If one of those things came at him, he would be shredded in an instant. But if they didn't get to the HEAV they would all be dead nearly as quickly.

He picked a rock up from the ground and hurled it at the hawk-monster. It bounced harmlessly from the beast's head, only now it was visibly angrier.

"Okay, wise guy," Nathan muttered to himself. "What now?"

He picked up another stone, this one just a pebble. The monster started toward him.

Then the stone they were standing on exploded in a burst of blue energy, hurling him from his feet. He saw Kong's throne implode, and the entire temple go up. A huge boulder smashed his antagonist, and the others of its species took flight, fleeing the destruction.

The ground lurched as Maia all but dove in to the HEAV, brushing past the remaining mercenaries. She headed up front to the pilot.

"Go, go, go," she snapped. "Move. Move. What the hell are you waiting for? Let's go. Go!"

The pilot was frantically flipping switches, and the HEAV jumped up, but then the pilot pulled back hard on the stick.

Kong loomed in front of them, looking dazed, blocking their way. In the distance she could see daylight vanishing as the temple continued to collapse. They only had seconds to get out.

"Get him out of the way," she screamed. "Shoot him!"

The pilot obliged; the HEAV's guns began rattling, blasting into Kong at point-blank range. The Titan spun away, and the path was open. The pilot saw this, too, and punched it, aiming them toward the huge pit that had opened in the ground. It was going to be tight, she saw, but they were going to make it.

Then the HEAV came to an abrupt and absolute stop, sending Maia lurching forward. She recovered, looking out the windshield. Kong was there, looking royally pissed off. He had snagged them in midair.

Oh, shit, she thought. "No, no, no—" she said.

Then Kong crushed the HEAV in his fist.

Nathan watched as Kong snatched Maia's HEAV from the air. Just before he closed his fist, before fire gushed from every opening, Nathan saw Maia's face, frozen in an expression of horrified indignation, her mouth working soundlessly.

Then the burning HEAV slammed into the stone floor.

He knew Maia had lied to him, had in fact been in the process of screwing all of them. And even before he was aware of all that, she'd been sort of a pain in the ass. She had been blunt and unapologetic and dismissive, and he had become used to her, even begun to like her—a little. And now she went on his list. The list of people killed on his watch, along with the pilot and other men whose names he had not even bothered to learn.

He felt himself sliding toward self-pity he didn't have time for, so he cinched it up. Ilene and Jia were still alive, and he cared about them a hell of a lot more than he had ever cared about Maia. If there was anything he could do to get them out of this alive, he had to do it. And after that…

Better not to plan that far ahead. He might lose focus.

They still had one HEAV, but at the rate the temple was collapsing, they wouldn't for long.

Jia and Ilene, of course, came to the same conclusion, sprinting through the shower of stone toward the vehicle.

They piled in the back as he climbed into the pilot's seat.

He looked up briefly and saw Kong watching them, concerned, but now that they were in the HEAV he seemed satisfied, so the Titan turned his attention to the charred hole on the floor. His axe lay nearby, the blade shimmering blue with radiation. Kong snatched it up, gripped it like a lumberjack and without the slightest hesitation leapt into the hole.

The temple was in full collapse now. Nathan could no longer see the entrance they had come in by; as far as he could tell, the whole mountain was coming down. He looked again at Kong's exit.

That's our only way out, too, he realized.

He gazed at the unfamiliar controls; then he started guessing, flipping switches and pushing buttons, anything to get a reaction out of the machine. Why hadn't he watched the pilot? Given his past luck, he should have guessed he would have to fly the damn thing.

"Hindsight, twenty-twenty," he muttered, under his breath.

"What?" Ilene said. "What are you doing?"

"I think Kong is going after Godzilla," he replied. "Hold on, ladies."

"Yes," Ilene said. "Let's go, *now.*"

Nathan nodded and pulled back on the stick, bracing for the acceleration.

Nothing happened.

What? he wondered, desperately. *What am I doing wrong? The stick makes it go, right?*

Jia stabbed her finger at the control panel.

"Nathan, how about the red one?" Ilene said. "The red one…"

"Which one?" Nathan asked.

"The red one," Ilene said, more frantically, as rocks

began pounding earnestly on the craft. "The huge red one that says 'Ignition' right there."

Oh. Yeah. He punched the red button, and the engines roared to life.

"Right," Nathan said. "Thank you." He nodded at Jia. It seemed someone had been watching the pilot, after all.

The HEAV lifted up, wobbling a bit. He tilted the stick up, then down, diving into the hole after Kong.

Apex Facility, Hong Kong

When Madison was sure the pilot was gone, she carefully opened the hatch she had noticed in the bottom of the skull and ascended the ladder into it.

Inside was pure weirdness, with all kinds of crazy wiring and consoles and keyboards—and yet a single focal point: the helmet the pilot had been wearing, and the chair he had been sitting in.

There was another problem she noticed immediately; in one side of the skull, a glass wall with a door set in it opened into another room, where several tech-looking types were gathered. None of them had noticed her yet, and she crouched down below their sight level to keep it that way. She found the door's keypad and locked it, flinching at the sound of the bolts sliding into place, but again, it seemed to go unnoticed by the techs, who were clearly busy at their tasks.

She motioned through the hatch for the others to come up.

"Stay low," she said, and then moved to the main console. There was lots going on, with a monitor showing POWER UPLOAD IN PROGRESS.

She remembered the Mechagodzilla and its sudden power down. That might explain the upgrade; whatever batteries it had been running on hadn't been enough to keep it going for long. Now they were trying to fix that.

Bernie came up and started taking pictures with what looked an awful lot like a flip phone. She didn't have to ask; he had done five or six episodes about the dangers of smartphones.

"Yeah, going viral," he said.

Josh poked his head up next, but Madison was still focused on the upgrade the system was processing.

"I wonder if we can shut it down from here," she said.

"I don't like this," Josh said.

"You know," Bernie said, looking around at the inside of the skull and its neon-pink lighting, "if this wasn't contributing to world destruction, this would be a great DJ booth. I know that it—" He broke off, then continued, frantically. "Maintenance!" he said. "I'm here for maintenance."

Madison realized that one of the techs outside had seen him, and now they were all staring through the glass.

"Madison, we should go," Josh opined.

Yet Madison dithered. The doors were locked. If Bernie could buy her enough time to figure this out, she might still be able to give Walter Simmons and Apex a very bad day.

Bernie was still at the window, shouting to one of the techs. "You don't have to alert the…" He trailed off, turning to Madison.

"She doesn't buy it," he sighed. "Madison, we need to go. The woman with the villain hairdo? She's getting security, so we need to leave."

On cue, two armed guards appeared at the window.

"Madison," Josh said, "they have guns!"

"Hey guys," Bernie said to the guards. "It's soundproof, so I can't really hear. I want to communicate."

"Open the door," the guard demanded, through the obviously non-soundproof door.

"Say again?" Bernie said.

Madison scanned the control panel, looking for something, anything that could help. If it was there, it didn't jump out at her.

Behind her, she heard the door crash open. As she turned, security guards poured in, their guns aimed at her and her friends.

Monarch Command and Control, Hong Kong

Why Godzilla was burning a hole in the ground was anyone's guess, but it bought them precious time for the evacuation. Ground vehicles streamed out of the area, and helicopters airlifted out those in areas already rendered inaccessible by the destruction. A path between the waterfront and the Apex buildings had been cleared and now peripheral areas were emptying. They had refrained from attacking the Titan while he was busy breathing blue, because as destructive as the effects of his drilling were, it wasn't as bad as when he was on the move.

But now, finally, he stopped, lifted his head, and seemed to search around.

"What was that all about?" Mark asked. He wished that Ishiro Serizawa was here, or Dr. Chen—anyone from the old team who might have a guess as to what the hell Godzilla was doing. Because he was clueless.

Whatever it was, he seemed to be done now, and for a moment it almost appeared that Godzilla was flailing again, trying to decide what was next. Then he took a step, and another. Toward Apex. But with a bit of hesitation.

"Just go home," Mark murmured. "Nobody to fight here."

"Holy God," one of the techs suddenly yelped.

"What?" Mark asked, moving to the screen. Director

Guillerman stood to his side.

The picture showed an enlarged view of the hole, its rim still glowing red from Godzilla's breath. Something had just come out of it. Mark wasn't sure, but it looked like an axe with a shining blue blade. Then his gaze tracked back to the hand holding it. Immense, human-like—furry.

Another hand reached out of the hole and slapped down on the half-molten surface.

And then, like some monstrous primeval deity of the Earth, Kong rose up.

"I do not understand what is happening," the director said. "Did Godzilla—"

"Kong was in Hollow Earth," Mark said. "We got word hours ago."

As impossible as it seemed, Godzilla had burned a tunnel all the way down to Hollow Earth.

They both fell silent as the Titan clambered out of the hole. He stood, wielding the glowing axe. He turned until he spotted Godzilla.

For a long moment, the two Titans locked gazes.

"Easy, boys," Mark said.

"Doctor, what's happening?" the director asked.

"They're both alphas," Mark said. "If they were two lizards, or two apes suddenly in the same territory, they might do threat displays. Make a big show of their strength, their power, their size. They wouldn't necessarily fight."

"That's promising," the director said, as Godzilla and Kong continued to stare at each other. Then Godzilla slashed his tail back and forth, and assumed a threatening posture. In response, Kong put his axe down and pounded his fists into the concrete.

"Threat displays," Guillerman said.

"Yeah," Mark said. "If they were both lizards or both apes. But they're Titans, so—"

Before he could finish the thought, Kong broke toward Godzilla in a dead-on charge, crushing everything in his way, knocking cars and buses out of his path, leveling a high-rise with a brush of his thigh.

Godzilla, in turn, rushed toward Kong.

"I think we're watching round two," Mark said.

"My money's on the ape," the tech said. "He has a weapon."

"Yeah," Mark said. The weapon was interesting—its glow was the same color as Godzilla's fins when they lit up. "See if you can isolate a radiation signature from that thing," he said.

"On it, Doc," the tech said.

Doc? Mark thought. Nobody called him that. Was everything turning upside down?

Kong came out strong, swinging the huge weapon in a blow meant to take Godzilla's head off.

But Godzilla ducked. The axe sliced into a building and stuck there. Enraged, Kong yanked it free, bringing most of the structure down with it. He swung again, and once more Godzilla avoided the blow, putting his head down and butting Kong into the still-collapsing building. Mark felt the jolt in the concrete floor and tried to imagine what a couple of hundred tons of Godzilla smacking into you would feel like. As Kong tried to recover, Godzilla bit his neck and worried him like a dog with a bone, smashing him into buildings. Mark noticed the blue light creeping up Godzilla's fins. He was charging up his beam.

Kong punched himself free, then brought his elbow down on Godzilla's back just as a blue ray shot from his mouth. Kong, recognizing the danger, grabbed Godzilla by the jaws and tried to pry his head apart, but another surge of atomic breath forced him to shift his grip to a hold on the reptile's neck. Kong then tossed Godzilla into a skyscraper. Before the saurian Titan could recover, the ape leapt, bounced off another building, and landed a haymaker on the side of Godzilla's head. Kong tried to renew his headlock, but Godzilla shook him off. Kong answered by clutching both of his fists together and hammering Godzilla down to the pavement—and when the giant lizard stood back up, he used nearby buildings to swing forward, slamming into his opponent with both feet and the full weight of his body.

As Godzilla reeled back from the hit, Kong paused to beat his chest a few times and recover his axe, just as Godzilla began charging up another blast. Kong lunged forward, jamming the handle of his weapon into the enemy's mouth. That worked for a few seconds, staving off the energy attack; then Godzilla hurled Kong back, finally giving him the range he needed to use his atomic blast properly.

That's it for Kong, Mark thought.

Godzilla let go, the beam jetting from his maw, straight toward the other Titan.

Kong jerked his axe up defensively.

The beam struck the blade and the beam stopped. They stood like that for a moment, Godzilla blasting blue fire and Kong using his axe as a shield. And the blade was glowing brighter, and brighter...

"Wait a minute," Mark said, leaning in to the monitor. "Is that—"

"Sir," the Tech said. "I've isolated the weapon like you asked. It's the same as Godzilla—"

"It's a fin!" Mark said. "See? That axe—the blade is a dorsal fin like Godzilla has!"

The blast forced Kong back, but he kept the glowing weapon in front of him. He seemed as surprised as anyone at the turn of events, staring incredulously at the glowing blade. While he was thus distracted, Godzilla followed, crashing into the ape and flipping him backward to the water. Godzilla levered up as Kong continued the charge, swinging the shining axe and sinking it deep into one of Godzilla's thighs. The saurian shrieked, slamming Kong again, hurling him into the harbor, leaving the axe buried in his leg. Godzilla reached down with his mouth, wrenched the weapon out and hurled it so that it stuck in a skyscraper half a mile away.

Then he swiveled and conjured another blast on the now-defenseless Kong.

Kong did the only thing he could do—he dodged. For all of his vast bulk, the simian Titan was incredibly nimble. He swung through the buildings as he might a jungle, staying just ahead of the deadly beam as it sliced through buildings like butter. He could only stay ahead for so long, though, and eventually the blue ray struck him in the back. He screeched, piling into another building, beating the fire off his back. He staggered back to his feet, but Godzilla wasn't done yet; he tore the fierce blue beam of energy through the city, aiming to cut Kong in half. Kong kept running, ducking, sidestepping, evading the terrible weapon, finally leaping to the top of the tallest building he saw.

Godzilla's breath sliced through the bottom, so it toppled, with Kong still clinging to it.

TWENTY

From the Notebook of Dr. Ishiro Serizawa

A Jewish legend speaks of Behemoth and Leviathan – the first, a terrible monster of the land, the second a massive creature of the water. It is said that one day Leviathan will come forth, and even the weapons of the angels will be of no use against him. But then Behemoth will arrive to fight Leviathan. They will inflict mortal wounds on one another, and both will die. Similar stories are recorded in our oldest texts, the clay tablets from the ancient civilizations of the Fertile Crescent, but they can be found scattered about the entire globe. In such stories, gods and monsters are often indistinguishable.

Hong Kong

The HEAV was bucking Nathan's direction, trying to slam them into the wall of the increasingly unstable tunnel. And his instruments, if he was reading them correctly, told him the worst was yet to come.

"We're about to breach the veil," he warned his passengers. He pushed the engines as far as they would go, and again they hit the strange space–time distortion, and HEAV turned into a bullet firing through the roughest musket in the world.

An eternity passed. No time passed at all. And suddenly they were rocketing from the passage into a kaleidoscope of colors and shapes; one shape in particular loomed large…

They were on a collision course with Kong, who was in midair.

They all screamed in unison as Nathan yanked back on the stick. He avoided the giant ape by a hairsbreadth, wondering what the hell was going on, when in his peripheral vision he caught sight of a beam of blue energy spearing through the air, and he was flying through clouds of shattered glass and concrete. Out of the frying pan and into … a much bigger atomic frying pan. He put the craft into a climb, desperately trying to get the away from the warring Titans. He avoided the energy beam by a matter of feet and had one very up-close-and-personal view of Godzilla's face before whipping past him into the sky above Hong Kong.

As Nathan fought for control and the craft gyred and ascended, Ilene couldn't tear her gaze from Kong, Godzilla, and the destruction of Hong Kong. Kong was running, leaping, climbing, swinging from skyscrapers, avoiding Godzilla's energy bolt with agility that was hard to credit to a creature so large, without seeing it first-hand. At first, she didn't understand his goal, but then she saw his axe, buried in the side of a building. He reached it, pulled it out, and raised it high to attack Godzilla, who was still a considerable distance away. Kong took a short run and leapt, the axe cocked over his head.

A blue beam shot from Godzilla's mouth, but Kong, sailing in a long arc through the air, blocked the ray with his glowing blade. And it worked.

But that would be the point, wouldn't it? Godzilla's energy beam made him almost invincible. Unless you had something to counter it. Like one of the very fins that charged and channeled the energy. After all, Kong had found it stuck in the skeleton of something like Godzilla.

As the HEAV started to level out, she saw Kong finish his arc, swinging the axe down to meet Godzilla's gaping maw.

Then everything turned blue-white as a sphere of energy expanded out from the two Titans, hurling them in opposite directions and leveling everything in its radius. She watched, horrified, as the explosion raced toward them. Nathan gasped, trying to force the HEAV to somehow go faster.

The edge of the shockwaves reached them, buffeting them hard. But when it was over, they were still intact.

Below, she saw Kong pulling himself up from the rubble.

"Looks like round two goes to Kong," Nathan said.

Ilene let her breath out and took another clean breath in, and saw the sun was rising from the South China Sea.

"Guy definitely has a flair for techno," Bernie murmured, as the guards pushed them into the room.

Madison knew what he meant. If the Skull Room was the nerve center, the launch pad, this place was mission control—but as designed by a nightclub architect. Everything had a neon cast to it; there was even strip-lighting buried in the translucent floor. A huge observation window formed most of one wall, and the others were covered in panels displaying various data sets, including the energy upload she'd seen inside the skull. Various workstations faced away from the window, maybe to keep the techs from being distracted by the carnage below, since Madison was certain they were now overlooking the arena.

A man turned from the picture window to watch them enter. He wore a black suit over a blue shirt unbuttoned to the third button. No tie. Casual shoes, salt-and-pepper beard, a drink in a glass tumbler. If you looked up "tech-company giant" in the encyclopedia, this was the picture next to it. Walter Simmons—CEO of Apex, genius, techno-logical savior. He watched them enter with an almost playful expression as he sipped his drink.

"Oh, no," he said. "More environmental crusaders?"

"Actually sir," Bernie offered, "I'm a level-two engineering assistant for this company. Uh, provisionally level two but my evaluation was very encouraging…"

A guard nudged Bernie with his gun.

"Just sayin'," Bernie said.

Simmons turned his quizzical gaze upon Madison. She straightened her shoulders and stared back as recognition dawned on his features.

"Where do I know you from?" he asked. He tilted his head fractionally. "Oh my goodness," he said, "Director Russell's daughter, yes?"

"You caused all this," Madison accused.

Simmons raised his eyebrows a little, then seemed to acknowledge the comment with a cock of his head and a lifting of his arms to take in the room.

"If by 'all this' you mean I and I alone have given humanity a chance against the Titans, yes, I will proudly own that title," he said.

"Godzilla had left us in peace!" Madison said. "You provoked him into war!"

"We couldn't have known he would react as he did to the Mecha's construction, that its energy signal would draw him like a whistle, but—there can be only one alpha, Ms. Russell ... it seems to have been providence."

"Providence?" Madison said. "He's probably trashing Hong Kong right now."

"Yes, as a matter of fact," Simmons said. "But, as you will see, we'll put an end to that in a moment."

"With that thing out there?" Madison said. "The real Godzilla will shred that."

"Oh, you've seen that too," Simmons said. "Well." He frowned. "May I ask what brought you here? Let me be more specific. How did you get here?"

"We took the fast train from Pensacola," Bernie said.

"And who are you?" Simmons asked.

Bernie straightened up. "Just a guy," he said. "A guy who has been onto you for *years*. And just so you know, all of this is out there now. Viral, baby."

"Wait," Simmons said, gesturing with his drink. "You aren't that blogger? Mad Truth? Oh, my God, you must be. This is just all so wonderful. I can't tell you. Oh. Huge fan. I loved that four-part series on chemtrails. Gave me some seriously promising ideas for future projects." He took another drink.

"Please," he said. "Consider yourselves my guests for now. We've got quite a show coming up."

He turned away, back to the window.

"He didn't even ask who I was," Josh grumbled.

But Madison was staring at one of the monitors. Godzilla was there, fighting ... Kong? Where had Kong come from?

From their aerial vantage, Nathan and the others now had an unobstructed view of how the fight was going. Judging by the state of the city, they had already missed a lot of it.

Following the explosion that sent both Titans flying,

Kong had stayed under cover, wary of the other Titan's energy attack.

Jia was busily signing in the back.

"She says we have to help him," Ilene translated.

"Yeah," Nathan said. "I would love to. But we're clean out of ammunition. No missiles, anyway. And I'm far from proficient at flying this thing. I'm afraid all I can do is get us killed. Anyway, it looks like Kong is doing okay."

"He's lost his axe," Ilene said. "Without that he's got nothing to protect him from Godzilla's morning breath. Maybe we can find it for him."

"Given the amount of energy released," Nathan said, "it might have been destroyed."

"We can try," she said.

He nodded. "I'll fly. You two look. Let me know if you see anything."

"Okay," Ilene said, as Nathan started a broad circle. From the air, it was clear Kong and Godzilla were no longer in each other's line of sight, but Godzilla, obviously searching for Kong, still tended to move in the right direction.

"He senses him," Ilene said. "Kong can't hide."

"Looks like that's what he's doing, though," Nathan pointed out.

Kong had found a tall building, had climbed it, and seemed to be lying in wait, holding very still.

"Clever," Ilene said.

"Clever is all he's got right now," Nathan said.

They watched as Godzilla stalked the city, drawing nearer Kong's hiding spot.

"He still doesn't see him," Ilene breathed. Godzilla was almost on Kong.

From his perch on the skyscraper, Kong tossed a spire he had snapped off from another building. When Godzilla turned at the distraction. Kong leapt squarely onto the other

Titan, throwing his arms around the big lizard and binding him in a headlock. Then he rammed Godzilla's head into a building. The reptilian Titan writhed like mad, trying to escape Kong's deadly embrace, but the ape held on, punching Godzilla in the head whenever he could get one arm free. The saurian snapped at Kong's face and savaged his arm, but the ape held on like a bull rider, refusing to be thrown. Ilene was beginning to think he could hold on forever, but then Godzilla clamped down on his arm and yanked his head down, throwing Kong over and landing him flat on his back. Godzilla tried to stamp on him, but Kong rolled aside, and then they were fighting again in such flurry of arms and legs, it was difficult to tell what was happening. But then Godzilla tossed Kong across the city, crashing through multiple structures until he fetched up hard against the base of a building. Kong reached for his shoulder, groaning, but Godzilla gave him no chance to recover his wind. He came at Kong like a bull, head lowered. The Titan rolled away, and the gargantuan reptile plowed headfirst into the building, but that hardly slowed him down; his tail swung and slammed Kong against the pavement; Godzilla lunged. Kong, still sitting, retreated crab style, kicking at Godzilla with his stumpy legs, clearly very much on the defensive. Godzilla pounced, absorbing Kong's kicks and slashing his claws across the ape's chest; then, towering above the pummeled Kong, the reptile slammed his hind foot down on Kong. Kong continued punching, but he had no leverage, and Godzilla, keeping him pinned, screamed his triumph at the heavens.

"That's it," Nathan said.

For what seemed a very long moment, the tableau seemed frozen. Godzilla stood there, dominating Kong, a threat display moving up and down his dorsal fins.

"Kong won't bow," Ilene said, softly. "Godzilla will kill him."

Nathan dropped the HEAV lower. He could see Ilene was right; Kong was down, but he glared up in defiance, as if daring the victorious Titan to finish him. Kong might have lost the fight, but he was not defeated; he wasn't giving in.

Godzilla, done with his victory proclamation, tilted his head down toward his beaten foe.

Maybe if I buzz him, distract him, Nathan thought. But a glance back at Jia, and he knew he wouldn't. The girl had lost so much. She was about to lose Kong. But Nathan wasn't going to be responsible for her death as well. He couldn't.

Ilene met his gaze, then looked at Jia. She nodded.

Then Jia pointed and signed.

Nathan looked back down in time to see Godzilla do something extraordinary.

The saurian leaned down, so his snout was in Kong's face, and roared. For a moment, Kong just stared back, as if finally acknowledging the fight was over. But then he lifted his head and howled back at the Titan, an act of purest defiance.

Godzilla straightened back up and then slowly, very deliberately, the reptile removed his foot, maintaining eye contact with Kong. Then he turned and walked away, moving once again toward the Apex building, knocking down everything that stood in front of him.

Kong, for his part, struggled to rise, but then his eyes fluttered, and he collapsed back into the street.

Nathan started the HEAV down toward the fallen Kong. He looked back at Ilene and Jia.

"I'm sorry," he said.

Ren looked over his readout; the energy upload was complete. And his doubts were stronger than ever. There was something weird going on, behind the numbers.

"Kong has weakened Godzilla," Simmons's voice came over the link. "It's time. Begin bio-integration."

Ren sighed. He knew what was expected of him; he knew why he was here. This was no time to be timid; Kong was down, and he wasn't getting up. The upload signal was all Gojira needed to find them, and Simmons wasn't going to let him power that down. It was either take control of the Mecha and obliterate the Titan or be crushed by him. Why was he even hesitating? He had waited most of his life for this.

You gave your life so that this monster could live, Father, he thought. *I now present mine to destroy him.*

He put on the helmet and started the link-in. He felt the life-energy, waiting.

No, not waiting, multiplying. Like living cells. And the artificial intelligence was going nuts, pouring out packets of nonsense information, swamping the system. And the skull itself—it seemed to be pulsing in rhythm with his heartbeat. Not just pulsing, but shrinking, closing in on him—but no, that wasn't it. He was growing larger as the cells multiplied. Filling it up, merging with the bone itself. He felt the connection establish, felt his will begin to filter over to the other skull, the control mechanisms of *his* Gojira, expanding all the while, filling it up, too.

But it suddenly wasn't one way anymore. It was not just him entering the machine—something was also entering him, oscillating, a feedback loop between his own consciousness and the AI. He felt a million years of rage rising in him, hatred that transcended time and space. He felt as if he was sinking into it, dissolving, as another mind full of terrible, alien thoughts began to take his place.

He tried to take the helmet off, but he couldn't feel his hands. He opened his eyes and realized he was in the Mecha, staring at Simmons through the glass. But when he tried to move the mechanical hands, they wouldn't move either.

At least not when he wanted them to. But the Mecha was moving; the *other* was moving it, and as it did so, Ren's field of vision began to shrink, pixilating at the edges. Images flashed in staccato bursts, recognizable for an instant, then gone. He saw a shadow in the distance, a man.

Dad? Daddy?

The man looked back at him and smiled, then he, too, broke apart, and the thing that called himself Ren was gone, and *it* had arrived. It did not know who it was, or what it was, but it was full of rage and the black joy of finally *being*, and having limbs, and teeth, a boundless, unending energy at its command. It saw everything as a blur, but as the one known as Ren died, its vision sharpened. It felt its hands, its legs, its fins, everything. And it saw a shape, a tiny shape, staring at it from behind a clear wall. One that believed they controlled it.

While Madison glared helplessly, Simmons walked to the observation glass to stare at his synthetic Titan.

"It's time to launch," Simmons said. "*Now* my Mecha is not just Godzilla's equal, but his superior. *The* apex Titan, of my own hand. It's time to show the world what he can do. This is how we, as a species, win."

Outside, Mechagodzilla was slowly pivoting, facing the glass and Simmons. But Simmons had turned to address them, so he didn't see. Madison began inching back, and so did Bernie and Josh.

"You see," Simmons went on, "ten years ago, when Gojira first revealed himself to the world, I had a dream. And in this dream, I saw one thing. And that beautiful, amazing thing was—"

Then he noticed them retreating. He turned to find Mechagodzilla filling the window—and still coming forward.

"Oh, shit," he said. There came a sudden flash of

movement, and then the window and the entire front part of the observation room was gone, including Simmons. Madison, Bernie and Josh were suddenly thrown back, half buried in debris. It was as if a meteor had just cut the room in half, but Madison's brain was running it all back, in slow motion—and in that replay she saw Mechagodzilla's claw, darting out, sweeping through the booth.

Just shy of them. Gasping, coughing, she pushed shattered metal and plastic off of herself, still staring at the gaping hole.

"No fair," Bernie gasped. "I wanted to hear the rest of that speech."

The guards and techs were gone, Madison noticed. Obliterated by Simmons's creation or running for the closest exit.

Was Mechagodzilla done? Or would it kill the rest of them?

But a look through the gaping hole in front of her revealed the mechanical Titan had turned its attention to the far end of the arena. It blasted the wall with its red breath and tore through the stone like it was wet papier mâché.

Beyond, the golden rays of the rising sun shone through the smoke on what was left of the city of Hong Kong.

"So much for Kong," Mark said, as Godzilla turned back towards his original target.

"Sir," the tech said. "We're getting that signal again. The weird one. It's coming from inside the Apex complex. But it's—it's really strong now. Off the charts."

"Maybe we're finally going to see what Simmons has planned," Guillerman said.

"Yeah," Mark replied. "I'm afraid you might be right

about that. If I were you, I would increase the evacuation radius."

"Already done," the director said.

Before Godzilla could reach the Apex building, a string of fireballs erupted on the hillside, opening up a huge breach in the stone beneath. A red beam blasted through, gutting the nearest buildings in eerie imitation of Godzilla's energy weapon. The mountainside collapsed, revealing a huge hole, and emerging from it, silhouetted against the fire and tumult was—something fantastic. Crackling with crimson energy, it stepped into the light, and roared, a sound like nothing Mark had ever heard, and he had heard his share of Titans hold forth.

But this thing…

He watched in horror as it "breathed" its red beam through the city, torching dozens of buildings.

"What in God's name is that?" Mark asked. As he watched, it crushed forward through the city toward Godzilla. And Godzilla began a charge. The new thing—it looked a lot like Godzilla. But it also looked *built*, not grown. And that set it apart from any Titan he had ever seen.

"It's like some kind of robo-Godzilla," he said. "Simmons, what the hell have you done?"

"More like a Mechagodzilla," Guillerman said. "But that's beside the point. What I want to know is—which one are we rooting for?"

Mark shook his head. It had been clear when Godzilla faced off against Ghidorah. And just now he had been rooting for poor old Kong. But this time…

"Heaven help me," Mark said. "I just don't know."

The mechanical Godzilla launched a fusillade of missiles at Godzilla, causing him to break stride, but not stopping him.

* * *

From the ruins of the control room, Madison, Josh and Bernie now had an excellent view of the fight via the huge hole Mechagodzilla had punched in the mountainside. As the two giants grappled, it quickly became clear the mechanical Titan was faster and stronger than the real Godzilla—and Godzilla was worn down from his fight with Kong.

The guy in the skull is controlling it, Madison thought. *All we have to do is get the helmet off of him.*

But when she tried to return to the control room inside of Ghidorah's skull, she found that it had also been annihilated when Mechagodzilla killed Simmons. She found no sign of the pilot.

So, nothing to be done there.

She glanced at the control panels that were still functioning. They showed a fully functioning Mechagodzilla and power readings that appeared to her to be ridiculous.

Something had happened. The mechanical Titan didn't need a pilot anymore.

She looked out through the gap in the wall in time to see the Mechagodzilla suddenly ablaze, as rockets on its back fired, giving it a power assist as it punched Godzilla again, hurling the flesh-and-blood Titan through the city.

"It's thinking for itself now," she told the others. "We have to warn Monarch."

"Or stop that thing ourselves," Josh said.

"How do we do that?" Madison asked.

Josh was looking at the control console.

"That thing is still linked to a satellite," he said. "If we can figure out the password, we can shut it down."

"Okay," Bernie said, as Josh started in at the console.

Outside, Mechagodzilla knocked the real one back once more—and then unleashed its own energy beam. Godzilla was hurled backward to sprawl in the rubble; the scales on his chest were now glowing like embers. He tried to get up, but the cyborg monster was there, grabbing Godzilla's arms and biting into his thick hide.

Godzilla roared, but to Madison's ears, it was more of a groan. He was losing.

Nathan found what seemed like a safe spot to set the HEAV down, and the three of them climbed out. He realized then that in concentrating on flying the vehicle, he had somehow missed something crucial. Kong was still down, but Godzilla was still fighting—this time with a weird, robotic version of himself.

"What the ... hell is that?" he wondered.

He stood, transfixed for a moment, watching the bizarre scene. The mechanical monster had claws that whirled like drill bits and blazed with energy. It punched Godzilla repeatedly, then grabbed him and began slamming him into buildings.

Then he realized Ilene was running off through the rubble-strewn streets. Further in the distance—ahead of Ilene—he saw Jia, racing toward the fallen figure of Kong.

Jia had never been anyplace so strange, so unsettling. Everything smelled wrong, like the machines back home, but *everywhere* and everything. What she had taken at first to be strange cliffs and rock formations she now saw were more like termite hives kicked open, filled with little spaces. Except here the termites were people; as if Awati buildings back home had grown and multiplied to fill up the whole world. Her mother had spoken of such places, but she had believed those were just stories to frighten her.

And the vibrations. On her skin, through her feet, even

in her skull, the place was alive with the awful tremoring and shuddering of machines, more of them than she could have ever imagined. The noise was worse than the storms that took her people. And that was without the fight, without the *wrong* thing that looked like the ancient enemy, that sent prickles up her back just to look at; and from it, the worst vibration of all, a sickening feeling in the middle of her bones that felt like illness come alive, like all of the hatred in the world put on two legs.

And in all of this horror, amidst all of the chaos and weirdness, in the stink of fire and the burning of unnatural things there were only two things she recognized as familiar—her mother and Kong. And Kong needed her.

She reached where he lay collapsed; she pressed her hand to the earth that wasn't earth. And there she felt it. His heartbeat. Slow. Getting slower, fainter.

Ilene found Jia next to Kong, her palms spread against the ground. She knelt by the girl.

What are you doing? Ilene signed.

His heart is slowing down, Jia replied.

Nathan caught up just then. "What's happening?" he asked.

"She can feel his heartbeat," Ilene told him. "It's slowing down. He's dying."

Nathan looked away, toward the ongoing fight.

"There's nothing we can do," Ilene said. "To start his heart, we'd need to produce a charge big enough to—"

"—light up Las Vegas for a week?" Nathan finished. He had a gleam in his eye as he looked back toward the HEAV.

TWENTY-ONE

The sun darkens,
earth in ocean sinks,
fall from heaven
the bright stars,
fire's breath assails
the all-nourishing tree,
towering fire plays
heaven against itself.

Völuspá, circa 1270 (an account of Ragnarök,
the Old Norse Apocalypse),
trans. Benjamin Thorpe, 1865

Hong Kong

Josh typed frantically at the keyboard as Bernie crowded
over him.

"Is that a password?" Bernie asked. "Is that a password?"

"I don't know!" Josh replied, exasperated. "It's all just evil jargon. I'm not used to this; I'm used to pirating movies online!"

"Do you see 'settings'?" Bernie demanded. "Look for 'settings.' Control-Alt-Delete. I thought you were a hacker!"

Meanwhile, Madison was working the phone. She finally figured out how to get an outside line and entered her father's number. The phone rang...

And he picked up.

"This is Mark," he said.

"Dad!" she said. "Can you hear me? I'm in Hong Kong."

"Madi ... son..." She heard his voice break up and then the phone went dead.

"Hello?" she said. "Hello?"

But the connection wasn't coming back. She looked over at Josh and Bernie, just in time to see "security lock" appear on the monitor. Josh was still typing, but nothing was happening anymore.

Nathan made it back to the HEAV and climbed into the cargo hold. He popped what he thought was the right panel. He rewired it, hoping against hope he was doing it right. Then the light on the panel changed and it closed.

That ... looked promising.

"Okay," he told Jia and Ilene, "you two better get some distance."

Nathan saw Jia hesitate. Tears streaked down her face.

"You're a very brave little girl," he said. He made the sign for "brave" as he remembered her making it what seemed like an eternity ago.

She smiled; it was like a little burst of sun in the middle of a storm. She shook her head and pointed at him.

"I don't know," he said. "Maybe we both are."

He watched as Jia and Ilene climbed out. Then he made his way forward to the controls.

Ilene watched the HEAV lift off, then turned her attention to the gargantuan battle still unfolding.

It wasn't going well for Godzilla. As she watched, he tried to swipe the mechanical monster with his tail, but his foe caught it, spun to gather momentum, and hurled the Titan across the city, where he crashed into Victoria Peak.

Godzilla wasn't out, though. He planted his feet and unleashed the energy beam that had tunneled through the Earth's crust and mantel to Hollow Earth. But the robot thing let loose its own energy beam—a red one—meeting and overpowering Godzilla's, blasting the Titan back through multiple buildings.

Nathan landed the HEAV on Kong's chest. Then he went to work on the anti-gravity engine, rewiring it, directing the immense charge that powered it to his purposes. He was just finishing up when he felt a tremor of movement. He looked over to see Kong's eyes were slightly open.

It wasn't the Kong he had come to know. He looked sad, beaten. Dying. He was glad Jia wasn't there to see it.

He made the final connection.

"All right," he said. "Good luck, big fella."

He flipped the final switch and ran like hell as a high-pitched whine began building up behind him. He'd made about two blocks when the engine exploded. He looked back and saw electricity pulsing through the Titan's body. Then his own muscles spasmed, seized up.

Oh, crap, Nathan thought as his knees buckled. *All*

I've done is electrocute him.

Then everything went black.

Jia saw the HEAV explode, felt the distant lightning on her face. She saw Kong twitch.

Then he jerked up, eyes wide, huffing frenetically. He opened up his mouth and she felt his roar on her skin. She broke away from her mother and ran back toward him. She didn't know what the man Nathan had done, but she could feel Kong's heartbeat again, even through her feet; strong, alive. She ran up to him, waving her arms to get his attention.

Finally he looked down at her, squinting. She started telling him.

Godzilla. Not. Enemy.

He snorted at her, roaring his disapproval at the very thought. He didn't believe. How could he? Their kinds had been at war for so long. Godzilla—like Jia, like Kong—he was an orphan now. The last. But this other thing—it had no people, and never had. And it was not right, not a thing that should be in the world. She could feel it all the way to her marrow.

It's true, she signed, emphatically. She pointed at the mechanical monster. *That is enemy. It's true.*

Mother was here, pulling her back again. Kong still looked dubious, but Jia thought maybe he believed her.

Please, she told him. *Be careful.*

Kong looked over to where the abomination-monster was beating down Godzilla. Then he pushed himself to his feet. He gripped his hurt arm, and then cracked his shoulder against a building. Jia felt the grinding crunch of his bone moving into place.

Then, battered, wounded, Kong went back to the fight.

* * *

Bernie, Madison thought, was losing it.

"I thought you were a hacker!" he yelled at Josh for the tenth time.

"I never said I was a hacker," Josh said. "I said I took HTML at camp."

"HTML?"

"Yeah. At summer camp."

"I knew it! Tap Water! Hah."

"Shut up and let me think," Josh demanded.

Mark swore at his phone, punching redial for the fourth time. The number was unfamiliar, but he was certain he had heard Madison's voice on the other end of that line.

And it was a local number. Was she *here*? How was that possible?

Because it was Madison, that's how.

Madison, he thought. *What have you gotten yourself into?*

Outside, things were not going well for Godzilla.

Mark had seen him on the ropes before, but not like this. For every attack the reptile launched, the machine countered faster, better, stronger. Maybe if Godzilla hadn't had to fight Kong first, if he had been fresh for this battle, things would be going better.

And Mark realized something then. Despite what he had told the director, he was definitely rooting for Godzilla. Why, he could not exactly say. Maybe for no better reason than because Madison would, because *she* believed in him.

The mechanical Titan knocked the reeling Godzilla back, and back again, stunning the Titan, dragging him across the city on his belly like a ragdoll. Then, with its mechanical hands, it grabbed Godzilla by the jaws and pulled his mouth open. Its fins began shining red, charging its own beam-weapon. Mark, feeling helpless, couldn't turn his gaze away.

Then Kong was suddenly there, wrenching Mechagodzilla's head back so the beam shot straight up into the sky. The construct heaved Kong from its back, but that gave time for Godzilla to clamber back up, and now it was two on one. They each took one of the mechanical Titan's arms and rammed it through a building, scrubbing its face on the city floor as it had just been doing to Godzilla. But the metal monster fought its way back to its feet, even with the both of them hanging on to its arms. Kong leapt up and tried to kick its head off, but although the blow rocked it back, Mechagodzilla was undeterred. It fired a missile at Godzilla, blasting him back, then hurled Kong away, before turning back to pummel Godzilla relentlessly with its spinning claws. Godzilla, already weak, could barely continue to stand. The metal Titan grabbed the reptile and flattened him against a building, then arched its tail toward Godzilla's face, like a scorpion—the tip of which was spinning, alive with energy.

Kong had vanished for a moment, but now he suddenly reappeared, once more wielding his glowing axe, grabbing the mechanical Titan's tail and swinging his weapon at the machine-monster. Kong beat it back and even managed to knock it off its feet, but then Mechagodzilla rallied, jamming its spinning tail into Kong's face. The ape strained, trying to keep it from biting into him, but his arms were trembling, while the robotic Titan seemed as powerful as ever.

Staring at the "security lock" message on the screen, Josh finally stopped typing. The keyboard was no longer accepting input.

"Josh, you have to do something!" Madison said, tearing her gaze from the battle outside. In seconds, the mechanical Titan would kill Kong with its tail, and then it would finish off Godzilla. Whatever Simmons had been planning after that was moot. Mechagodzilla now had plans of its own. She was certain of one thing; something that beat Godzilla and Kong in the same fight would not be stopped by anything else. Once they were dead, Mechagodzilla could do what it wished with impunity.

Josh shook his head in defeat.

"We tried to take down those Apex bastards," Bernie said, "but looks like this is as far as we go."

Madison looked at Bernie, and Josh, and realized he was right. They were at a dead end. There would be a new alpha, with the power of Godzilla and more, from whatever source Simmons had discovered and maybe the soul—if you could call it that—of Ghidorah. What if Mechagodzilla brought back Rodan, and Scylla, and some of the other really nasty Titans? The horror of three years ago might end up looking like a common cold compared to the bubonic plague.

And she couldn't think of a single way to help.

Bernie sighed, and a look of resignation settled on his features. He reached to his holster and pulled out his flask. He uncapped it and looked skyward.

"Sara, my sweet," he said. "You know we tried our level best. But I think this is as far as it goes. I was hoping to die with adults, but bottoms up." He paused and looked down at Josh, who was still staring at the nonfunctioning controls.

"If you ever wanted a drink, kid, now's the time."

"Drink?" Josh said. He suddenly snatched the flask from Bernie.

Bernie jerked as if stung, and Madison didn't know what Josh was doing.

But then she saw, as Josh poured the contents all over the controls.

"That's your solution?" Bernie erupted. "I have to die in here with you *and* sober?"

The keyboard began smoking, then sparks spewed out.

Outside, Mechagodzilla's tail suddenly stopped spinning and went limp.

Well that's something, Madison thought.

But then, just as suddenly, the control screen sputtered back to life.

"Wait," Mark said. "Something just happened."

He pointed to the zoomed monitor. For a second, the glowing red eyes of the mechanical Titan dimmed, and the tail, set to drill through Kong's forehead, dropped. But even as he said it, the eye flickered back on, blazing as brightly as before, and the tail swung back. Kong, taking advantage of the slight lull, pushed back, raising his axe, but the machine began overpowering him again.

In the background, Mark saw blue light. Godzilla lifted his head.

Azure light blazed from the Titan's mouth, but it didn't strike Mechagodzilla. Instead it burned by him and hit Kong's axe, which suddenly took on a life of its own, absorbing and then transcending the now-faltering beam.

Kong roared, pushing back on the Mechagodzilla, wrenching free of the machine's grasp, and hewed his weapon straight into his opponent's arm. Sparks flared and red lightning snapped as the weapon sheared off the appendage as if it were a palm frond.

Without pause, the mechanical Titan launched a punch at Kong's face with its remaining arm, but Kong, it seemed, had had enough. He flew into a berserk rage, whaling away with the glowing axe, cutting the mechanical Titan into pieces. It tried to charge up, to blast Kong one more time with its energy weapon, but Kong buried the edge of his weapon in the monster's face. Then he let go of the axe and leapt on the pile of metal. He put both hands on the mechanical head and wrenched it off, holding it up like a trophy for the world to see. He roared again, savage, triumphant, as the red glow in the metal skull faded.

Then Kong swayed on his feet and stumbled. Blood hemorrhaging from a dozen wounds, he sat down heavily against a building, his eyes closing.

For a moment, Madison wasn't sure what she was seeing. She switched her gaze from the hole in the wall to the monitors with closer views to be sure she understood. And it finally sank in; Mechagodzilla was destroyed, and Kong was holding up its head like the statue of Perseus and Medusa. Then she started to yell, and Josh and Bernie joined her wild cheering. They celebrated, and they laughed, hugging one another. It was over, and they had won. Somehow.

Madison realized, after a moment, that she was maybe hugging Josh for too long. It was getting weird. She let go, stepped back—and with a grin hugged him even harder. Let it be weird.

Bernie looked skyward again. "Thank you, my sweet," he said.

In all of the tumult of the fight, Ilene realized she hadn't seen Nathan since he had used the HEAV to start Kong's heart back up. She had seen him leave the vehicle, but he had never made it back to her and Jia. Of course, they had also been a moving target running toward Kong. Maybe he'd just lost sight of them. But she feared much worse.

She and Jia made their way through the debris, circling toward where Kong has been laid out. In the wake of the fight, an eerie stillness had settled over the wreckage of the city. The quiet *after* the storm.

It was Jia who spotted Nathan, face-down in the street. *You stay here*, she signed to the girl. *I'll go see if he's okay.*

Jia shook her head stubbornly. *I know what dead is*, she signed. *I'm not a little girl anymore, remember?*

Tears glistened in the girl's eyes, but they stayed there, contained. Ilene wasn't sure she could be so controlled. From here, things didn't look so good. If Nathan was dead, it might be a little more than she could handle at the moment.

So she approached slowly, looking for some sign he was okay, for a twitch or the rise and fall of his ribs. But the nearer she got, the less promising it looked.

She knelt next to him, Jia by her side. She gripped the girl's hand. Then she prodded Nathan. She felt for a pulse at his throat.

She found it, and carefully rolled him over. His eyes popped open; he looked confused, disoriented.

"Nathan," she said. "Nathan, are you okay?"

He seemed to recognize her, then he looked at Jia, who was smiling wider than Ilene thought she had ever seen the girl smile. He nodded.

"Come on," she said, helping him to his feet. Around her, the ruins were coming alive again as helicopters arrived, bringing military and relief workers into the stricken city.

Jia's sunny disposition broke a moment later, when she saw Kong still slumped senseless or dead against a building.

Kong, she signed. *Make better again?*

"We'll see," Nathan said. "Maybe you two can fill me in on what happened?"

* * *

It took a while for Madison and the others to squirrel their way through the Apex headquarters, but they didn't encounter any resistance in the way of guards; the place was almost entirely empty. Once on the street, Madison guided them toward the area where the Monarch control and relief process was most evident, near where Kong had fallen. As they approached, she saw who she was looking for.

"Dad!" she shouted.

He turned, saw her running toward him.

"Madison," he shouted. "Madison!"

"Dad! Dad!" she yelled back.

She bounded across the distance, and a moment later they were wrapped up in a hug.

"I'm sorry," she said.

"Me too," he replied.

"Mr. Russell," Josh interposed, "It was Madison's idea to—"

"Shut up, Josh," he said, gently.

"Okay," Josh agreed. "I'll shut up."

Madison pulled back a bit and saw Bernie standing there, looking somewhat lost.

"Dad," she said, "I want you to meet the man who saved our lives. Bernie. Meet Dad."

The two shook hands.

"Bernie, Dad," Bernie said. "It's an absolute pleasure to meet you. I have a podcast and I would love to have you on to talk about the Monarch facility in Roswell. I have some theories—"

"No, stop," Madison told him. "Is this the right time?"

Jia stared up, glassy-eyed, at the unmoving figure of Kong. Nathan wished he knew what to say, but he figured that even if he were fluent in sign, he would never find the words. Jia must feel like an orphan all over again.

Across the crowd he saw Mark Russell and his daughter Madison. He understood why Mark was here, but Madison? Well, she tended to get into things, didn't she? There was a story there, and he was sure he would hear it soon enough. Then he could tell his own story about how Walter Simmons had duped him into all of this, nearly destroying the world as they knew it...

Mark saw him and lifted his chin in acknowledgement. Nathan nodded back. Yes, he had screwed up—again. But he had also come through, this time. If he hadn't jump-started Kong ... anyway, things seemed to have all worked out, more or less. At least it was over.

Then the earth shook, and a familiar screech filled the air, and the gathering crowd screamed along with it. Nathan jerked his head toward the sound and there, emerging from the smoke, was Godzilla; bruised, injured, but very much alive—and headed right toward them. Or, more likely, toward Kong.

Jia got that right away; she broke free of Ilene's grasp and sprinted toward the fallen Titan. Nathan and Ilene ran after her, managed to grab her and try to hustle her out of the way, but by then Godzilla towered directly above them.

That woke Kong, though. He pushed himself up, doggedly determined to finish the fight if he had to. He lifted the glowing axe and bellowed at Godzilla. For a moment they stood like that, two Titans from a lost age, the only survivors of an ancient war, face to face.

Then Kong looked down at the axe. He let it slip from his hand. He straightened a little and regarded Godzilla.

Godzilla held that gaze for a moment. Nathan felt as if he was watching something important, something passing between the two Titans. Then, with a slight growl,

Godzilla turned and began walking seaward, unleashing a roar of triumph. Kong joined in, pounding his chest, and together they created a strange—well, if not harmony, at least a welcome cacophony.

At the water's edge, Godzilla paused, looked up at the sky, then turned back toward Kong. Kong acknowledged with a huff, and then they all watched as Godzilla vanished beneath the waves.

EPILOGUE

In the most ancient times, animals and people did not live on the surface of the earth. They lived below the ground with Kaang, the master of life. People and animals were the same then and lived together peacefully. Although they lived underground, there was always light and plenty to eat.

But Kaang desired that they should move to the World Above. And when this happened, everything changed.

From a tale told by the San People
of Southern Africa

Kong Monitoring Station, Hollow Earth, Two Months Later

Ilene Andrews had spent the morning studying a form of proto-writing inscribed on ruins that preliminary dating suggested were older than the Sumer civilization by ten thousand years. If she was right, that made it the oldest form of graphic communication ever to be discovered. And they had only been back in Hollow Earth for a couple of weeks. Who knew what she might discover in a month, two months, a year? At this point, it wasn't even clear to her who or what had made the inscriptions. Ancient humans, possibly, or some race of beings entirely unknown to science. This was the place where the myths came from, after all—the prototypes of the gods, the demons, the monsters, the heroes. The tales of hell and paradise and everything in between.

Behind her, she heard a slight sound and turned.

Good morning, Jia, she signed. *Good morning, Nathan.*

She smiled. Behind them, the Monarch team was still setting up equipment, for what was to be an ongoing, open-ended project. They had been fully funded this time, and she meant to make the best of it.

Good morning, Mother, Jia signed.

I am incontinent, Nathan signed. Ilene smiled wider, then laughed.

"What?" Nathan said. "Did I get it wrong?"

"Has Jia been teaching you?" Ilene asked.

"Yes, I…" He broke off. "Okay," he sighed. "What did I just say?"

"Nothing we can't iron out later," Ilene replied. "Come on, how about a walk?"

"That sounds good," Nathan said. But Jia tugged on his arm.

"Right," he said. He took his walkie-talkie off his belt and spoke into it. "All right. Is he ready for his morning walk?"

A moment later, Kong landed ahead of them with a tooth-rattling *thud*. He turned back, and for a moment he and Jia stared at one another. Then Kong raised his hand.

Home, he signed. Then, with a happy roar, he swung off ahead of them.

He is *home,* Ilene thought. Then she glanced over at Jia. *And so are we.*

In the distance she heard Kong beating his chest, and his triumphant cry echoing through the valley.

ACKNOWLEDGEMENTS

Thanks to my editor, Sophie Robinson and copy editor Sam Matthews. Kudos to Natasha MacKenzie for getting the cover design together in record time. Thanks once more to Legendary and Toho for such a great playground to cavort in. Special thanks to Jann Jones, Mary Parent, Alex Garcia, Jay Ashenfelter, Zak Kline, Robert Napton, Barnaby Legg, Josh Parker, Brooke Hanson, Rebecca Rush, Spencer Douglas, and Chris Mowry. Thanks to Adam Wingard, Eric Pearson, Max Borenstein, Terry Rossio, Michael Dougherty, and Zach Shields for such excellent source material.

For more fantastic fiction, author events,
exclusive excerpts, competitions, limited editions and more

VISIT OUR WEBSITE
titanbooks.com

LIKE US ON FACEBOOK
facebook.com/titanbooks

FOLLOW US ON TWITTER AND INSTAGRAM
@TitanBooks

EMAIL US
readerfeedback@titanemail.com